“I-I don’t understand a thing you’re saying, yet I feel like I need to.” Isis kept her tone as calm as possible. “Please, explain to me what you saw in your dreams.”

“You must understand.” Domina’s eyes looked to the night sky. “I see it each night in bits and pieces. I knew it was coming, but now I know my dream is here. Everything changes when it arrives.”

“What changes, Domina?” Isis’ fists clenched. “What is coming?”

Domina’s mouth popped open. “You need to go through time again. Only one minute ahead. That should be enough. Yes, in that minute, you avoid the change.”

Lightning shot through the sky. It forced Isis to look up. The gray smog that covered the village had disappeared. It was the first time in a decade Isis saw the stars. Another lightning bolt passed, then several crisscrossed from all directions. There were no clouds, just stars. Which meant no rain or thunder, either.

“What’s going on?” Isis frowned. “What is this lightning?”

“I do not know about lightning, only that it is about to come!” Domina shouted with an intensity Isis had never heard from her. “You need to go now!”

“I don’t understand. Go where?” Isis could barely hear her own voice over the weather overhead. “What’s about to hit—”

“*Time!*”

Domina lunged and shoved Isis, knocking her to the ground. Everything blurred around her and, even though she was falling backward, a sensation overtook her body as if she were being forced forward.

Praise for Mark Rosendorf

Awards For THE WITCHES OF VEGAS

2021 RONE award winner in the Young Adult category
Shelf Unbound's 2020 Best Indie Book – Notable Indy
2020 International Digital Awards' finalist in the 2020 Young Adult Category.

Awards For JOURNEY TO NEW SALEM

2022 RONE award nominee in the Young Adult category
InDTale Crème De La Cover's Cover of the Month award

"My teen, Moxie, really digs The Witches of Vegas series and is looking forward to the next book."

~Penn Jillette
Penn & Teller: Fool Us!

~*~

"Spellbinding, captivating, and enchanting…A fast-paced adventure that readers will want to devour front to back without pause."

~InD'tale Magazine
Five Star review, Crowned Heart Recipient

~*~

"The Witches Of Vegas series is simply screaming out to be a movie series. The glamour and sparkle of Vegas juxtaposed with the magic and dark undertones of the story would convert so well on the big screen. One can only hope that Hollywood snaps up this incredibly engrossing adventure."

~Doctor Who Online

~*~

"(Journey To New Salem is) another fast paced, action packed story. If you love witches and vampires, you're really going to enjoy this story."

~Bedside Book Review

~*~

"Hands-down Journey to New Salem is an excellent continuation of The Witches of Vegas series. It's a fast-paced read that is touching in places and has a few unexpected surprises that I appreciated. Highly recommended."

~Dan's Sci-Fi and Fantasy Blog

~*~

"The Witches of Vegas is both unique and utterly engaging. With endearing characters and an adventure-filled plot, readers will surely be clamoring for the next book in the series!"

~ Nicole Kilpatrick
Author of Clover

~*~

"For those who love an innovative witch story, this is an action-packed fantasy series that will thrill everyone from twelve to a hundred!"

~Susan Sewell for Readers' Favorite

Witch's Gamble

by

Mark Rosendorf

The Witches of Vegas Book 3

This is a work of fiction. Names, characters, places, and incidents are either the product of the author's imagination, are used fictitiously, or were caused by a witch messing with time. Any resemblance to actual persons living or dead, business establishments, events, or locales from this timeline, is entirely coincidental.

Witch's Gamble

Contact Information: info@thewildrosepress.com

Cover Art by *Jennifer Greeff*

The Wild Rose Press, Inc.
PO Box 708
Adams Basin, NY 14410-0708
Visit us at www.thewildrosepress.com

Publishing History
First Edition, 2022
Trade Paperback ISBN 978-1-5092-3992-4
Digital ISBN 978-1-5092-3993-1

The Witches of Vegas Book 3
Published in the United States of America

Dedication

To my wife, Sue, if I could go back in time, I'd fall in love and marry you all over again.

Prologue

Valeria hovered miles over the Earth, trapped in a vortex formed by five enchanted crystals. Her creation stared her in the face. Isis Flores Rivera, the sixteen-year-old powerful, but naïve, witch was now immortal. Turning her into a vampire had been a calculated risk. It was also one Valeria had needed to take. Their combined Wiccan power over the course of centuries would have reshaped the world. Plus, it was her one way out of the purgatory Isis' family damned her to for what would have been all eternity. Granted, it was a merciful and somewhat comfortable place, but it was still a prison.

The planet was ripe for re-creation, and Valeria would be its artist. She had waited long enough to begin her conquest. Now was the time. All she had to do was remove this one coven that stood in her way. It should have been easy. But instead, after four hundred years of plotting and planning, she found herself at the mercy of a damned teenager. Isis was too immature to understand that Valeria was saving this population from itself. Now her fate was in this girl's hands. It was as humiliating as it was infuriating. Why didn't she kill her when she had the chance?

"I'm going to send you away." Isis' voice trembled. "Far away."

"To where?" Valeria's tough tone had intimidated

the girl in the past. But not this time. Although Isis was new to immortality, it had given her a huge boost in confidence. She had a plan and, based on those narrowed eyes, she was fixated on it. Damn this girl and her naïve heroics.

"Nowhere," came the reply. "I'm going to give you a push through space so you will keep floating far away from Earth."

So much for mercy. In all her time, Valeria had never found herself in such a hopeless situation. She was trapped, powerless, and facing a deathtrap she could not escape. This was new territory, and not one she appreciated. If Isis was truly about to do what she claimed, then at least Valeria would not have to live with the indignity for long. Not unless she could use her wits and experience to escape.

"Hurtling through space." Valeria tried to raise her arms but to no avail. At the moment, trapped in a veritable coffin of energy, she could barely shrug a shoulder. In the past, she handled Isis through fear and intimidation. But right now, the girl had too much advantage, and a belief of righteousness. Valeria needed a new strategy, and quick. Otherwise, the black lacy dress she teleported out of a store window in Sweden would become her permanent covering.

It was time to be smart, not angry. Now was not the time to allow her temper to take over.

"I guess you do intend to murder me," Valeria said. "Even a vampire cannot endure the freezing temperatures of space. I may float away for eternity." And so would her crusade. The world would continue as-is, with humans as the dominant species, while witches—their superiors—stayed in hiding, as they had done so for hundreds of years.

Isis was the type who believed she could save the world, one person at a time. People like her could be controlled by guilt. She was, after all, a child, and an emotional one at that. Valeria needed to get her to break concentration just for a moment. But so far, the little brat's resolve would not budge.

"I was right about you, after all, young Isis," Valeria said, hoping shame would distract Isis enough to break her control where all else failed. "You are ruthless and would have made an excellent apprentice. We would have changed this planet and ruled for all eternity."

Isis' gaze dropped to her feet. Was she considering it? Either way, this was the moment Valeria needed. She focused her will on the enchanted crystals, trying to use her far longer relationship with Earth's energy to overtake Isis' control. The attempt failed. The crystals denied her call. Even lost in thought, Isis kept her focus and wouldn't give it up. Her Wiccan connection had just reached a new level.

Isis picked up her head. "I don't want to do this. That's why we're different. You like hurting people. I don't want to rule the world. I have to save it from you."

Valeria's vision went red. This girl was truly a damned fool. In "saving the world," she only denied her fellow witches their rightful place at the head of natural selection. She damned them all to persecution upon discovery. They were constantly under threat by inferior beings, yet none ever took a stand. After hundreds of years, Valeria was the only one willing to change this. Now the world would no longer have her to put things right. She'd scream at the top of her lungs if she thought it would relieve her of the rage that coursed through her body.

"And once that deed is done, what happens to you, young witch?" Valeria slammed her forehead against the energy shield. Her neck was the only part of her body she could move. The head-butt didn't crack the crystals' shield. "Do you travel back to Las Vegas and hide your true self behind the cheers of mortals as you play the part of jester? Or will you bury yourself in that quarantine for witches directly below us?"

"Your path is filled with death!" Isis shouted. "Your way hurts innocent people. I know what it's like to be an innocent person and be hurt. To suffer for no good reason—"

"Innocence is a fairy tale!" Valeria shouted, unable to hold her composure. "You will learn this over time, once you experience humanity through a long-term perspective."

"You're not my teacher, and I'm not your student!" Now it was Isis losing control of her temper, but not of the crystals' energy dome. "You're evil! Maybe you don't want to be, maybe you don't mean to be, but it's what you've become. You're obsessed and blind. This is the only way to stop your evil."

It was clear Isis would not be swayed. She had made up her mind and refused to be coaxed, manipulated, or intimidated out of this decision. There was nothing left for Valeria to do but capitulate. But she wouldn't go out begging like a mere mortal. At least she'd keep her dignity in the face of her own extinction.

"If you're going to damn me to such a fate, then do

it," Valeria snapped. "But do not lecture me. You haven't lived long enough to realize the horrors humanity has brought onto our kind. You know nothing of what you speak."

Isis did not respond. The two stared at one another for what felt like an eternity. Finally, the girl's nostrils flared. "I have no choice," she said in what sounded like genuine sorrow. "The world is better without you. I'm sorry."

To Valeria, it looked like Isis was moving away, perhaps backing off on her declaration. She realized that it was her floating backward. The girl was really going through with it, and all she could offer was an apology. "You are sorry," Valeria said. "Small comfort for one you are about to damn for all eternity."

"I know." Isis pointed a finger forward.

Valeria focused all her will on the crystals. If ever she needed the Earth's energy to come to her aid, it had to be now. Soon, the Earth would be out of reach. Still, nothing. She couldn't keep the energy shield from dragging her back. There was nothing she could do except wait to lose consciousness in the frigid vastness of space.

Valeria felt the rage begging to come out of her. But it would do no good. Anger wouldn't help her escape this death trap. It seemed nothing would. Besides, as angry as she wanted to be, she was also impressed. To the girl's credit, it actually was a brilliant plan, and one only she could have pulled off. No mortal witch could use the energy to float out of the Earth's atmosphere and survive without air or oxygen. But Isis was no longer a mortal witch, thanks to Valeria. An irony worthy of her mission's end.

Both Isis and the planet Earth appeared smaller as Valeria moved farther from it. She wanted to kick a crystal away, break the pentagon that trapped her in a transparent coffin, but her legs couldn't move any more than her arms. The crystals would separate soon enough due to the distance from Earth breaking their connection. Unfortunately, once that happened, Valeria's connection would be broken as well. She was doomed.

Within seconds, Isis had fallen out of the line of Valeria's vision. She was just a light in the dark created by the glow that emanated from her body. The enormous planet once underneath Valeria's feet was now in the distance and barely the size of a basketball. The crystals floated in different directions. Valeria's body shivered. She tasted the frost—sweet, yet acidic—on her tongue and face. She was no longer trapped in its dome, yet she still could barely move her arms and legs. For the first time in Valeria's existence, time was no longer on her side. She was damned, and without her intervention, so was the future of her kind.

Valeria poked her head forward. The slight movement made her throat burn. She could make out Isis, who floated downward, back to Earth. The light she created faded. Twice now the girl had hindered Valeria's plans. But it wasn't just her; it was also the boy, her young lover, Zack Galloway. He had no Wiccan connection at all, yet he proved to be an even bigger hindrance to Valeria than Isis and her coven. Now the two lovers were vampires; they'd be around forever to assure Earth's status quo. "Wait…" Valeria widened her eyes.

She saw the girl through enhanced vision—a

Wiccan ability only the greatest of witches could use on instinct. That meant, even miles from the Earth, she was still close enough to tap into the energy. The connection was weak, but it was there. With her experience, she could call to it, use it, and survive. Maybe.

With enough focus, Valeria could teleport herself back onto the planet, perhaps somewhere warm so she could thaw out and resume her mission. But that wouldn't be enough. Even if her undead existence were to continue on, what would be her next step? How could she prevent yet another failure?

Valeria shut her eyes and focused. Escape from this icy prison was her priority, but she couldn't forget her purpose. The world needed to be changed. Unfortunately, it could not be accomplished here, not now. She needed to go elsewhere…or maybe else when…before it was too late.

"Yes, I know what I must do." With each word, ice crackled around Valeria's jaw. "Help me succeed, Mother Earth. Guide me on my path."

Energy flowed through Valeria's body, or did it? Was it truly her connection to the Wiccan energy that she sensed, or was it a hallucination caused by her brain solidifying? Would this be her final thought before a living death?

The answer would come immediately as she focused her thoughts on her intended destination. At least there was still a chance for survival.

Part One

Chapter One

Two hundred years later...

To think, life was supposed to be calm and mundane. But, once Isis hovered high above the village of New Salem, she knew today wouldn't work out as she hoped. Their soothsayer was right. An attack was coming. A horde of reanimated corpses, turned into mindless vampires, were heading toward New Salem, pushing through the swamp jungle's shrubs and bushes. A few collided with trees that stopped them in their tracks. Many others, however, had enough instinct to shuffle their way through and resume their path. They smelled blood, and they were determined to get their hands on it.

Isis eyed the village below. Most were indoors, standard protocol before an impending threat. The few who were outside gazed at her as if she was a bright star in the sky. Isis' primary job as of late was to turn away attacks. Today would be no different. Well, maybe a little different. Despite her protests, she was about to have help in securing the borders and protecting lives.

Isis held out her arms and allowed her body to glide to the ground, into the middle of the quad where a crowd awaited her return. One person stood in front of the others. She landed before him.

"So, what's the deal?" Zack asked.

Isis focused on Zack's green eyes and blond hair. After all this time they were still his best features. "They're coming," she said in a huff. "They're five minutes away." A collective gasp filled the small crowd.

"Then Domina's vision about the attack was accurate?"

"There's around two dozen of them." Isis eyed the short and rotund girl standing to Zack's right. Her hair was box-braided down her back. "But she was off about what direction they're coming from. The North is clear of any threats. This horde is coming from the East."

"Then what are we waiting for?" shouted Elian, the youngest of the group. "Let's go kick some mindless vampire ass!" At least one in the group was excited, maybe too excited, to charge off into battle. The rest had widened eyes and were tense. A few kept taking deep breaths.

"Wait until we get the word," the taller and redheaded Cindi snarled at him. She returned her attention to Isis and Zack. "We have to be ready, right, Mister President?"

"You are ready," Zack replied. He looked upon the entire group of six. "Listen to me. This will be no different than what you've been practicing in our class. Yes, they are vampires, but they work on impulse, not thought. You will need to use your cunning and your ingenuity. But, most importantly, you will need to use the energy to fend them off. You're the best we have here in New Salem. I believe in you. Your families believe in you. We all believe in you!"

Elian jumped up with two fists clenched. If Zack was looking for excitement from the others, they weren't giving it to him. At least they were taking their first task as New Salem's latest protectors seriously. It was finally Cameron, Cindi's twin brother, who stepped forward. "We will make our people proud, Sir." Two of the witches behind him nodded their agreement.

"Let's head east," Cindi shouted.

The twins and the other four grabbed the wooden spears lying at their feet. They ran for the east border. Isis watched them all with a skeptical eye. They had been both her and Zack's trainees for a few years, and now they were being put on the front lines. Were they truly ready to turn away the horde of savages heading to New Salem looking for thirst-quenching blood? Of course, they were anxious. It was just what Isis expected from them. These kids could barely handle being trained by a pair of vampires. Now they'd have to engage vampires in battle? This was the main reason Isis wore jeans and a pink T-shirt while Zack wore jeans with a blue T-shirt. They thought it made them look less like the undead.

Cameron and Cindi took the lead. They strode with confidence that may have been staged. Zack always spoke to them about looking poised in front of the others. It seemed both siblings, especially Cameron, were always looking to impress Zack. At seventeen, they were also the oldest members of the team. For the others, however—two boys and two girls—they were no older than fifteen. Elian was only thirteen and just started his training three months ago. When he wasn't running around the entire village, Elian moved with a strut and a dance in his step. He never looked nervous, especially around the older kids in the group. Isis did notice, however, that he always wore his white baseball cap, passed down through a number of generations, like a security blanket.

"Nice speech," Isis whispered. Zack replied with a nod and a smile.

Domina's gasp had them both spinning around. "They come from the east, not the north. I beg forgiveness for my flaw." Her voice shook as she spoke. "I try, but a full understanding of what I see, it is hard for me."

"In that case." Isis raised a finger in the air. "Off with your head!"

Domina shrieked. "My head?" She grasped her neck, her face turned as white as Zack's. "What do you mean? What is off with my head?"

"I'm making a joke." Isis placed her palm against Domina's exposed forearm. "Relax. It's all good."

Domina jumped back. Isis' arm fell to her side. The girl was never relaxed, especially around Isis. It wasn't because Isis was a vampire, not when there were two others in the village. But, whatever the reason, the obvious fear began the moment her Wiccan abilities manifested three years ago at the age of thirteen. As was the case with her ancestors, Domina's connection manifested as psychic visions. Isis had been hoping her fear would subside, but it had only grown over time.

"Okay, then. I thank you for understanding."

Zack chimed in. "You did well, Domina. You let us know the threat is coming, and we appreciate that. Now, it's time for the rest of our team to do their part."

"I should get there, too." Isis stepped forward. Zack's ice-cold fingers wrapped around her wrist. She stopped in her tracks. "What are you doing?" she asked.

"They need to do this themselves, Isis," he said.

"*By themselves*?" Isis threw Zack a wide-eyed glance. "They're so young. Do you really want to risk their lives by having them fight those things without us?"

"We have to," Zack replied. "The village relies on your connection too much as it is. They need to know this team can keep them safe and turn away threats without you."

"Zack, there's a bunch of monsters heading here!"

"Twenty plus one," Domina said. "That's what I saw."

"They looked nervous. Real nervous," Isis said. "That could play havoc with the energy, maybe even sever them from it."

"I get that," Zack replied. "But with each generation of witches we trained, they hung back while you did all the heavy lifting. This group needs to see they can use their Wiccan abilities on their own. If not, they'll fall into the same pattern. It's time this village started relying more on each other and less on you all the time."

Isis opened her mouth to argue but then stopped herself. She hated it when they disagreed, especially when she knew he was right. People called on her for even the most menial of tasks about ninety percent of the time. After two hundred years together, she had learned to trust Zack's gut just as he trusted her Wiccan connection. But she still couldn't stand by and watch the six students they trained get slaughtered. There had to be something she could do, even if it was in a subtle manner.

The sound of dozens of the undead snorting and growling came closer. They were less than a minute away. With her enhanced vision, Isis saw the six defenders standing in a straight line, each a few feet apart. They held their wooden staffs with the sharp ends aimed forward. Isis smelled the sweat on all of them, even Elian. An idea suddenly hit her. Isis knew exactly what she had to do.

"Okay." She wrapped her arms around Zack's waist. "But let's at least stay close and keep an eye on them. Just in case."

"That's a good idea. You'll teleport us there?"

Isis touched her nose against his cheek and smiled.

"Unless you became a witch since this morning, I'd better handle the travel."

Zack moved back, keeping hold of Isis' hand. "Domina, you want a lift?" Isis had almost forgot the girl was still standing there.

"No, no, no." Domina waved her hands in protest. "Walking is best. Walking is what I shall do to transport."

Isis shut her eyes and focused on the New Salem's eastern border. Once she opened them, Isis and Zack stood in the middle of the cemetery, which lined the village's border. The mindless vampires' feet scampered their way. Each of the six stood ready, although a few swayed as if caught in a strong breeze. The undead horde came into view. Their eyes were pure black, and their mouths hung open, displaying corroded teeth. Some of the older ones even had the sharp ends of teeth, the beginnings of fangs, protruding. The noises they made sounded more like pigs snorting than anything human.

Three of the undead were steps ahead of the rest. They charged forward with hands stretched out, reaching for the human beings in front of them. Kim, a fifteen-year-old girl they found and rescued in Taiwan, aimed her wood staff and attacked. She let out a loud scream. Cameron and Cindi did the same. The mindless vampires marched directly into the three staffs, becoming impaled through their chests. Each staggered, but they stayed on their feet.

Cindi stretched out her arms. "Rise!" she chanted. "Rise!" But nerves and stress interfered with her witchcraft. The vampires stayed in place.

Isis, realizing what Cindi was trying to do, focused on the energy around each of the three vampires. "Rise," she whispered, copying Cindi's chant. The vampires levitated up, over the trees, then shot off into the horizon and far from the village. Cindi faced her brother with a face filled with relief. That relief melted at the sight of several undead attackers charging at full speed from behind the trees.

"Heads up!" Zack shouted. "Do not let them enter New Salem!"

For a moment, the entire team stood frozen in place as more of the vampires approached. Elian finally lunged, pointing his palms outward. "Fire, light up!" he shouted at the top of his lungs.

Isis focused on the two creatures in front of him. Smoke rose from their backs and shoulders. The smoke burst into fire that spread across their bodies. The undead ran in circles while the flames grew. They scurried away from the village border squealing like pigs the entire way.

"Did you all see that?" Elian threw his arms in the air and cheered. His head darted back and forth. "Who's next? I have more where that came from!"

An arm across her shoulders filled Isis with pride. "I see what you did there," Zack whispered in her ear. "Clever misdirection."

"I knew you'd like that," Isis responded.

Cameron and Cindi clasped hands. Cameron pointed to the fattest tree in the area. "Fall and roll," the twins chanted in unison.

Isis prepared herself to bring down the tree, but the energy around it crackled. In response to the siblings' spell, the massive tree ripped from its roots, slammed against the ground, and rolled over three of the undead. The vampires let out high-pitched screeches as they were sandwiched between the bark and the ground. To Isis, the tree looked like the wheel of an old tractor running over long strands of grass.

Confidence in the young team grew, as did their Wiccan control of the Earth's energy. Kim stood with her shoulder facing her attackers. Her fingers shook toward the ground. "Grass grow!" she said over and over. Isis focused on Kim, making sure the connection obeyed her command.

The blades of grass around two of the undead attackers grew. The strands reached out and wrapped around their feet. Then it weaved together up the leg and to the knees. The ever-persistent vampires groped in a futile attempt to get their hands on their meal. Kim flung her hands downward. Her victims slammed the ground face-first. It was an excellent display on why she had the potential to be the strongest witch within their group.

"Are you still doing this?" Zack asked.

"Nope, not me anymore," Isis answered. "This is all them."

"That is great!" Zack pumped his fist. "They got this!"

The final two, a brother and sister one year apart, leaped in the path of two of the undead and waved their hands in circular motions. "Air!" they chanted. The vampires hovered straight up as a gust of wind lifted them off the ground. The two invaders were suddenly flung at the trees, bouncing off and hitting the ground. The two stood back up, grunted, then ran in the opposite direction of the village. The two siblings exchanged a well-deserved high-five. Isis clasped her own hands together with pride. This time, she didn't need to offer any assistance.

Each member of the coven kept a safe distance while using their power to fend off the horde. It was exactly the way Isis had trained them, and now they were confident enough to do it on their own. After several minutes, all the mindless invaders were either fully dead corpses on the ground, or they were retreating. A sense of warmth filled Isis' cold body.

"Who says you're not clever and able to think outside the box?" Zack said with a tease in his tone.

Isis shrugged. "Usually, I say it."

"I think you just proved that statement false," Zack replied. "I've never been happier to be wrong. Without your involvement, this could have really gone bad."

"Great job," Cindi said to the teen witches around her. "Twenty vampires up, twenty sent running or beaten, Wiccan style."

Facing the group, Elian raised his arms over his head like a soccer player who just scored a goal. "Yes!" he shouted with an ear-to-ear smile across his face. "We rocked it. Go, team!"

A rustle along the grass made Isis' head spin left. Another threat? No, it was Domina taking a slow jog their way. "Mister President, Madam Vice President," she said between huffs and puffs.

"What happened to you, Domina?" Zack asked. "Did you get delayed?"

"Yes, yes." She stopped in place. "My papa, he says you meet with him right away. He and Simon, they wait for you in the laboratory."

Domina's head scrolled back and forth at the group of victorious witches. A few were out of breath, or relieved to survive their first encounter. But for the most part, there were smiles and cheers across the group of witches. Domina ran over and waved her hands. "Please, listen, all show caution," she called out. "Be ready. The battle is still here."

"What are you talking about, Domina?" Elian said through a laugh. "The fight's over. You missed the whole thing. We did it. There were twenty, just like you said, and we took out every single one of them. First time out, we won."

"No, I did not say twenty." Domina's body shook. "I said twenty plus one."

"Twenty plus one. You mean twenty-one?" Cindi asked. "Look around. I'd say we took out about twenty-one of them."

"No, not twenty-one," Domina lashed out. "Twenty plus one."

"You're being weird again, Domina." Cameron leaned down to look Domina in the eyes. "What exactly are you trying to say?"

"I…I don't know…my dreams, they confuse—"

"I'll tell you what she's saying," Elian shouted.

"She's saying we just rocked it out here and she's sorry she missed it!"

Elian's body swayed back and forth as if he were listening to dance music inside his head. His midsection swung in a circular motion. Elian had the attention of everyone, and he reveled in it. He never noticed the single vampire dashing through the trees behind him. The female undead looked like a teenager, and her teeth were aimed directly for Elian's neck. Cindi shrieked.

"Elian, look out!" Kim shouted over all the gasps from her teammates.

The vampire snorted.

"Isis!" Zack shouted.

The mindless vampire leapt in the air and lunged for Elian, its closest source for blood. Elian spun around in time to see it coming. His baseball cap flew off his head. He raised his arms on instinct, but it was too late for him to come up with a spell, not while he was clearly in panic mode. Evidently, the others were too shaken to use their witchcraft as well.

Elian would be dead within seconds. This time, Isis couldn't be sneaky with her help or wait for the others to react. She needed to do something, quick.

Isis shot forward with her right palm outstretched. "Freeze!" she shouted, focusing the energy on Elian and his attacker.

The mindless vampire was in mid-leap with its teeth showing and its hands aimed for Elian's throat. The intended victim's face was pointed upward. From the shape of his lips, he was about to scream. Both were frozen in time one moment before Elian became an early morning snack. Lucky for him, he had a two-hundred-year-old witch watching his back.

Isis levitated the vampire high over the trees. The energy carried it far from the village, then dropped it. The time freeze spell broke. Elian fell on his back with terror filling his face. “Holy crap!” he cried out, grabbing his throat.

He looked around, confused at first. Then, flashing his gaze at Isis, he exhaled loudly. It was clear he realized why he was still alive and not a vampire’s Slurpee. “That was a close call. Thanks a lot.”

“Yeah, it *was* a close call!” Cindi stood over Elian with her hands smack against her hips. “That’s because you let your guard down.”

“Hey, chill out,” Elian said from the ground. “I said thanks.”

“Thanks, nothing.” Cameron ran to the side of his sister. “You got cocky, and you were almost that thing’s supper because of it.”

“Lucky he wasn’t.” Kim jumped in front of Elian, facing the twins. “We all got cocky. We all let our guard down. You two are supposed to be our field leaders. This falls on you!”

“If you’re going to blame us, then give us credit too,” Cindi snapped. “We worked as a team, and we protected our land. We should be celebrating, not fighting about it.”

Elian scurried away from the argument. He grabbed his hat off the ground and shook off the dirt before placing it back on his head. Cameron and Cindi, meanwhile, argued back and forth with Kim. Isis wanted to separate them or chastise them. Or something. The last thing she wanted was to see her newest team of trainees falling apart after their first test. But she wasn’t the village’s president. That fell under

Zack's jurisdiction. For the moment, he seemed content to stand back and watch.

"Are you going to step in?" Isis whispered into Zack's ear. "Say something to them?"

"Nah. It looks like they have it under control," Zack replied. "Kim's right. They did get cocky and let their guard down. But Cameron and Cindi are also right. This was a win."

"What do *you* think?"

"What do *I* think?" Zack folded his arms across his chest, watching the back and forth continue. "I'm just glad I listened to you and that you were close by."

"Yeah," Isis replied. "Because then this wouldn't have been a win. It would have been a horrible tragedy. But they did need the confidence to see they could do it on their own."

"That solution you came up with all on your own." Zack rubbed Isis' lower back. "Keep coming up with ideas like that, and pretty soon you won't need me anymore."

Isis giggled, but inside she cringed. Zack made that joke a lot. "I promise, that'll never happen—"

"Mister President, Madam Vice President." Domina tugged on Zack's arm. "I remind you of your meeting with my papa. He says he prefer you not keep him waiting for long."

"Let me guess. Another emergency he wants us to attend to, or another idea he wants to present?" Zack's tone filled with snark. "I guess it's a good thing everything worked out here and no one was killed. Now we can make his meeting."

Picking up on Domina's slumped shoulders, Isis grabbed Zack's hand and yanked him. "Thank you for telling us. We're on our way."

Isis threw Domina a smile. It was not reciprocated.

Chapter Two

Isis could have teleported herself and Zack to the medical center for their meeting with Doctor John. Doing so would have saved a lot of time. But she enjoyed the slow walk through the village with Zack, especially after helping their students fend off the mindless vampires. With their administrative schedules keeping them busy, their strolls from one meeting to the other were the only times they had to spend together in private. Their conversations were usually light and fun. But sometimes they took some serious turns.

"It feels like all we do is attend meetings," Zack said. "The worst part is when they explain things to us like we're children who haven't been around long enough to have watched their great-grandparents grow up."

Isis snickered. They walked through the cemetery that circled the village. Three tombstones always made her stop in her tracks. They were old and had seen some terrible weather over the years. But they held up after all this time, almost as if the three buried in front of them were protecting those pieces of monumental stone. Sebastian, Selena, and Sacha. Without seeing those names carved into the granite, would Isis have forgotten them by now? Not a chance, she told herself.

"The dandelions around those graves are dying," Isis said. "I remember Sach loved dandelions."

Isis held her hand over Sacha's grave. Through the grass, several dandelions, with bright yellow flower heads grew on all sides. "There, that's better."

"Hey, are you okay?" Zack asked her.

"Yeah, I'm good." They resumed their stroll. Isis waved a hand at each tombstone they passed. The moss that had formed slithered off.

They left the cemetery and walked through the circle of cottages. At one time, the small houses looked new and vibrant. But since the war, New Salem's focus was spread thin on everything they needed to survive. There was no time to apply fresh coats of paint or even groom the grass around the cottages. Despite her enhanced connection, Isis couldn't do everything in the village, even if too many of the residents thought she could.

"I'll tell you, Zack, even after all this time," Isis said, "not a single day goes by that I don't think about them."

"Your folks?"

"Yeah. Mom, Dad, and my Aunt Sacha. Even Luther." Isis wiped a hand across her eyes, an instinctive action since she couldn't form actual tears. "From the day they took me in and made me their own, they kept saying they wanted big things for me." She made a shaky chuckle. "I'm sure this wasn't what they had in mind."

"I know what you mean." Zack put his arm across Isis' shoulders. "I think about them, too, and of course my Uncle Herb. He always said he wanted me to become something important. Now I'm the undead president of the last group of people still alive in the world. It took two hundred years and getting turned into a vampire, but Uncle Herb got his wish."

Isis stepped in front of Zack. She put a hand on his stomach to stop his pace. "Tell me something, Zack, and tell me the truth." The conversation was about to that serious turn. "Do you regret any of it?"

"You mean our life?" After Isis nodded, Zack raised his shoulders. "Well, sometimes I think we had it easier before they put us in charge of the village. But that's what the people needed and wanted. It was the least we could do for them, even if it is a never-ending task."

"That's not what I mean." Isis' eyes locked onto Zack's. She pressed a hand against his cheek. "I mean giving up your normal life, not being able to grow old like everyone else…You let yourself get turned so you could save me. Do you ever regret it?"

"I regret that since the nukes ruined the atmosphere, the cow blood tastes kind of funky."

"Zack, stop." Isis pulled her hand from his cheek and gave him a playful slap on the shoulder. He liked to joke, but was he doing so now to avoid the question? "I'm looking for serious convo. However you feel about this, I can take it."

"Serious convo. Fine." Zack took Isis' hands and squeezed. "Not for one moment have I ever regretted our existence together. Not when we were alive, not since we've been undead. Every day, for the last two hundred years, I enjoy looking at those cute dimples, that long brown hair, your beautiful brown eyes, and adorable smile."

Isis' grin stretched across her face. If she were still capable of blushing, her cheeks would have turned a bright red.

"We may not have met under normal circumstances," Zack said, "but it was the best thing that ever happened to me. *You* are the best thing that ever happened to me."

Isis leaned in, tipped her head up, and kissed him. There was a time her lips against Zack's caused a physical reaction for both of them, not just an emotional one. Yet another disadvantage of being a vampire.

"Zack, I couldn't have survived all this time without you, and I wouldn't have wanted to, either."

"Aw shucks, it was nothin'," he responded to her through a wide grin. He waved a hand. Isis obliged, staying at his side with each step. "But there's one thing I've never understood."

"What's that?" Isis asked.

"Throughout all those years Luther mentored your coven, there's so much he could have taught you about being a vampire. I'm surprised he never did."

Zack had stated that thought to Isis several times spread out over the last two centuries. Yet another disadvantage of immortality was how often topics of discussion repeated themselves, even between the two of them. Nothing ever felt new. Did Zack really forget their conversations on this subject, or were they just running out of fresh subjects to talk about?

"Luther probably never thought I'd need to know," Isis said, giving him the same answer as the last time they discussed Luther.

"Yeah, he probably didn't. Back then, you were just a witch, and I was a magician." Zack looked up to the gray-covered sky. "Who would have thought this was going to happen to us?"

Isis stretched her arms out like an actress on the

stage. "Surprise!" she shouted as loud as she could.

"Yeah, no kidding," Zack replied. They had finished their walk through the maze of cottages and ended up in the quad.

He looked upward at the four-story school building. The huge old-fashioned clock was nailed against the wall, overlooking the quad. There was some resistance to the clock's presence at first, not because it was ugly—it wasn't—but it was something new. Isis found that people, witches or otherwise, had a natural resistance toward change. But Isis liked it and thought it gave some character to New Salem's antiquated structure. Over time, the huge clock had become the quad's focal point. Thanks to a Wiccan spell by Isis, its Roman numerals could be seen from anywhere within the area, even in the middle of the night. Despite all New Salem had gone though over the last half century, the clock still hung and ticked away.

"I really do love that clock," Isis said.

"I'm sure you do since you teleported it here all the way from London when we found it." Zack laughed. "Very few souvenirs come that big."

Isis rolled her eyes. "You don't like anything you can't palm in your hand and turn into a magic trick."

"My real magic trick is looking interested during all these meetings." Zack waltzed to the medical center door and pulled it open. "I'm not looking forward to this one. You know Simon and Doctor John will have some crazy idea involving witchcraft that they'll want *you* to try out."

"I can't fault them for wanting to keep New Salem as safe as possible," Isis said.

"But we can fault them for seeing you as their

guinea pig."

"We don't know that's what they think. Let's at least hear them out, okay?"

"Fine." Zack threw his arms up in defeat. "Let's hear them out. But I think you're way too trusting of people."

"I consider that a strength."

"We'll see."

Isis strolled past Zack and toward the open doorway. She smelled Doctor John's body odor which meant he hadn't gone home all night to sleep or shower. It was a habit he developed thanks to Simon's bad influence. Simon sometimes forgot that the non-vampires—particularly the doctors—needed sleep. Simon, meanwhile, had become lazy about keeping his vampiric body clean. He developed a strong "old man" smell to him. It was like being around a human-sized sliced onion. From Zack's scrunched face, he smelled it as well, even from out here.

A young voice shouted at Isis, which made her pause mid-step. "Madam Vice, Madam Vice!" She about-faced and saw Elian waving to her from the middle of the quad. The boy was covered in sweat, which made sense. Isis had never seen him go anywhere unless he was running at full speed. Somehow, that baseball cap always stayed on his head.

Elian was running backward as he passed by the front of the medical center. He waved to Isis and Zack, then pointed east. "Thanks for saving my ass back there! But please don't tell my mom what happened, or she'll pull me from the team! She already thinks I'm not old enough."

"You're welcome," Isis shouted. She wanted to

reassure him what happened with that last vampire would remain their secret, but Elian was already out of range. He had made a beeline for the school. Maybe better that Isis wasn't able to make the promise since she couldn't vouch for the rest of the team who loved to gossip. Their training sessions rarely remained a secret from the village residents.

"We should totally rat him out," Zack said. "It would serve him right for being so impulsive."

Isis placed a hand on Zack's chest. "Maybe we should let it go. I think he learned a valuable lesson today."

Zack kept an eye on Elian, who fired a force blast at the ground. It propelled his body high into the air. He flew across the quad and landed on his feet in front of the school's double doors. He stopped his momentum in just enough time to keep from crashing through the doors. Elian grabbed the handle, yanked the door open, and ran in.

"I'm glad *you* think so," Zack mumbled.

Isis snorted, then walked into the medical center.

Chapter Three

Isis sat at the rectangular table in the center of the lab and eyed the two gentlemen across from her. With a clear smirk, Zack dropped into the matching wood chair on Isis' left. At one time, this laboratory was the main examining room in the medical center. The room held special meaning to Isis. It was where she was cared for when Zack and her family first brought her to New Salem. The doctor at the time, Mac, was an amazing and knowledgeable doctor and also a witch. Isis almost died in this room. In fact, she did die, because it was the only way to save her. The metal table stood in the exact spot where Isis was laid out on a gurney. That was many generations ago, but for her, it may as well have been a few decades ago.

Doctor John, the man directly across the table from Isis, was now the head of the medical facility in New Salem. He, too, was knowledgeable and good for New Salem, but he was no Doctor Mac. In fact, he was low on Isis' list of favorites among all the doctors who ran the medical center. Doctor John had an interest in the Wiccan arts to the point it was more of a priority to him than his medical duties. His favorite test subjects were Isis and his own daughter. The man was most definitely overcompensating for everyone in his age group not being gifted with a connection to the energy. It never made sense to Isis that an entire generation would get skipped over like that, but Mother Earth sometimes had a wicked sense of humor.

"Thank you for coming." Doctor John folded his hands and rested them on the table. "Simon and I wish to discuss an experiment that would add additional security for our beloved village."

Zack's smirk grew. "I'll bet it has to do with Isis. Am I right?"

"It does." Doctor John motioned to the two glasses in front of Isis and Zack. "Please allow me to explain."

Of the four glasses sitting on the table in front of each member of the meeting, three were filled with the one substance vampires needed every twenty-four hours to survive. Isis was sure this supply came from the pigs they roasted for the village barbecue the night before. Doctor John's glass was filled with water, the village's choice of beverage since all other liquid supplies were exhausted four years ago.

From the seat next to Doctor John, Simon clapped his hands together. "I think you two are really going to love this idea," he announced in his overexcited high-pitched voice.

"Go ahead," Isis replied.

Zack's arms folded over his chest. His lips were slightly open. Isis was sure the word "no" was ready to pound its way out of his mouth. Isis, however, tended to give Simon the benefit of the doubt. He was, after all, the only other vampire in the village, and their one constant throughout the generations. Simon lived in New Salem when Isis and Zack first arrived. He trained them on how to survive from the moment they were both turned. They owed him at least an ear whenever he asked for it.

Once Isis and Zack no longer needed him for survival skills, Simon found other ways to occupy his immortal existence. One such way was developing new theories on how to improve New Salem's security and way of life. He had many "partners" in these escapades over the centuries, the most recent being Doctor John.

"Do fill them in, Doctor." Simon's body twitched. He was clearly making a strong effort to remain seated at the table.

"Yes, please fill us in," Zack said with more than a hint of skepticism.

Doctor John sat up in his chair. "Isis, you have shown an amazing use of your Wiccan connection to freeze time around a person or object. It has been a saving grace on many occasions, particularly in the defense against our recent invaders. We believe that manipulation of the energy…the utilization of chronic influence can be enhanced—"

Simon jumped out of his seat. "We want you to travel through time."

"I'm sorry. What?" Isis' head tipped back.

Doctor John cleared his throat. "What we are saying is that when you freeze time around a contained space, you are doing so by manipulating the quantum energies that surround the area. Much as you can teleport through space, which you do with ease, we believe you can similarly use the energy to travel through time as well."

Sometimes, Doctor John and Simon's ideas were inspiring. Other times, they were confusing at best, insane at worst. Zack's scrunched face spoke volumes as to which side of the fence he thought it fell.

"Let me see if I am following all of this." Zack

slapped a hand across his forehead. "The two of you believe Isis can use the energy to move through time, and you want her to try this. Is that really what you're suggesting?"

"That is exactly what we are suggesting." Dr. John's voice was deep, but assured, as always. "We are not saying she take herself far through time, but rather try to move within a couple of minutes. It is a use of the energy no witch has ever been able to accomplish. Of course, none have been using their gift as long as Isis."

"Travel though time." Zack's head flipped to Isis. "Is that even possible?"

Isis thought back to all the lessons from her family on how everything is made of energy, which meant a witch could theoretically do anything. They taught her everything from telekinesis, to hypnosis, and even thought projection. But time travel? That was impossible, but impossible was a concept witchcraft proved wrong for centuries.

Isis did have the ability to freeze time around people or objects. It was something any witch could learn, but most needed enchanted crystals to accomplish such a use of the energy. Unfortunately, crystals no longer existed. Isis was the first to pull it off on her own without them, but only because she had the advantage of two hundred years' experience. But to physically travel through time? The idea hadn't ever occurred to her.

Isis sipped from her glass. "I've never heard of any witch being able to do that," she finally answered. "I'm not even sure how that can be done."

"No witch has, no witch ever could." Dr. John pointed a finger across the table at Isis. "But you are different from any other witch, perhaps in history."

"We've put a lot of discussion into how far your power can stretch." Simon leaned over and slapped his hands against the table as if it were a drum. "We believe this is within your scope."

Isis wanted to respond, but the words wouldn't come to her. She couldn't get past knowing her connection was such a huge discussion between these two. It made her feel violated, like a piece of meat the chefs wanted to find new ways to season.

"Within her scope?" Zack threw his palms up. "What does that even mean?"

"Isis is an immortal witch," Doctor John said. "It gives her a connection beyond any other witch alive. I—we believe we should see how far that control can go."

"Told you," Zack whispered at Isis. "Guinea pig."

Isis' body twitched. She hated that term "immortal witch" almost as much as "guinea pig." It always made her think of another immortal witch, Valeria. Isis sent her hurtling through space to assure the safety of humanity, or at least that's what she had told herself. It sounded better than she did it because letting Valeria live scared the hell out of her. "Traveling into the past or future," Isis said, more to herself than the men around the table. "I wouldn't know how to do that."

"What a coincidence." Simon raised a finger. "We've discussed that question in depth."

Zack's eyes rolled. "Of course, you have."

"The witches along my family line see into the future. They do so through dreams," Doctor John explained. "They are unconsciously tapping the power just enough to propel their minds into the future and see how events play out. It is my theory, Isis, that with your level of connection, you could do the same, but with your physical self. You could conceivably move forward or backward in time."

Over the years, as Isis grew stronger in her connection, she often wondered what she could do with this sort of power in protecting New Salem. She had to admit, this wasn't an idea that came to her…and she had a lot of time to work on ideas.

"Let's say you're right and she is capable of time traveling," Zack asked. "To what end?"

Simon wandered around the table. His hands flailed as he spoke. "For a moment, imagine we are under attack by the mindless undead at a moment we aren't ready. What if we are all guarding the eastern border, but the horde comes from the west?" Simon leaned in behind Isis and brought his lips near her right ear. "Isis, you could go back in time and head off the attack—or simply warn us—before lives are lost. This is so important considering we guard possibly the last of humanity. This would be a chance to redo a lapse in our system. A safeguard, so to speak."

"We already have that with Domina," Zack responded. "That's exactly what she does with her connection, forewarn us so we can be in the right place at the right time." He eyed each of the men in turn. "She is that safeguard."

Doctor John shook his head. "Over the years, Domina has missed details in her visions. A large group of the undead, if we are caught unexpected, could ravage this village within minutes, unless we can change the events prior to those minutes. Domina is the latest of my family to serve as New Salem's first safety measure. Isis could be our last resort."

"Of course," Simon added, "we would need to test this theory. Preferably, before we have an actual crisis that needs to be stopped before it starts."

"So, this is just about stopping a crisis?" Isis asked.

"It's not just about crisis," Doctor John added. "Our plants grow best when the sun shines through the gray cloud that covers our sky. Unfortunately, we never know when the window of natural sunshine will come. Now, if you could move back in time and plant our seeds—"

"Yeah, I get it." Isis did understand the practical uses but, at the moment, she was only getting annoyed. Their plans for time travel were helpful to New Salem, but it wasn't like they would be the ones doing it. To think she argued with Zack over giving them the benefit of the doubt. That they didn't see her as a guinea pig, although Isis still didn't think that was the case. Maybe he was right about her being too trusting.

But, whatever their motivations or lack of consideration toward her safety, they did have a point. It would be a huge benefit to go back in time, even by a day or two, and prepare the crops before the natural sun shined through the few holes that formed throughout the vapors above. Doing so would help feed her people with fresh food. From what she had been told, fruits and vegetables grown through witchcraft and artificial sun didn't have much taste. Her people endured it out of necessity.

"I'll tell you now, I don't like this idea at all." Zack placed his elbows on the table and leaned his chin against his fists. "It sounds like Isis would be taking a dangerous, and unnecessary, risk—"

"Maybe we should think about it," Isis interrupted. "We don't have to make a decision now, right?"

Zack threw her a surprised and disapproving glance. "Isis, it was you who always tell our students that the energy is not meant to be abused in a frivolous way. This sounds exactly like that."

"I do tell them that," Isis responded. "I'm not saying I should attempt it. I'm just saying we should at least…talk about it."

After a long pause, Zack's narrow-eyed glare lasered on Doctor John and Simon. "Okay, let's talk about it. Do either of you know how this would work?"

"We do have theories," Simon answered.

"Theories," Zack repeated, "but no idea how she would do it, or even what would happen to her. For all you know, the attempt alone could end her existence."

"Oh, no, no, no!" Simon gasped. "We don't think *that* would happen, not at all."

"But you don't know for sure, right?"

"Nothing is ever for sure when it comes to utilizing the Earth's energy," Doctor John answered. "All witchcraft is theoretical until someone with a strong enough connection and an imagination makes it happen. This has never been done. Isis would be the first."

"What are you worried could happen if I try?" Isis asked Zack. It was a genuine question. Even though Zack wasn't a witch, he'd certainly been around them and learned more about witchcraft than anyone else in history.

Zack rotated his head to Isis. His hand slammed against the table. "What if you get stuck somewhere in time and can't find your way back?" He blinked his eyes in a rapid fashion, an attempt to calm his rage before the vampire inside of him took over. "This village can't afford to lose you over an experiment." Zack's head dropped. "I don't want to lose you."

Doctor John cleared his throat. "If I may. A witch teleports by focusing on a location. They mentally picture themselves somewhere else, and their physical forms transport via the energy. Distance is limited to the strength of their connection. Isis, you can teleport to any location in the world. So, why not to a specific time? Moving to the past, future, or returning to the current time. Theoretically, it should be the same premise."

"Should be." Zack rubbed his temples with his right thumb and forefinger. "Isis, are you absolutely sure you'd want to try this?"

"Please, Isis, it is necessary that you consider it." Doctor John's tone suddenly became more forceful. Perhaps even a bit desperate.

"Yes," Simon added. "For New Salem's future we should at least try—"

Zack raised a hand at Simon and Doctor John. It was a signal for them to settle down, and one he had used in too many meetings. It was clear there was something neither was sharing. Isis could have easily pulled it from their minds—if she was that kind of witch. But, despite the fear many in New Salem had of her, Isis never used her connection in an abusive way on anyone. She certainly wouldn't start now. Right now, based on Zack's fluctuating eyes, it was time to end this meeting.

"How about we put this discussion on hold?" Isis took Zack by the hand. "For now."

"It's okay. I'm fine." The vampiric darkness in

Zack's eyes faded. His green irises were now showing. "In the end, Isis, it is your decision."

Isis threw Zack a slight grin. She did agree that time travel, if she could do it, was a great defense to an incoming threat. It also had countless benefits to the village. But that was only half the reason she wanted to try. A decade ago, Isis had to stretch her control of the energy beyond what she had ever done before. While the rest of the world was decimated by the nuclear war, she stood on that rooftop for three straight days and held back the radiation, saving the lives of every man, woman, and child in New Salem. It was perhaps the greatest achievement of her two-hundred-year existence.

But for a long time before that, and since then, things had been stagnant. She loved her life in New Salem, especially with Zack, but it was kind of dull. It was why she talked him into running for president; it gave them something new to occupy their time. Unfortunately, that thrill wore off quickly, and training yet another set of witches barely excited her now. Even chasing off the mindless undead at the borders stopped being a challenge years ago. Maybe this was exactly what she needed to feel alive again. Still…

"We don't have to do it right now," Isis said to Zack. "We can talk about it and come to a decision at a later time." She didn't want to get into an argument with him. After all, his concerns for her safety were justified.

"Then, perhaps we should resume this conversation once you are sure," Doctor John said directly to Isis. He stood from the table.

"Do let us know." Simon offered a huge smile.

"After all, we have plenty of time."

"The three of you do," Doctor John replied. "However, I'd appreciate it if you'd consider conducting the experiment sooner rather than later."

Isis' eyebrows rose. She wanted to believe that despite Doctor John and Simon's eccentricity, they shared a mutual respect in trying to improve and save lives. Was it possible Zack was right about them seeing her simply as a guinea pig?

Chapter Four

Isis spent each morning, including this one, on the dining hall's rooftop watching the youngest of New Salem enter the school. To her, it was the most normal thing that happened in the village. Despite being both a witch and a vampire, Isis liked normal. She felt a sense of pride seeing the students walk along the quad, a few alone and some in groups, with knapsacks over their shoulders. The pride came from the fact that it was on her insistence that education continued for everyone in New Salem under the age of seventeen.

Most of the council didn't see the point. They argued that, considering how the world around them had essentially ended, it would make more sense for the younger generation to learn from their families at home. But no one wanted to push hard against the Wiccan vampire that just saved them from sharing the world's fate. It was an especially ironic request from Isis considering her adopted family, The Witches of Vegas, homeschooled her.

Enhanced hearing and the scent of an overuse of deodorant told Isis that she was no longer alone on the rooftop. She didn't need her Wiccan connection to figure out the other person's identity. He tried to sneak up on her all the time even though it never worked. After two hundred years, she thought that game would have gotten old by now.

"Don't you have a meeting with the farmers this morning?" Isis asked never turning around.

"I postponed it." Zack wrapped his left arm across Isis' shoulders and stood at her side. "President's prerogative."

Zack also had a thing about dressing in a similar color as Isis. This morning, she decided on a light blue crew necked T-shirt with black jeans. With his twisted sense of humor, Zack wore his black button-down shirt and light blue jeans. She knew he was waiting for her to make a remark so he could claim he wasn't dressed similarly, but opposite of her. The joke lost something around a hundred and fifty years ago, but she loved him for trying.

"What are you doing instead of your meeting?" Isis asked, ignoring the color coordination.

Zack held out his empty right hand with the palm facing Isis. He waved his wrist up and down. When he stopped, a red playing card with the queen of hearts printed on the front appeared between his fingers. The card had rips at the edges and brown lines across the front.

"Now, watch carefully. No witchcraft behind it. Just two hundred years of practice." Zack waved his hand again. When he stopped, the card had disappeared, until it suddenly slipped from behind his closed fingers, landing on his sneaker. "That was a lot more impressive before the cards got old and worn out."

Isis giggled. "I'll bet today's New Salem villagers would be impressed if they knew what playing cards were."

"That's a good point." Zack kneeled and picked the card off the top of his sneaker. "I guess magic is a lost art form. So much for a Witches of Vegas reboot coming anytime soon."

"I wouldn't expect one." Isis felt her grin melt from her face. God, was Las Vegas still there? Isis could teleport anywhere in the world, but she couldn't bring herself to go back there and see what the strip looked like since the war.

Zack stopped in his tracks and faced Isis. "Hey, can we talk about that meeting yesterday with Doctor John and Simon?"

"What is there to discuss? You made your feelings clear," Isis said. If her answer came out with some attitude, it wasn't with intent.

"I'm sorry I was so forceful with my insistence that you don't do it." Zack took Isis' hand. "Of course, it is your decision. It's just—"

"I do get where you were coming from, Zack, I really do." Isis moved in a bit closer. "You've been my conscience for a long time, and all of your concerns made perfect sense. Especially about the risk to me."

"It's not just that. It couldn't have been more obvious that they were hiding something. I've wracked my brain, but I can't figure out what it might be."

"I got that sense, too." Isis shrugged. "I don't know what, but the way they didn't want to take no for an answer, you're right, something's up."

"But you still want to try it, don't you?"

"Yeah, I do." Not like she could hide anything from the guy who knew her longer than anyone else alive, or undead.

"Why is this worth it?"

"Because it's never been done." Isis flashed wide eyes his way. "Centuries of witches manipulating reality, yet no records of any of them using it to travel through time. I know it's a risk, but Doctor John and Simon are right. This could save lives. We could use it to give our people a better life. If I can move through time, shouldn't I at least try in case we ever have a need?" Yeah, definitely a better explanation than admitting to boredom.

"Just because you can do something doesn't mean you should." Zack leaned in and kissed her right temple. "You remember who used to say that to you all the time?"

"Yeah. Paul." Isis tipped her head to the sky. "Then my folks. I don't know what any of them would say about this if they were still alive."

"I have some idea. This is a lot of risk all for the sake of Doctor John's experiment." Zack's voice rose. "We don't know the first thing about time travel. How could we? What if you go to the past or the future and you get lost? What if you end up going nowhere and can't get back? There's so much risk in this to you, Isis. You need to consider that, and they should, too."

"Is it really about the risk, or is it about Doctor John using me for my strong connection again?"

"It's both," Zack snapped. "And can you blame me on either?"

Isis shook her head. "No, I can't, and I really appreciate how you're looking out for me. You've been doing that ever since we were fifteen."

"We look out for each other," Zack replied. "It's what we promised your family a long time ago. I know your connection is strong and you don't really need me to keep you safe, but still—"

"That's not true." Isis took both of Zack's hands. "I

always need you, even when I can take care of myself. I needed you back when we were alive in Vegas, and I need you now. We look out for each other, and we protect each other. I feel we owe it to New Salem to do the same for them."

"How sure are you that you *can* do this?" Zack asked. "If no witch has ever done it, it can't be as simple as Doctor John and Simon made it out, can it?"

Isis considered her answer. Zack did make a good point. What if time travel wasn't as straightforward as teleportation? Right now, teleportation was second nature for Isis—it was an easy manipulation of the energy—but she still remembered as a kid the first time she ever tried it. She tried to teleport from one side of the hotel room to the other but found herself in a couple's suite down the hallway. She ended up in the bathroom while the occupants were in the bedroom making noises that she knew weren't meant for her ears.

When she first learned the technique, teleportation wasn't so simple. But Isis now had lifetimes of experience using the energy. Trying something new would certainly be a nice change of pace. But this wasn't the hill she wanted to die on when it came to being at odds with Zack.

"Isis, I know you really want to try this, and I get it," Zack went on. "Just make sure it's for the right reasons. We have a relatively safe life here. Do we really want to take an unnecessary risk? If it works, great, but if something goes wrong, you could disappear forever."

"I know, I don't have to take that risk. Although Doctor John and Simon both think I'll be able to pull it off." God, even Isis wasn't buying that argument.

"I don't think they have your safety in the front of their minds," Zack responded. "I don't get why they want you to rush into this. We're talking about time travel. Why don't we discuss it a bit further? Let's make sure you're sure you can pull it off without a problem before trying it. At least, that's my feeling on the issue."

Zack was making perfect sense. They were discussing an unknown, and their lives, despite everything, had been pretty good in New Salem. Maybe boring wasn't such a bad thing.

"Okay, Zack, that's fair. We can give the idea more thought. Maybe give it a few years then discuss it again."

"Thank you." Zack flashed a grin. "That makes me feel better about it."

Isis nodded, then refocused on the quad. Most of the students had already entered the school building. A few stragglers were still making their way inside.

Domina waddled toward the school balancing what looked like two textbooks and three spiral notebooks on her palms. They were stacked higher than her nose. The books had to be blocking part of Domina's line of sight, but she kept moving forward.

Two girls around her age walked side by side a few steps behind her. It was Penelope and Holland. Domina being late for class was a rarity. Penelope and Holland, not so rare. Both sets of eyes were fixed on Domina. The chuckling showed they were taking great pleasure in Domina's balancing act.

"I really hate those two," Isis mumbled. "The prom queen and her disciple."

"Hate's a strong word," Zack replied. "We've seen their attitudes in others. Eventually, they all grow out of it."

"I sure hope so, for everyone's sake."

Zack's eyebrows rose. "How do you know about proms? You never even went to school."

Isis smirked. "I read a lot of those magazines in the hotel gift shop. That was back before they were considered trash."

"They were always that."

The two girls giggled as if one had just shared a hysterical joke. Penelope wasn't a particularly strong witch. Holland's connection hadn't yet manifested, if it ever would at all. But both had natural charm among their peers, and the boys liked Penelope with her long legs and blonde waist-length hair. Holland was far shorter with shoulder-length brown hair. She, too, had a charisma much like Penelope's. Both girls took full advantage of their popularity.

Unfortunately, some of that popularity came at the expense of fellow schoolmates who were outside the social circle. This was especially the case with Domina, who was a contrast to both their physical appearances and outgoing personalities. The fact that the last group of teens left on the entire planet still had cliques irked Isis to no end.

"You're the witch," Holland said, "and I'm daring you to do it."

"Okay, Hol, watch this." Penelope rotated her wrist while chanting under her breath. Then she raised the hand over her head.

Domina's books flew into the air. They landed in a muddy patch caused by the rain from a few nights ago.

"Oh, no!" Domina cried out. "My books." Both girls burst into laughter.

"Did you see that?" Isis growled. "Did you see what they just did to her?"

"Horrible." Zack shook his head.

Domina dropped to her knees, reaching for her books. She picked up one notebook. The cover was soaked in brown water.

"Oh, Domina," Penelope sang, standing over the poor girl's shoulder. "You dropped your schoolbooks. How come you didn't see that coming?"

"She looks like one of those pigs playing in the mud." Holland laughed.

The girls' giggling rang through Isis' enhanced hearing. "Teleport to ground," she snarled. Zack and her rooftop view faded out. The two girls, inches from her face, faded in. Both backed up. Holland shrieked.

"I hate bullies, and you two are the worst." Isis let her fangs protrude from her mouth. The light around the girls darkened, meaning Isis' vampiric black eyes had sneaked out. "Don't let me catch you bullying anyone in this village again. You hear me? *Anyone*!" Isis nudged a thumb over her shoulder. "Especially her."

Isis noticed another mud puddle behind the girls. One simple force push or even a sudden wind would knock them both off their feet. They'd suffer the same fate inflicted on Domina's books. The difference was that they'd deserve it. Every instinct in Isis' head told her to do it. But the momentary joy she'd get from covering them in mud wasn't worth compromising her principles. Using the energy on village residents was wrong on every level. Isis wouldn't let herself become that kind of witch, even if these two deserved it.

"S-sorry, Madam Vice President." Penelope held her hands out in front of her face. "It…it was an accident."

"Yeah, we didn't know you were watching," Holland sobbed.

"I'm always watching. Don't ever forget that." Isis pointed to the building. "Now, go to school!" she screamed.

The two ran to the school doors. Isis turned around to see Domina, who was still on her knees, using her hand to wipe the mud off one of her notebooks.

"I'm sorry they're such jerks," Isis said. "Are you okay?"

Domina looked up at Isis, her eyes wide like melons. "It's all up to you." Her voice rattled. "You're the one who can fix it. The only one."

"Fix what?" Was she referring to the bullying? Was it a bigger problem than Isis realized?

Isis reached out. Instead of taking her hand, Domina fell backward, landing on her rear end. Damn, this girl was actually more afraid of her than she was of the two school bullies. "Domina, what are you talking about?"

"You need to be my papa's experiment," Domina whispered. "You need to save yourself before it comes."

"Before what comes?" Isis suddenly realized that everything around Domina was still dark. She focused on calming down so the black in her eyes would fade. "What am I saving myself from?"

"I do not see exactly what will come, but it is." Domina rolled over, pressed her hands against the ground, and brought herself to her feet. "It is coming soon." Domina grabbed Isis' wrist. "You must believe me." Her hands tightened. "Most people don't, but for this, you must."

Isis yanked her wrist out of Domina's grip. Before she could answer, a loud thud sent dirt in all directions. It was Zack making a perfect two-point landing from the roof. "Domina, did you see something in a dream?" Zack asked.

"Not a dream. A vision but no image. More of a feeling. It will come. You can't stop it now. It's too late."

"Please, Domina," Isis shouted. "You need to be straight with us. What do you know—"

"Please don't blind me!" Domina screamed.

"Don't what?" Isis froze in place. Blind her? Did she hear that right? Isis had never felt more confused than in this moment. "I would never, ever…what does that mean?"

A loud snorting echoed. A lone vampire must have stumbled into the village. Isis spun around. She straightened her back and clenched her fists trying to sense the intruder, but she couldn't pick up anything. She eyed Zack, who turned in every direction. He faced Isis and shrugged his shoulders. Isis looked back to find Domina had run in the opposite direction from the school. Her books remained on the ground in the mud.

Isis faced Zack. She tilted her head. "Did she create that?"

"Her power is premonition," Zack answered. "That should not be within her scope."

"But you heard what she said?"

"Every word, although I didn't understand it at all." Zack eyed the path Domina had run. "It does change everything. At least now we have some idea of what Doctor John and Simon weren't telling us."

"That it all started with one of Domina's dreams." But could they trust her dreams? Domina's visions had been wrong before, although she'd never expressed one on this magnitude. So much for debating the risk or waiting years to resume discussions. Isis took Zack's hand. It was ice cold as always. "I guess we know what we have to do."

Zack responded with a reluctant nod. "Let's check the perimeter, make sure that snort was just an illusion. Then I'll tell Doctor John and Simon we'd like another meeting to readdress their experiment. I really hope we don't end up regretting this."

"Me, too."

Chapter Five

After searching every acre of New Salem and finding it intruder-free, Isis and Zack strolled to the front of the medical center. She couldn't hold in her smile. The idea of traveling through time excited her like she hadn't felt in a long time. To connect with the energy in a way she had never fathomed before. How cool was that? How had she not come up with the idea herself in the last two hundred years? Zack's concerns still lingered in her head, but those anxieties took a backseat to the alarms of the village's resident clairvoyant. Her warning was clear, and they couldn't ignore it. Whatever Domina was seeing scared her so much she chose to run rather than talk about it.

"It's pretty early. Is Doctor John in there yet?" Zack asked.

Isis shut her eyes and focused on the laboratory. She sensed two people inside, one alive and one undead. "Yeah, he's up and working. Simon's in there with him."

"Of course he is." Zack rolled his eyes. "So, you're definitely ready to try this?"

"I am. I have to." Isis about-faced. "Just give me a minute."

"Take your time. I'll head in and let them know. I'm sure we can imagine how thrilled they'll be when I give them the news." Zack yanked the door open and walked in but said over his shoulder, "Maybe too thrilled to put you at risk, if you ask me."

"I'm sure they mean well," Isis said, even though Zack was no longer in front of her.

Isis didn't want to stray from her morning routine. Once the quad was empty of students heading into the school, the farmers came out. Isis enjoyed seeing them work. Six farmers, made up of five men and one woman, all wearing dirty overalls, stood at the quad's edge, ready with tools such as shovels, rakes, and plows.

Each morning, the twins, Cameron and Cindi, were excused from classes because they had an important job. They hovered on opposite sides of the quad with their hands high above their heads utilizing a complex manipulation of the Earth's energy taught to them by their grandparents. It formed a dome over the quad's area. Sunlight filled the dome. It was artificial, of course, but it gave the crops the light they needed to grow.

Within that dome, the farmers spread out and moved like lightning. They planted seeds and tended to the crops. Isis loved the fact that, even after two hundred years, the residents of New Salem still worked in unison, like a well-oiled machine. Today, that work meant the survival of every resident in New Salem. With the world around them nearly desolate, those crops, along with their animals, were responsible for all the food they had, or could have, available.

A hand pressed against Isis' shoulder. "They're ready for us," Zack whispered in her ear. "And they're about as thrilled as we expected."

"I'm ready," Isis said as a breeze lifted her hair and

whispered it across her face. “Let’s do this.”

Isis and Zack entered Doctor John’s laboratory. The doctor rushed them back to the table where two mugs were refilled with fresh blood. Simon sat across the table with a larger-than-life smile across his face. Both were a lot more excited about conducting this experiment than Zack. Maybe even more than Isis. Figures. It wasn’t their lives on the line if it didn’t work out. Doctor John walked up to the table with a notebook and pencil in his hands.

“I am very happy that you have reconsidered.” Doctor John leaned forward against the table. His focus was directly on Isis. “I believe this will be a fruitful experiment of your Wiccan abilities.”

“But you didn’t come up with this idea, did you?” Zack said. “It was Domina.”

“I see she said something to you.” The doctor shook his head. “It is true, Domina foresaw the need in one of her recent dreams. She confided in me, and immediately after I met with Simon to propose this experiment.”

“Maybe you should have met with us,” Zack replied. “Or been more forthcoming in our initial meeting yesterday morning.”

“Yes, you are right, and I apologize for that.” Doctor John bowed his head. “We felt it best Isis participated by her own choice, not because of a vision that may or may not be accurate.”

“Domina told me it’s coming, and I need to save myself,” Isis said. “What does that mean? What’s coming?”

“I do not know.” The doctor folded his arms across his chest. “My daughter sees the future, but her visions are never clear. Therefore, her explanations of what she sees are not clear either. It is a detriment of her Wiccan connection, and one that has followed my family for generations. I'm sure the three of you know that better than anyone else in this village."

Isis narrowed her eyes. The attitude in Doctor John's tone when discussing his daughter and her visions was not unlike the ones Domina endured from the school bullies. Isis' heart went out to the girl. As Vice President, she'd need to have a discussion with Doctor John on showing his child and her gifts a bit more respect.

"Oh, this is going to be so wonderful!" Simon exclaimed with enthusiasm in his voice that didn't fit the moment. Not that it ever did. "We should get started right away."

"Isis." Zack cupped his hand on her knee. "If you have any concerns, you don't have to do this. You can back out if you want. You could also wait on this, just like we discussed doing before."

"I don't think I can," Isis replied, her mind occupied with Domina's warning. "I'll be okay. I can go back, like, five minutes, then jump ahead to now. We'll know right away if I can do it or not."

"Five minutes would be a good test," Doctor John said. "I would not recommend any farther, at least not on your first attempt."

"I understand."

Isis, Zack, and Doctor John all stood from the table. She noticed Zack mouth the words *first attempt*? with his nose scrunched. "Zack." Isis wrapped her arms around his waist. "I'll be okay. If it doesn't feel right, I'll pull out before making the jump."

"I'm still not crazy about it," he answered. "But I get it. Just be careful, and make sure you come back to me."

"Always." Isis downed the remaining contents of her glass, then used the back of her hand to wipe away the blood mustache above her lip. Best to be at full strength before using the energy in such a new and unique way.

"Come." Doctor John led Isis and Zack across the room and placed Isis against the only bare wall. He took her hand and wrapped what looked like a watch with a screen around her wrist. "This will keep a recording of your journey," the doctor explained.

Isis held her wrist up under her nose and examined the screen. "What kind of recording?"

"It will track your coordinates," Doctor John explained. "It has a timer so we can see how long you were actually gone, even if, for us, it is a matter of seconds."

"So, you were prepared for this." Zack's fists pressed against his hips. "And long before yesterday's meeting."

Doctor John's head lifted with pride. "I have nothing but time in here. I have been preparing for many possible eventualities."

Isis held her wrist with the screen facing out. "This looks like a man's band. You couldn't use something a bit more fashionable?"

"Science rarely considers fashion," the doctor replied. "That's especially in these days, but it will do the job of recording your journey for study."

"Speaking of recordings…" Simon, from across the room, waved an old-fashioned hand-held camcorder.

"This is going to be a New Salem first. It will be a good addition to our library."

The small screen on Isis' wrist lit up. The monitor was full of digital numbers, including the date, time to the tenth of a second, and what she presumed were longitude and latitude coordinates. There were several other numbers constantly changing, although she couldn't begin to guess what they meant. There were also a few zeros, which Isis guessed were meant to record her vitals. She didn't expect they'd pick up anything from a vampire.

For Doctor John and Simon, this was all about testing their only immortal witch's limits with the Earth's energy. But Isis didn't care about any of that. At first, she had seen it that way, but not anymore. Now, this was about a threat Domina claimed was on its way. Maybe others didn't respect the girl because of how weird she came off—and she did come off in an odd way—but Isis always trusted the energy. To her, Domina was the energy's latest messenger, and she needed to be heard.

"Let's do it," Isis said. She couldn't remember such anxiousness coursing through her body. Isis placed her back flat against the cool white wall. "So, I just focus like I'm teleporting?"

"Precisely," Doctor John responded. "Except you are focusing on a time as well as a place. Aim your focus on the hallway, but as of five minutes ago."

"The hallway?"

"Yes. If you were to appear in this room five minutes ago, it would have already happened. We would have already seen you."

"Or so we think." Simon pressed the Record button

and aimed the camera outward, aiming the lens at Isis. "We really don't know much about how time travel works."

"What does that even mean?" Zack's eyebrows rose. "How much research have the two of you put into this?"

"It's not like we have background to base this on," Simon explained. "This has never been done before by any witch. There's no point of reference."

"We cannot be sure that, even with two centuries of experience, Isis can accomplish this," Doctor John added.

"I can," Isis said. "And I will."

"Very well. Let us begin." Doctor John stood in front of Simon and the camera. "It is now 10:15 a.m. and Isis is about to make New Salem's first Wiccan attempt at time travel."

"Remember our agreement," Zack said from across the room. "If it doesn't feel right, trust your instincts and pull out."

"I know." Isis flashed Zack a huge cheese-faced smile. "Don't worry. I'll see you soon."

"Actually, if our theory is correct," Simon chimed in, "he will see you momentarily."

Isis nodded, then folded her hands against her chest. She focused on Earth's energy. Normally, she could access it on instinct, but with what she was about to do, Isis needed to sense it flowing around and through her body. "Five minutes ago, in the hallway," she muttered over and over until a euphoria ran through her. It forced Isis' eyes shut. "Five minutes ago, in the hallway," she said again, addressing the energy.

Her arms tingled, as did her legs. It was as if every

muscle in her body fell asleep all at once. The sensation of falling backward overtook Isis, but she was pretty sure her feet were still planted on the floor. Then, for a brief moment, she couldn't feel anything underneath her. It was as if her body was standing on air. Then, the ground was once again against the soles of her shoes. But it wasn't the hard tile that made up the medical center's floors. Her shoes seeped down into what felt soft like grass and mud.

The euphoria left her body, as did the tingling. A slight wind tickled her forehead. Isis opened her eyes. This wasn't the hallway, but she knew that just from the smell of fertilizer coming from all sides.

She stood in the middle of the quad.

Chapter Six

Somehow, Isis missed the mark. She aimed for the hallway but ended up several feet from the medical center. But was it five minutes in the past, or did she just end up teleporting herself? She had teleported literally a million times before. This felt different, like nothing she had ever experienced before, but did she really travel through time as well as space?

Isis gasped at the sight of Zack holding the medical center's door open for…what appeared to be herself. It was the two of them when they entered for their meeting, but that wasn't five minutes ago. That blue shirt she wore yesterday morning was now in her laundry basket. Isis darted her eyes toward the clock on the school. The hands showed 9:14, one day and twenty-one minutes before the time she used the energy to move five minutes back.

The longitude and latitude numbers on Doctor John's monitor had changed since she last looked, although she didn't really know what they meant. But the time said 10:18 a.m. "I actually moved through time," Isis said to herself. "It worked—"

"Madam Vice! Madam Vice!"

She jumped at the sound of the young voice. Elian ran up to her. Over his shoulder, she saw Zack and the other Isis enter the medical center. The door shut behind them.

"Thanks for saving my ass back there," Elian said. "But please don't tell my mom what happened, or she'll pull me from the team! She already thinks I'm not old enough."

"Yeah, no problem."

Isis' mind drifted back two hundred years, long before her turn, to the time Valeria abducted her. The old hag took Isis back to past moments from each of their lives so they could witness them firsthand. But Valeria used her power of illusion to create those scenes. "Did I just create an illusion?" Isis asked herself.

Elian's face scrunched. "Um, say what?" Isis grabbed Elian's arm. The flesh felt real. This wasn't an illusion.

Isis threw a glance at the medical center. The door swung closed. "This time, you were focused on me, so you ran right over," she mumbled. "You didn't see them over there."

"See who?" Elian asked, yanking his arm from Isis' grip and then taking a huge step back. "Uh, I need to go to my class. Am I dismissed?"

"Yeah, go ahead." Isis waved him along. Elian straightened out his baseball cap and ran for the school as if his tail was on fire.

It was time to go back before anyone else saw her. No need to take the chance that two of her would be seen in New Salem, or that they'd see each other. No one discussed what would happen in that situation. But first, she wanted proof. Right now, no one else knew that she had traveled through time. She needed some sort of evidence. For all everyone knew, all she did was teleport across the village.

Isis eyed the hands on the clock. Perfect. She pointed an outstretched hand toward the clock and focused on the hour hand. It was on the three, but that was about to change. Isis moved her hand downward. The hour hand moved with her, stopping on the six. Soon, the quad would be filled with the farmers. No one would have been able to change that clock without someone else noticing.

The time on the clock suddenly being different would serve as proof, or would everyone remember the clock being wrong for the entire day? Then again, it could have been construed as a teenage prank caused by one or more of the students skipping school and having fun with their Wiccan connection. Still, it was better than nothing. Time to go back…or forward.

Isis shut her eyes and focused on one day and a few minutes forward. "Travel ahead through time, back to from when I came," she said to the energy flowing through her body. She pictured Zack, Doctor John, and Simon in the laboratory. The euphoria swept through her body once again. So did the tingling in her joints.

This time, she had the sensation of falling forward. It felt like her body was being sucked through a wind tunnel. Isis' non-beating heart dropped into her stomach. She stamped her foot, trying to keep herself from hitting the ground. The sensation stopped. Isis opened her eyes. Rows of tombstones faced her. Apparently, traveling through time was not as straightforward as traveling through space. It wasn't even close.

Isis closed her eyes and focused her thoughts on another mind, the one she knew almost as well as her own. "Zack."

His voice shot into her head like a bullet. *Isis! Where the hell are you? Are you okay?*

I'm outside the village in the cemetery, she thought in her head. *Why are you freaking out*?

YOU'VE BEEN GONE FOR OVER TWELVE HOURS!

"What?" Isis tipped her head up. She could barely see the gray fog over the night sky. Isis held out her wrist. It still showed only a few minutes had passed since the lab. "I…I'm heading to the quad. I'll meet you there."

Guess Zack was right again; this was way too dangerous to try. Isis got lucky. All things considered, she could have ended up a hundred years in the future instead of twelve hours. The thought made her body shiver. Should she dare try it again?

How could this experiment lead to her eventually saving New Salem, anyway? Maybe Doctor John's frustrations with Domina were justifiable, at least on one level. Isis straightened her back, then focused on the quad. Straight teleportation was something she could do on instinct. The swamp jungle and the tombstones blurred until they disappeared. Within seconds, she was standing on the grass surrounded by the four buildings.

The medical center's doors swung open. Zack sprinted to Isis with Simon and Doctor John on his heels. Domina was with them as well, skulking several steps behind. Zack wrapped his arms around Isis and squeezed her for a passionate hug.

"I'm all right," she said to him.

"Are you sure?" There was a slight croak in Zack's voice.

"Yeah, I am." Isis wrapped an arm around the back of his neck. "As far as I know, I was only gone a few minutes."

"You were gone a lot longer than a few minutes, Isis." Zack's head snapped back. "I told you I didn't like this from the beginning. It was just too dangerous."

"But it did work," she exclaimed. "I was in the past. Not five minutes. I went back a whole day. I guess my aim coming forward was off too, but I did it. I actually traveled through time."

"The old adage does say that time works in mysterious ways." Simon clapped his hands together. "I guess that applies to traveling through it as well."

Isis placed her hand against Zack's cheek. His eyes examined her as if he was looking for some sort of injury. The concern on his face sent a chill down her spine. "Zack, I'm okay," Isis whispered to him. "I really am."

Doctor John joined Zack at his side. He gripped Isis' wrist and studied the monitor. As the numbers scrolled along the screen, Isis noticed Domina kept a distance from the group.

"From what I am reading, the watch has only been running for a few minutes, but it did record the spatial distances of your jump. This is interesting, but not surprising. It was always a possibility that time travel would not work so precise—"

"Hold on," Zack interrupted. He threw a narrowed glare at the doctor. "You expected this to happen?"

"Not precisely." Doctor John unlatched the monitor from Isis' wrist. "Our knowledge of quantum mechanics is limited. We considered every theoretical possibility, but we did not know what would actually happen."

"You should have mentioned some of those possibilities before using Isis as a test subject," Zack growled.

"Did you change anything in the past?" Simon asked, in what was an obvious attempt to change the topic.

"I moved the hour hand." Isis waved a hand to the big clock. "I figured we're experimenting with time, so I changed the time on the clock." Isis' proud grin only received confused expressions on everyone's faces. She peeked up at the clock. It should have been three hours ahead. Yet it was the correct time. "I don't understand," she said. "I remember moving the hour hand ahead."

"How interesting that it is not changed now." Simon scratched his lower chin. "Is that all that changed while you were visiting yesterday?"

Isis gave it a quick thought. "Nothing major."

"But there was something besides the clock?" Doctor John asked. "Specifically, what?"

All eyes locked on Isis. "I didn't change anything else, but Elian didn't see Zack and me at the medical center doors." Isis waved a hand at the building. "This time, he saw me in the middle of the quad, and we had, well, mostly the same conversation."

Zack did a double take. "I remember the conversation with Elian by the medical center doors. I said we should have ratted him out to his mom."

"Oh." Isis clutched her forehead. She clearly remembered both conversations with Elian, but how could they both have happened? And what happened with the clock? Isis shut her eyes and rubbed her temples. This was all so confusing. A headache formed in her reanimated brain. "I don't understand. I know what I remember."

"And it does serve as proof you went through time," Doctor John said.

"Luckily, they weren't major changes," Simon chimed in. "But there were changes, which means this experiment was successful."

"What changed?" Isis asked. "The clock is still the same, and Zack remembers the first conversation, so it must have happened, right?"

"What first conversation?" Zack asked.

"The one we had yesterday with Elian before we walked into the medical center."

Zack stepped back. His eyebrows touched his hairline. "We never spoke with Elian when we entered the medical center. Not yesterday or today."

"But you just said…" Isis flung around to face Doctor John and Simon. "You both remember him saying he remembered, don't you?" The blank expressions answered her question. "That is so weird. He just said it, but none of you remember?"

"Because I didn't say anything like that," Zack replied. "At least, not that I can recall."

Isis backed away from the group and eyed them with suspicion. Did time just shift around her? If it did, it was clear no one remembered their conversation changed midway. No one, except for Isis. But, if her presence in the past altered when her conversation with Elian happened, why didn't the clock—

Isis picked her head up and looked up at the school's rooftop. The clock's hour hand was three hours ahead. She squinted her eyes. "The clock," Isis said. "It's changed…how?"

"You said you changed it," Zack replied. "While you were in the past."

"She did, and it was a clever change, indeed." Simon said. "It is certainly tangible proof that you traveled back in time."

"Isis." Zack wrapped an arm around her waist. "What's going on? What's the matter?"

"A second ago, the clock's hour hand was showing the right time like I never moved it." She poked Zack in the chest. "You said you remembered the conversation with Elian. Now you don't, and you don't even remember saying that you did. It's like, everything just changed around me."

Awkward silence filled the quad. It was clear they all believed Isis, and now they were pondering the mystery. Simon spoke up. "You changed an event in the past. Perhaps such an alteration takes time to catch up?"

"This is fascinating," Doctor John said with a hint of joy. "It is most definitely a topic for discussion, then study. But we should put it off until first thing tomorrow. It has been a long day for all of us, so I will close up my lab." The doctor strolled in the direction of the medical center. He looked to his daughter who remained a distance by several feet. Her hands were cupped behind her back. "Domina, the Vice President has been found. Thank you for your assistance. Now return home and go to bed. If your mother is still awake, tell her I will close up my lab and be there shortly."

"Yes, Papa." Domina trotted in the opposite direction of Doctor John.

"Good night, Domina," Isis called. "Thank you for

searching for me."

The girl paused mid-step like she was avoiding a pile of horse manure. She resumed her path. Isis was glad everything worked out, although the experiment brought about more questions than answers. The biggest question Isis wanted answered was why Domina wanted her to make that jump in the first place. What did she see coming? Did they somehow prevent it, or was this simply a practice run for when the danger does arrive?

There was only one way Isis could get those answers.

"Hey, Zack, I'll meet you back home." Her eyes never left Domina, who disappeared behind the school. "I need to speak with her."

Zack put his arm over Isis' shoulders. "You know you can't take her standoffish attitude personally. Who knows what's going on inside her head?"

"This is true," Simon added. "Her abilities allow her to see things in a way the rest of us cannot."

Simon's comment didn't make Isis feel any better. "You're right, Zack. I don't know what's in her head, so I need to ask. I need to ask her about everything. I want to know what she sees in me that makes her so nervous, and why she thought I was going to blind her. Mostly, I want to know why she needed me to test my connection this way."

"That young lady was a nervous Nellie even before her connection manifested." Simon waved his hands at Isis. "You may look her age, but the last two centuries have built your confidence beyond what Domina could ever pull out of herself. Maybe she finds that a bit intimidating."

Zack snorted. "She should have known you when you really were her age."

"It's not that," Isis said. "It's something else. I know it is. I have questions, and she may be the only one who has answers. She and I need to get it all out in the open. I'm sure it won't take long."

"I get it. Just tread lightly with her."

"Um, about the clock?" Simon chimed in. "It is a few hours ahead now."

"Right, I have to fix that," Isis replied.

"Have Kim do it in the morning. She could use some practice with the energy." Zack threw an angry glance toward Simon. "Meanwhile, I'll have a talk with our resident doctor. I want it known that Isis is not to be used for any more of these experiments." Zack marched toward the medical center.

"I did volunteer to do this, Zack."

He looked back. "The last twelve hours have been hell for me, Isis. For a while, I didn't think I'd see you again."

"I'm sorry," Isis said in a low voice.

"I'm just glad you're back and you're okay." Zack about faced and made a beeline for the medical center.

"I am, as well," Simon said to Isis. "We shouldn't have been so quick to push you into this. But, after Domina's warning, we thought it was necessary."

"Maybe it was. I don't know." She suddenly realized that Simon was staring at her with a huge grin. "What?"

The older vampire let out a chuckle. He brought his palms up and waved them. "Don't mind me, Madam Vice President. I'm reminiscing."

"About?"

Simon pressed a hand against his heart. "I have been keeping an eye on you and Zack since the day you came to this village two hundred years ago. Your love has never wavered. In fact, it has only grown stronger over time."

"Yeah, it has." Isis' smile stretched across her face. "Zack's the cinnamon in my cereal."

Simon's eyes opened wide. "An interesting analogy from one who does not eat."

"I guess." Isis eyed the direction Domina had disappeared. "If you'll excuse me?"

Simon waved her along. Isis had a feeling her next conversation wouldn't be so jovial.

Chapter Seven

Isis knew the path Domina always took to go home; the girl was a creature of habit. Among all homes surrounding the quad, Domina's family lived in the second row of cottages behind the dining hall. She never took a straight path. She walked through the entire line circling the quad before crossing through and changing direction.

Isis hoped to catch Domina before she made it to her cottage. This was meant to be a private conversation and wasn't for her mother's ears. Once around the dining hall, Isis jogged straight through. She stopped short once around the first cottage when she nearly ran through Domina who stood directly in Isis' way.

"Damn, girl, you almost gave me a heart attack!" The irony of Isis' statement wasn't lost on her. "What are you doing standing over here in the dark?"

"Y-you wish to speak with me." Domina's voice shook like a tuning fork. "So, so I w-wait for you."

"How did you…" Right. Clairvoyant. "I do."

"I have done something to upset you?"

Domina stood with her back straight and hands cupped against her stomach. Her head pointed down at her feet. Isis did have the power to look inside Domina's mind, or even use hypnosis to influence her actions, but if she wouldn't use her connection to interrogate Doctor John and Simon even when she knew they were hiding something, she certainly wouldn't use it against an innocent and bullied teen. Better to engage in conversation and hope for the best.

"Hey," Isis said in the softest voice she could muster. "Domina, please look at me, okay?"

Domina's head lifted. Her eyes were wide, like a child about to be scolded. Isis stepped back, hoping distance would alleviate the intimidation the girl clearly felt. To think, at one time Isis had doubts she could even intimidate a kitten.

"Can we speak openly and honestly with each other?"

"If we must, Madam Vice President, now would be a good time."

"Um, okay." Isis raised her hands and shrugged her shoulders. "Domina, I have lived in this village for two hundred years. In all that time, I've never harmed a soul. You must know that."

"I do know this. Here you have not harmed a soul."

Here? "Then why are you so afraid of me?" Isis held her arms out. "You must know I wouldn't hurt you—"

"Now is no longer the time to guess." Domina looked into Isis' eyes, or through her eyes. "We can no longer stop it. Happen soon and happened quickly. That's what it will do."

"What's going to happen? I'm not getting you..." Isis took Domina's hand and cupped it. "Please, help me understand. Is this what you were trying to tell me the other day?"

Domina's eyes went wide as if she had been confronted by a mugger. Then, before she could answer, Domina pulled back her hand, about-faced, and ran off as fast as her plump legs would allow.

"Are you kidding me?" Isis whispered through a clenched jaw.

After running two steps, Isis leaped in the air. Her body propelled above the cottages. She twirled around in mid-air and landed directly in front of Domina. The girl stopped in her tracks and stumbled backward. Domina was about to fall on her back, but Isis created a wind behind her to keep the girl on her feet.

Isis lunged forward and threw a hand on each of Domina's shoulders. Domina tried to back away, but Isis kept a firm grip. "Look at me," Isis screamed. "I need to know what you're talking about. What do you see? What is coming? *Why are you so afraid of me?*"

Domina's bottom jaw shook. "I see…I see…the other you in my dreams."

"The other me?" Isis leaned in. Her hands melted off of Domina's shoulders. "What other me?"

"The one who evolved from a simple change. The one who led the destruction of New Salem and the world. I cannot see her, but I've dreamt about her for as long as I can remember."

"Destruction of New Salem?" Isis' head tilted. "What do you mean? When does all this happen?"

"It already has, a long time ago."

God, Isis hated Domina's cryptic answers. Maybe she should have brought Zack with her; he was far better at helping the girl get to the point. Isis backed away, but this time it wasn't for Domina's comfort; it was for her own. The last thing she needed was for this nervous wreck to see her eyes turn black.

"I-I don't understand a thing you're saying, yet I feel like I need to." Isis kept her tone as calm as possible. "Please, explain to me what you saw in your dreams."

"You must understand." Domina's eyes looked to the night sky. "I see it each night in bits and pieces. I knew it was coming, but now I know my dream is here. Everything changes when it arrives."

"What changes, Domina?" Isis' fists clenched. "What is coming?"

Domina's mouth popped open. "You need to go through time again. Only one minute ahead. That should be enough. Yes, in that minute, you avoid the change."

Lightning shot through the sky. It forced Isis to look up. The gray smog that covered the village had disappeared. It was the first time in a decade Isis saw the stars. Another lightning bolt passed, then several crisscrossed from all directions. There were no clouds, just stars. Which meant no rain or thunder, either.

"What's going on?" Isis frowned. "What is this lightning?"

"I do not know about lightning, only that it is about to come!" Domina shouted with an intensity Isis had never heard from her. "You need to go now!"

"I don't understand. Go where?" Isis could barely hear her own voice over the weather overhead. "What's about to hit—"

"*Time!*"

Domina lunged and shoved Isis, knocking her to the ground. Everything blurred around her and, even though she was falling backward, her body felt as if she were being forced forward. "Domina, what did you just do to me?" she screeched, but she couldn't hear her own voice.

Isis' entire body tingled. It was the same sensation she experienced while jumping through time. Domina insisted Isis go a minute ahead. Did she somehow activate Isis' connection to propel her forward through time? This should have been beyond the ability of any mortal witch. This was especially the case with Domina who, up until now, only connected with the energy through her dreams. How did she do it? And more importantly, why?

Isis sat up and opened her eyes. Her vision cleared. Domina was no longer standing nearby. Isis cringed from the acrid aroma that came from all directions. "What is that?" she asked. It smelled like death.

A long glance around gave Isis her answer. The four buildings that surrounded the quad were no longer standing. Instead, there were piles of wood and gravel protruding from large holes where the structures once stood. The barn that covered the area between the school and the dining hall was nothing but more destruction on top of unkempt dirt.

Isis climbed to her feet. All of New Salem, as far as she could see, was destroyed. Domina insisted that she go ahead in time by a minute. But this much destruction couldn't have happened in a mere sixty seconds. She had to be much farther ahead, but how far? And where was everyone?

Isis focused her thoughts on one mind other than her own. *Zack?* She awaited a response. None came. A second attempt to connect garnered the same result. She then called out, "Zack, where are you?" Still no response.

Isis didn't think vampires could experience panic. Until now, nothing in her afterlife had ever tested that theory. She had even kept her calm when facing the nukes that brought about the end of the world. Isis had been taught panic was a physical response caused by the heartbeat speeding up. A vampire's heart didn't beat—one of the few advantages—but her brain worked just fine. Right now, Isis' brain felt like it was about to explode inside her skull. She held up her hands. They were shaking. *Zack, tell me where you are,* Isis screamed in her mind, attempting the mental connection they'd had for so long. Nothing. She tried again, saying his name softly. Still nothing. Not a single sensation of his existence.

"Zack!" Isis screamed. "Is anyone here?"

Isis focused on the energy around her mouth. "Echo," she chanted. A tickle rippled up her throat, lodging in her esophagus so when she shouted, "*Hello?*" it came out more like a frog's croak. She cleared her throat and tried again. This time, her call repeated several times. She waited, but there were no responses. No voice, no animals scurrying, not even the sound of leaves rippling in the wind. The entire village was deserted, or exterminated.

How long had it been since Domina forced Isis to travel in time? Even if New Salem was attacked by hundreds of the undead vampires, they couldn't have wiped out the entire village in the span of sixty seconds. But whether it was a minute or a hundred years, Zack was a vampire just like her, meaning he had to be somewhere. God, what happened to New Salem, and did Zack suffer the same fate as their infrastructure? Was that why she couldn't sense him anywhere?

"Get a grip, Isis," she said to herself. "You can figure this out."

A thought crossed her mind. When she first came to New Salem with her family, the Wiccan members of the village created an illusion of destruction in an attempt to turn them away. Luckily, her folks saw through it. "That's it," Isis said. A nervous smile crossed her lips. "This has to be an illusion. It's the only thing that makes sense."

Isis walked forward. She only made it three steps when her foot hit something solid. It knocked Isis off balance and face-first into the dirt. A quick peek behind her revealed that she had tripped over a mound of dirt. From the pain in her foot, she knew whatever was under there was solid, and it was real. This wasn't an illusion. The mound was crude, but she suddenly realized what it was meant for. "Oh my, it's a grave," Isis said.

She spun her head from farthest left to farthest right. The grave was one of many that filled what used to be the quad. There were a few dozen, maybe more, but none of them had tombstones. They did, however, have objects across them. Some had shirts and pants, others had rakes and hoes standing straight up. One grave had a white baseball cap, which Isis knew well. It was Elian's.

At least it meant there had to be people still alive. These graves didn't dig themselves.

Isis shut her eyes and focused on every part of the village she had lived in almost her entire existence, trying to sense the thoughts of others. "Please, let Zack be one of them," she whispered.

Isis sensed movement…footsteps were tapping against a wood floor. It had to be coming from one of the cottages. Isis wasn't alone after all. Making an exception to her rules, Isis tried to read the person's thoughts, but they were rapid and chaotic. Isis couldn't make out an identity or even a single thought flowing through that brain. She couldn't make out the voice in the person's head, but Isis was sure it belonged to someone young, possibly in the teens, and female. That ruled out Zack, but was this a friend or foe? Only one way to find out.

Behind the rubble and destruction, a few rows of the cottages still stood. Only the ones that circled the edge of the quad had been destroyed. The other presence was somewhere around there. Isis stood up and ran for the cottages, zigzagging around the graves. Hopefully, whoever this girl hanging around a destroyed village by herself was had the answers Isis so desperately needed.

Chapter Eight

Isis walked through the rubble trying her best not to disturb the layers of insects that covered the area. She couldn't help but swat at the gnats, flies, and mosquitoes that buzzed around her in every direction. They were a sign that the devastation was not a recent happening; the destruction must have been sitting like this for years.

Each cottage she walked past was dark and empty; they looked abandoned, and not by choice. Doors were wide open or off the hinges completely. Windows were smashed, with glass all over the ground. Many roofs were collapsed. Others were completely demolished, most notably, the quad's four buildings.

An even bigger sign was that the plantation around the cottages was brown instead of green. The plants were dead and had been for a while. They lay flat to the ground looking as though they'd been trampled. By what? It was as if New Salem had been completely abandoned. This had to be the future, and not the near future, but the far future. Didn't it?

Isis couldn't remember the last time there was such a hesitation in her step. She stopped in front of a cottage three rows from the quad. It had been her home for the last two centuries. Luckily it was one of the few still intact. Like with the few cottages still standing, the glass in the windows were broken or removed completely, and the door had been broken off its hinges. This couldn't have been a mindless vampire attack; there were too many signs of intent. Whoever destroyed New Salem went out of their way to hit every single building, no matter how small. Nothing in the entire village escaped unscathed. She could only hope that some of its people got away. Which made her think of Zack.

Isis and Zack agreed a long time ago that if they were ever separated, they'd meet up at their home. What were the chances he was either in there waiting for her or would be around soon? If anyone could catch Isis up on what happened to New Salem, and help her save the place, it was Zack. But how much time had they been apart, at least from his perspective? Hopefully not so long that he either despised her or moved on completely. Isis peeked through the doorway and scoped her eyes around the scene. Of course…no sign of him.

The damage to Isis' home wasn't just on the outside. The inside smelled like a barbecue took place in the middle of the living room and spun out of control. The furniture was torn apart and charred as if a blazing inferno tore through the place. It also warped what was left of the ceiling into what looked like charcoal-covered Swiss cheese.

More concerning was how nothing in the living room looked familiar. The black couch, flipped on its side with rips across the back, was made of leather. Isis and Zack never had a couch made of leather. The window shades, which lay across the carpet and scorched, had a pattern of large flowers. Isis would never have chosen that pattern; she preferred solid colors. Zack would never have agreed to flowers either. He would have found them too "girly." As much as Isis liked flowers, she would have agreed with him on not wanting them on the walls.

With each step, dread multiplied throughout Isis' body. Nothing they ever owned was in this cottage. She entered the master bedroom, the one Isis and Zack cuddled in every single night as an attempt to feel like human beings. Everything was burned and destroyed as well…except for a framed painting, which still hung six inches above the bed frame. It was untouched by the fire. The painting was of a couple, both with gray hair and wrinkled skin. The man, with hair only on the sides of his head, was seated on the black leather couch. The woman was also in a sitting position, but her body floated a few inches above the cushion.

"Am I in the wrong cottage?" Isis asked herself. But even if that were the case, she still should have recognized the couple. Isis knew the faces of everyone who lived in New Salem, at least up until the present. How far in the future did she end up? Did she and Zack switch cottages at some point? Or did they move away from New Salem altogether? Damn. If they did leave, then Zack could be anywhere in the entire world.

Isis again closed her eyes and focused on him. She knew how to connect to his mind no matter where he may have been. Dammit, still no luck. But connecting with his mind wasn't her only option for finding him. Time for Plan B. Use the energy to locate him. "Find Zack," Isis mumbled. "Find Zack, wherever he is."

Moments passed. It was another fruitless endeavor. Zack wasn't in a neighboring land, or anywhere else as far as Isis' senses told her. It could have been nerves interfering with the connection. The Wiccan energy was hard to control when emotions were running high, especially when those emotions were ripe with anxiety. They certainly were right now. God, he had to be alive.

She needed to stay focused, stop thinking the worst. If the village was attacked—and from what Isis had seen, that was the case—maybe some of the residents escaped. Zack could have been among them. In fact, as president, it was likely he led the escape from New Salem. He could be surrounded by witches who were hiding their location. Yes, better to believe Zack was among the escapees rather than underneath one of those graves.

Time to refocus. She couldn't stand around waiting for him or worrying that he was no longer among the living. Besides, even though this cottage was where Isis lived, she felt as if she were trespassing in someone else's home. She would certainly try to locate Zack later, but right now, it was best she focused on the only lead she did have. It was time to find the girl. From the erratic thoughts which Isis could barely make out, she had to be scared, maybe even hurt, or trapped. Yet Isis couldn't hear a heartbeat or even heavy breathing. She called to the energy for teleportation. The bedroom blurred, replaced by the outside of the cottage.

"Where are you?" Isis asked, concentrating on the girl's presence, whose emotions were all over the place. Within seconds, she sensed anger, depression, and sorrow, yet she couldn't decipher her identity. Who was this?

Another cottage about a half mile away was still intact. Isis teleported there; it was the only one she had seen that still had a door on its hinges. This was Doctor

John and his family's place. Isis' vampiric senses picked up movement on the inside. More powerful than that though…a terrible stench like sweaty armpits that hadn't seen soap in years. It meant the girl was in there. Did she hear Isis calling for Zack? If so, why wouldn't she come out and see who entered this desolate village? So bizarre.

It was time to let her know that she wasn't alone and find out what happened to New Salem. At the very least, she hoped the girl could tell her the year. If this was the future, and Isis was pretty sure it was, she could try to return to her own time and then prevent this disaster from ever happening. That was the reason for the time travel experiment in the first place. Isis didn't think she'd need to implement that plan so soon, but right now, disaster was exactly what New Salem had suffered.

Normally, Isis never entered a home without permission. During her first year under his tutelage, Simon explained that it was an old superstition that vampires needed a formal invitation. There was no real reason for it, but he believed it was out of ancient courtesy. Whatever the reason, Isis always followed that protocol. However, under certain circumstances, she made an exception.

She grabbed the doorknob and turned it. The door was unlocked. Isis walked in. The odor was even worse inside. It was as if the room was filled with rotten eggs or milk that had been left out for years. The living room was bare except for one gray swivel office chair on wheels. Isis was right about the girl's age. That was a teen sitting in the chair facing the wall. She wore a thin green short-sleeved blouse that was soaked with sweat.

"Yes, you came back," the girl called out. "It's okay. I did what I must, and I am now ready to die. End my existence. Let me join my family and villagers."

The girl's voice was angry and a bit hoarse. Her black hair was tied in dreadlocks and hung down to her waist. Even from behind, Isis recognized her immediately. It was the last person she expected to see, but maybe she should have been the first.

"Domina?"

Chapter Nine

"Domina, I knew that was you." But seeing her only added to Isis' confusion. She wasn't older; she still looked around sixteen. That meant this wasn't the far future. It wasn't even a near future. As impossible as it sounded, this was either the same year or close to it.

The girl rotated her chair to face Isis. "You speak. This is the first moment I know you could."

Isis' mouth hung open. Not from the mud that covered Domina's hands, but from the two dark holes where her eyes were supposed to be. It looked like her eyeballs had been dug out of her skull. "My God, what happened to you?" Isis shrieked.

Domina's head tipped to the left. She stood from her seat and staggered across the room until Isis grabbed her by the arms. "Domina, what happened here? What's going on?"

"You…you, so different." Domina placed a hand on Isis' face. "You are same, yet you are not."

Isis clutched Domina's wrist and pulled down her hand. "I don't understand what you're talking about. Domina, please tell me what's going on. Who took your eyes? What happened to New Salem?"

"New Salem was bad!" Domina let out a loud sob, then paced back and forth along the floor. "The queen discovers us. She say we join. But our witches, they say we do not. They say Queen had the world, no need for us. Queen disagreed."

"Queen?" Isis wiped mud left from Domina's hands off her face. "What queen?"

"We put big shield over the village, one even she could not penetrate. But then, a mistake was made."

Isis placed a hand against Domina's chest, stopping her in mid-pace. "I don't know what you're talking about. Who is the queen?"

Domina sucked in her lips. "She who has always been queen, of course. Queen Valeria."

Isis gasped. "Valeria?" A pain the size of a tennis ball shot through her chest. "How…how long has she been…?"

"Queen?" Domina responded. "Don't know. Generations before my birth."

Isis wanted to throw up. Of course, as a vampire she couldn't puke, which meant the sensation that had come over her body wasn't a physical illness. Either way, she hadn't felt this ill in two centuries. Valeria was supposed to be somewhere in space, floating far away from Earth. By now, she should have been beyond the solar system and on the other side of the galaxy. But she's back, and she's queen? How was that even possible?

"This is a nightmare," Isis cried out.

"It always was." Domina resumed her back and forth pacing.

"Valeria is queen, and she did all of this to New Salem?"

Domina stopped short just inches from the wall. She placed her muddy hands against the sides of her head and pressed her forehead against the wall. "Never before, never now."

"Meaning what?"

"Queen Valeria, she would not travel all the way here. The royal apprentice. It is she who travels. It is she who always does the queen's bidding."

"Who is…?" Isis dropped her gaze to the floor. "It's me, isn't it? I'm the royal apprentice."

"Of course, you are not," Domina said, still facing the wall. "I sense your soul. I realize now, you are not her. But she is most definitely you." Apparently, this Domina was just as puzzling as the one from Isis' reality.

"Domina," Isis said. "You said there was a shield. How did I…the other me…how did she get through?"

Domina slapped her hands against the top of her head. She let out a loud moan. "It shouldn't have happened," she screamed. "The village, we were safe! The apprentice, she could not get through. The world is huge. Eventually, she would move on."

Domina's jaw shook like it was in the middle of an earthquake. That's when Isis realized, "You let her in, didn't you?"

"I sensed a good soul," she answered. "But I did not sense her. I sensed you, protector of our village."

"You sensed me?"

"Yes." Domina slid down to her knees. "I was mistaken. I beg her. I say to her, please, do not make me watch everyone I know die. So, as her witch army destroy it all, the apprentice, she takes my eyes. When they finally leave, I am all that is here."

"And you've been burying the bodies ever since." Isis leaned in and took a good look at Domina's face. Even if the girl could overcome her blindness by feeling around, all of New Salem's plants and crops were destroyed. The animals were gone. She still had the same body weight as the Domina Isis had always known. The question knocking around her brain slipped off her tongue. "Domina, how have you survived all this time? What are you eating?"

"Survive? Is that what I did?" Domina let out a sad laugh. The smile faded from her face as quickly as it appeared. "I sense the animals throughout the forest. Some are ours. Others, they are native to the swamp. I grab them, I bite them, I drink their blood, and then I face another day."

Isis widened her eyes. There were no immediate signs—Domina's skin hadn't faded—but it wouldn't have, at least not yet. "Domina…are you a vampire?"

"You…no, *she* took my eyes." Her head popped up. Her face pointed to the ceiling. "The apprentice, she kill me. I was so happy to suck in my last breath. But then she wake me. She give me blood…she put it in my hand and raise it to my mouth. It was so I'd know how to feed."

"How long ago did all this happen?"

"Thirty-six months and a day, I think." With her right thumb, Domina tapped each finger on her left hand. She did this while mumbling to herself. "I could be off, maybe by a week? Perhaps two. But I know at least that amount of calendar, it went by."

Isis put a hand across her mouth. "And you've been here burying the bodies all this time?"

"Early one time, I find a blade. I feel it while crawling around the floor. I slit my throat, but it did not take." Domina covered her face with one hand. "I try to deprive myself of blood, but the craving, it was too much to resist. So, I bury bodies instead. It fill my time and satisfy the fate I deserve for leading death to our village."

Isis pulled Domina's hand off her face and squeezed it. This poor girl. There was only one reason the Isis of this reality would turn Domina and then show her how to survive. It was Domina who opened New Salem to her, which led to mass destruction. Now, for whatever insane and demented reason, the royal apprentice—the other Isis—wanted Domina to live with it. She wanted her to suffer for all of eternity, blind and guilt-ridden. It was a fate worse than death, an eternity of torture.

The thought of the fate this other version of herself created for Domina made Isis cringe. Was she truly capable of such soulless cruelty? The answer to that question surrounded her all throughout what remained of New Salem. She destroyed the place without a shred of mercy.

"Oh God," Isis sobbed. "I'm so sorr—"

Domina leaped back to her feet. She lunged, took two handfuls of Isis' shirt, and slammed her against the wall. It was an aggression Isis had never seen out of Domina, which is why it caught her completely by surprise. She had no idea the girl was so strong.

"I knew hope would come. I see you in my dream back when I still sleep. It was what I held onto, that you would arrive before her return." Domina leaned in, touching her nose against Isis'. "You can fix this!" Wet dirt smacked Isis in the face. "Go back, change it all, make things so it never happened."

"Go back," Isis repeated. "To where?"

"Where it all began." Domina's voice was barely above a whisper. She released her grip of Isis' shirt.

Domina's head and shoulders slumped, leaving no trace of that strong and aggressive girl. "The moment that opened the path to her queendom."

"When was that moment?" Isis whispered back. "What do I have to do?"

Domina shrugged, which didn't help. She clearly had no idea what event Valeria changed. She saw the future, not the past, and she certainly didn't live through hundreds of years of history. But Isis did. It suddenly hit her.

"I know the moment I have to change," Isis said. Her voice rose with enthusiasm. "It was after my family and I battled her here in New Salem. I sent Valeria into space, but I made a mistake. I left too early. But, if I fix it, make sure the past me succeeds, then she can never go back in time. That's it, right?"

Isis widened her eyes with excitement. They drooped when she realized that Domina's sad expression did not change.

"You were never here," Domina said.

"Sure, I was," Isis exclaimed. "I beat Valeria right in the middle of the quad. With my family. And Zack, he tricked Valeria and trapped her in the crystals!"

"Zack." Domina shook her head. "I do not know that name."

"Are you sure? It would have been long before you were born."

"I am sure," Domina answered. "I study names on graves before I lose my eyes. I pay close attention in our history class before village destroyed. No big battle in New Salem. No one here named Zack, ever, or you."

Damn. Isis was hoping for a quick path to make things right. But that wasn't happening. She traveled through time twice. She was sure she could use the energy to make it happen again. Maybe this time, with enough focus, she could even aim it at a specific place and time. But that didn't help if she didn't know when or where to go. But she did know the one person who would. It was a confrontation Isis had thought about for two hundred years. Each time, it made her body shiver. She hated the idea that even with all her experience, something, or someone, could still frighten her, especially one who she thought was long gone. To succeed, she'd have to put aside that fear.

"I have to face Valeria," Isis said.

"I see no other way," Domina responded. "It is where your journey begins."

"I've never faced her alone."

"There is always a first time."

Isis shut her eyes. "I…I don't know if I can."

"Then this will be your reality as much as my own."

Isis peeked out the open doorway, at the ruins that were once New Salem. This version of Domina held herself responsible for the destruction. The guilt was evident on her face. But Isis knew it was all her own fault, on many levels. This entire reality existed because Isis was careless. It was for only a moment two centuries ago, but that moment was all it took to change everything. The responsibility for the destruction, and of fixing this, was all on her.

"Domina," Isis said, "where is Valeria?"

"Where she has always been." Domina's head shook. "At the heart of your roots."

"You mean Las Vegas?" Of course, she did. Isis should have figured that out on her own. Where else would Valeria want to rule than from the home of the witches who defeated her?

Domina made her way across the room with her hands straight out. She stopped once her fingers hit the chair. She spun it around so she would once again face the wall, then sat. “I know we would have this conversation,” Domina shouted. “It was the last dream I have before I can no longer sleep.”

“What are you going to do?” Isis asked.

“I will wait for you to replace time,” Domina answered. “I wait to no longer exist.”

The last thing Isis wanted to do was leave Domina behind. She was blind, alone, and surrounded by death and destruction. But without her sight, she’d be more of a hindrance than help in a confrontation with Valeria. Although this was a personal hell for Domina, it was still better that she stayed.

Isis focused on the energy around her. “Las Vegas,” she chanted. “Take me to Las Vegas.” A picture formed in her mind of The Sapphire, the resort she and her family called home before coming to New Salem. It was in the heart of the strip and the best place to start. She quickly formed a two-step plan. Step one was to find Valeria. She had no idea what the next step would be, although it had something to do with getting the old Wiccan vampire to spill.

“Great success, please,” Domina shouted as everything around Isis blurred, then faded.

Chapter Ten

Isis broke the first rule she ever learned about using the energy to teleport…she let her mind wander. She couldn't help it, the idea that Valeria was back in her life made it impossible to focus on a single thought. No one ever caused more stress for Isis than Valeria. Running from a foster family that wanted to set her on fire at the age of nine paled in comparison. At least her foster parents weren't corrupt witches, or four-hundred-year-old vampires. Valeria laid claim to both.

Two centuries had passed since Isis sent Valeria hurtling through outer space—or so she thought. The world should have been safe from Valeria forever. She never thought the old witch could survive, especially separated from the Earth's energy. Damn. Isis thought she had stayed up there long enough to make sure Valeria was gone. Apparently, she found a way to escape into the past and change history. Now Isis would have to face her again, and this time she'd have to do it alone. Her folks and Sacha were long dead, as was every single witch from New Salem including her recent trainees.

The twins, Kim, even Elian…she could really use them for backup against a powerful witch like Valeria. Then there was Zack; she had no idea what happened to him in this new timeline. Isis knew that whatever Valeria changed, it had to do with him. That had to be why she couldn't find him. Time to suck in her gut and find out.

Everything around Isis unblurred, meaning she had succeeded in teleporting. She expected to be surrounded by large skyscraper hotels. Or, if this reality suffered the same apocalyptic war, perhaps Vegas would be miles of rubble. At the very least, Isis expected to be standing on concrete. She couldn't have been more wrong.

The ground was covered in grass for as far as her enhanced vision could see. There were no skyscraper hotels, no streets or neon signs, not even a lamppost anywhere in what should have been the Vegas strip. Isis cupped a hand over her forehead like a visor. The sun was bright and strong without any buildings to block the rays. A shadow to her left forced Isis to spin 180 degrees. That's when she realized there was one tall building. It was at least thirty floors high, complete with a drawbridge and surrounded by a moat.

"I told you to take me to Vegas, but this can't be Vegas," Isis said to the Earth's energy. It had been a long time since her last visit, but she was sure there were no moats on the strip.

Isis ran toward the castle. God, the structure was ripe of ego. It had to be Valeria's home. In this reality, she set herself up as queen, so of course she'd have a castle with a moat. Good chance there was a conjured dragon under all that green slush around the castle.

Isis crept closer. It was unlike any building of that size she had ever seen, but the rooftop stood out to her. As a child, Isis rarely wandered too far from her home, The Sapphire Resort. It was the first place in her entire life where she felt safe and wanted. When she finally started exploring the strip, Isis always stayed close enough to see The Sapphire's top floor. It was recognizable even from a few blocks away because, unlike all the other hotels, the top floor stretched out beyond the rest of the building. Just like the top floor of this castle.

"That's the Sapphire," Isis mumbled. Valeria turned The Witches of Vegas' old home into her palace and wiped out everything else around it.

Three figures materialized in Isis' path. Three teens—two Caucasian males and one Asian female—wore matching camouflage uniforms. Their heads were shaved clean. The one in the middle was the tallest by several inches. He had a boyish face but the physique of a professional wrestler. The black leather leash in his hands had a metal collar hanging at the end. Isis raised her eyebrows, then moved a step back.

"Apprentice," the tall soldier said in a high-pitched squeaky voice that didn't match his impressive body type. "Her Majesty demands your presence immediately."

"Um, how about no?" Isis answered.

The three witches in uniform paused. The girl glimpsed over at the tall, muscular one. "What? All this time, she can speak?" Isis knew that voice. Was that Kim? "And look at her face. It's different, clear."

Isis' eyes widened. This was definitely Kim, but it was not the one Isis watched grow up in New Salem. She was harder, like someone who had spent a lifetime in training. This Kim was a soldier through and through. She wasn't the type who would defend Elian for breaking concentration while acting like a fool after a battle.

"Just another illusion." The big guy, clearly the leader of the group, tightened both hands around the leash. "What matters is the queen demands her presence, so we bring her in."

Kim and the smaller boy disappeared, then reappeared on either side of Isis. They each grabbed an arm. "Kim, what are you doing?" Isis whispered. "Why are you here?"

"Where else would I be?" she responded. "This is where *you* brought me."

"Enough talk!" the leader shouted. "Apprentice, we have our orders. Please do not make this difficult."

Isis sensed the powerful connection in each of them, but they didn't have her experience with the energy. She focused on an idea, one that would help her escape. "Force!" Isis shouted. Energy shot from three sides of her. It slammed her would-be captors against the ground. Isis' instincts told her to check on Kim and make sure she was okay. But this wasn't the Kim she and Zack found, then watched a loving New Salem family raise within that close and caring community. This version of Kim was found only by Isis and then placed into Queen Valeria's servitude.

Although Isis' force blast took out two of the guards, the big one stayed on his feet. He lunged and snatched Isis under her chin.

"Stand down, Apprentice," he roared. "You know there's no choice. It is her majesty's orders."

Isis focused on the end of the leash hanging from his other hand. It wrapped around the big man's wrist. She sent the metal collar backward. It yanked its owner with it, dragging him along the ground.

Time to run, although there was nowhere to hide,

not without any other structures in sight except for that huge castle. Still, Isis needed to collect herself before storming it and confronting Valeria. Her plan came to a halt when four more witches, dressed in the same camouflage, appeared in front of her, blocking every possible direction forward. Like the first three, they were also in their teenage years. The energy's connection must have skipped a generation in this reality as well.

Isis was ready to attack until one of the new guards made her pause. Unlike the others, his head wasn't clean-shaven. It was more of a red-headed buzzcut. It matched the red in his cheeks. He stared down Isis through two rage-filled eyes. It was Cameron. Apparently, Domina wasn't the only one in New Salem the other Isis spared.

The initial three witches were back on their feet and standing behind her. Rage filled their tensed and sweat-covered brows. Isis couldn't run. She couldn't take to the air either since they all had the power to shoot her down. None of them had guns, but they didn't need them, not with the Earth's energy as their weapon. Teleportation was an option, but to where? This was a Las Vegas Isis didn't know at all.

"I ask of you again, Apprentice," the leader shouted. "Please comply with the queen's orders."

The seven Wiccan soldiers approached her from all directions. There was nowhere to go…except down. While in Vegas, Isis learned about the underground tunnel system where many of Vegas' homeless resided. It was an unexplored world, and one she had never seen. Well, better late than never.

"Phase and drop," Isis chanted. Her body floated

through the ground while the faces of the witches looked on, baffled by her actions.

The bright sunlight faded and then disappeared. Isis landed on her feet. The smell of grass was replaced by a combination of sulfur and what had to be human waste. She held her right hand in front of her face. "Light," she said. Her hand lit up, which allowed her to see. The world underground was exactly what she imagined it would look like. The dark tunnel had several narrow corridors on all sides, and each had multiple paths of their own. It was a huge maze down here, easy to get lost. Did Valeria know about it after all this time as queen? She had to, meaning Isis wasn't out of danger yet; she only earned herself a reprieve.

A naked person lay across the floor in front of her. It was a boy in his teens with eyes open wide as if he had seen a ghost. His skin was pale like every drop of blood was sucked from his insides. The bite mark in his neck, which exposed his carotid artery, confirmed Isis' suspicions. This boy, who couldn't be older than fifteen, was another vampire's meal. The blood all around him meant little care was taken in the consumption.

The echo of a footstep brought her alert. "Is someone there?" Isis called out, which was probably a mistake since she was, for all intents and purposes, on the run from local authority. Of course, that's assuming those soldiers above ground were "local authority."

A girl slithered out from around the closest corridor. For Isis, it was like looking into a mirror, but a dark and demented one. It was her face and her body, but the eyes were blank, empty of emotion. Her hair was shorter and tied into braids. The skin on her face was faded from two hundred years of aging. At least they had that in common.

The doppelganger wore a black tank-top which exposed the dark red markings covering her arms from her wrists to the shoulders. They made her limbs look like a checkerboard. They also matched the streak that crossed her left cheek and chin. At first, Isis took it for tattoos, but on closer inspection, she realized the skin was distorted by severe burn scars. They probably covered her entire body. This girl had been set on fire, and since the damage was all still there, it happened prior to being turned into a vampire.

"Oh God, you're me, aren't you?" Isis asked in disbelief.

For a moment, the two stared at one another puzzled by what they saw. Then the other Isis threw out her arms. A wind snatched Isis and slammed her against the wall. The back of her head bounced, sending a stinging pain down her spine. Isis tumbled face-first onto the floor. She clutched the back of her head. Isis wanted to fight, but this wasn't a mindless vampire or one of those witches above ground. This was herself, but a version who suffered the torture Valeria had in mind for her two hundred years ago.

Isis picked her head up to find the doppelganger kneeling in front of her. The other Isis said one word. "Sleep." Her voice was hoarse.

Isis' eyelids grew heavy, like weights tied to her lashes. She couldn't remember the last time she slept. But now there was no choice.

Chapter Eleven

Isis had forgotten what it was like to be unconscious, or how hard it was to wake up. Grogginess was something she hadn't experienced in two centuries. Same with the sand inside her eyelids. It was a weird sensation, which was coupled with waking up on a bed she didn't recognize. It didn't even have a mattress, just a wooden board.

"Where…where am I?" Isis groaned. She had a strong hunch the answer wouldn't bring her any relief.

Isis grabbed the back of her head where she felt a lump that should have healed. After the other Isis slammed her into the wall, she must've used a sleep spell. Still, as a vampire, even unconscious her body should have healed. Not that she'd ever known a vampire who had been forced to sleep, so maybe that wasn't the case.

How long had Isis been out of it, anyway? It had to be less than twenty-four hours since the last time she drank blood. Any longer and it would have been a struggle for her to move. She'd lose feeling in her body, and soon she'd expire.

Isis stood from the bed and rubbed her eyes, trying to pull herself out of the daze that enveloped her body. No doubt she'd need her faculties intact to handle whatever came next. First step was figuring out where she ended up during her forced slumber.

Metal bars faced Isis six feet from the bed, which meant she was in a cell. Isis sat up, realizing her neck felt heavy. She pressed her hand against the metal wrapped tightly around her throat. Isis rubbed a hand along the collar. It was like the one Valeria's witches wanted to use before taking her in…or maybe it was the exact one. A padlock in the front just under her chin clinked when she moved. A quick yank confirmed it was thick and not coming off easily.

An incredibly tall man in a black robe and long white hair marched past the cell. He had a thin black staff in his hands. It was an unusual outfit for a prison guard. "Hey," Isis called out to him. The guy glared Isis' way. He had a young and clean-shaven face. He had to be somewhere around twenty years of age. That made his height and girth even more impressive, just like the huge soldier outside. That couldn't have been coincidence. Perhaps they were being enhanced by Valeria?

"Where am I?" Isis asked him.

"*Quiet,*" the young guard snapped. He stopped in front of the cell and gave Isis a stink eye. "The queen will summon you when she is ready."

"I just want to know where I am—"

"I am not to engage you in conversation." The guard held up the black staff. "If you speak to me again, I will be forced to enter your cell and use this. You wait until Queen Valeria requests your presence."

"What is that?" Isis asked.

The guard jabbed the end of the staff against the bars. Blue sparks fired in all directions. Isis backpedaled. "You just keep your mouth shut and wait until you're summoned," the guard shouted.

Isis responded with a nod, but she needed a heads-up as to what was going on. So much for her principles. Isis focused on the man's thoughts. Nothing popped into her head. Her connection was cut off. It had to be the collar, although she had no idea what sort of technology could cut a witch's connection to the energy. Was it somehow lined with enchanted crystals?

Isis rubbed a finger along the bottom of the padlock. There was a keyhole, which was perfect. Hanging around a magician for as long as she and Zack were together had its advantages. He liked teaching her the tricks of the trade. A few of those lessons were on how to use lockpicks. For her one hundredth birthday, Zack gave her a pair of lockpicks that he made from two thin pieces of metal. He requested that she always keep them in her back pants pocket just in case. "Better to have them and not need them than need them and not have them," he said to Isis numerous times. Apparently, he was more clairvoyant than he realized.

Once the guard resumed his stroll, Isis reached into her back pocket. Her head popped up, and her hand pulled away at the sound of a deep, familiar voice. "Now you wish to have conversation. How interesting." The voice was full of fury.

Isis walked up to the bars of her cell. Across the thin hallway, a man glared back from the opposite cell. He was dark skinned except for the right side of his face, which was discolored with one eye swelled shut. His hair was long and gray.

"Doctor John?" Isis' eyes opened wide at the sight of him.

"So, you *do* know my name," he scoffed. "Did you know it when I begged you to spare my people while you held my daughter by the throat? You stared right through me while your Wiccan soldiers brought our buildings down to the ground!"

"I'm not who you think I am," Isis said. "I'm not your enemy."

"I know exactly what you are, Apprentice," Doctor John responded. "You are the one who led an assault that destroyed my village and killed every man, woman, and child in New Salem! You are, in every way, my worst enemy."

Isis looked away. What Doctor John described may not have been her doing, but it was a version of her that committed these atrocities. Sure, it was a sick and twisted version, and she couldn't imagine herself becoming the type who would cause so much death and destruction no matter what horrific torture Valeria put her through. But she'd seen it with her own eyes. Not to mention what had been done to poor Domina.

"Look at you now," Doctor John said with disdain. "For all your loyalty and longevity to your master, here you are, collared and imprisoned like every other witch that ever dared stand up to the queen's cruelty. You are not so different than the rest of us. Let me assure you, life in this dungeon is brutal."

The guard smacked his staff against the bars of Doctor John's cell. Sparks flew. The doctor dropped to the floor. "Enough talk!" The guard's voice echoed throughout the hallway. He glared at Isis. "The queen is ready for you now."

"Oh, great." Isis bit her lower lip. "Thanks."

"You would do well to curb that sort of attitude with her," the guard snarled. "You know well enough her tolerance for insolence is limited."

The guard went out of focus, as did everything around her. Isis was teleporting, but it wasn't her doing. She shut her eyes tight, then reopened them. As expected, she was no longer in her cell. She was now in the middle of what looked like the resort's huge rectangular ballroom circled by picture windows instead of walls. There were no doors, just large open entrances on all sides. Isis expected to be surrounded by guards. To her surprise, there was only one. Cameron. He held one of those long black sticks that shot sparks at the end.

Isis remembered those picture windows with the various shades; they hadn't changed. The windows once surrounded The Sapphire Resort's casino. Isis never liked walking through the noisy and smoke-filled casino, but it was the heart of the hotel's ground floor, which made it unavoidable. She had a habit of walking briskly and staring at the black and white tiled floor whenever she passed.

The room now lacked the gaming tables, the slot machines, and the smoke. But the ceiling's height and the tiled floor hadn't changed. Now, the only thing in the room was that huge throne a few feet behind the guard.

"Cameron, what are you doing?" Isis whispered. "Why are you here?"

"Is that supposed to be a joke?" Cameron responded. "On your knees! You are about to be addressed by her majesty, Queen Valeria."

When Isis didn't drop, Cameron pointed the end of his staff at her. His scrunched, dimply forehead sent a clear message that he intended to use it. With the collar around her neck, Isis was left defenseless against the boy she once trained and recommended as field commander over his fellow students. Plus, Cameron wasn't wearing a collar, which meant his connection was well intact. With little choice, Isis dropped to one knee.

"After what you did to us," Cameron leaned in and whispered in Isis' ear, "I hope you get what you deserve." He stood at attention and faced the throne. "Your Majesty, your audience is here as you ordered."

"Excellent."

The woman on the throne stared down at Isis with a wicked grin across her face. Her fingers were well manicured with green polish and covered in diamond rings. The dress she wore was made from lavender silk. Her face was covered in heavy make-up, and her hair glowed as it hung behind her head. It was clear this woman took advantage of her royalty. The queen smiled, revealing corroded teeth.

"Hello, Valeria," Isis said.

"It is Queen Valeria," she responded. "And I've been anticipating your arrival for a long time, Isis Flores Rivera."

Chapter Twelve

"You were expecting me?" Isis had the crazy notion that she could catch Valeria by surprise and have an advantage in the event of a confrontation. But instead, it was she who was caught by surprise and was at a clear disadvantage.

The queen stood from her throne. She disappeared, then just as quickly, reappeared in front of Isis. The surprise knocked Isis off her one knee and onto her back like a turtle. Valeria cackled.

"Soldier, you are dismissed," she said, her powerful eyes never leaving Isis.

"Your majesty," Cameron said with a slight quiver in his voice. "If I may, I've displayed my loyalty to your rule. May I see my sister?"

Valeria's eyes rolled. "Your sister tried to form a rebellion. She does not get visitors. But fret not, young witch. Once her reeducation is complete, she will join you as a fellow member of the royal guard. Now, I will have time alone with my guest." Isis didn't even want to think about what horrors Valeria referred to as "reeducation."

"Your majesty, please—"

Valeria's angry glare snapped his way. "*Begone!*"

Cameron bowed, then marched out of the ballroom, down one of the long hallways. Isis recalled that at one time it led to the main lobby. She couldn't imagine what that area had warped into.

Queen Valeria stood over Isis staring into her eyes while tapping her heel against the floor. "You do not strike me as much of a threat," she stated. "You certainly did not benefit from the training my own apprentice received."

"H-how do you know about me?" Isis asked.

Valeria snatched a lock of Isis' hair, examined it, then let it drop from her hand. "The other me left a rather detailed letter where I would find it shortly after I escaped The Other World."

"How did she know—"

Another cackle echoed throughout the throne room. "That Valeria had long ago done exactly as I had, so she knew where I would go to collect myself. That is where her message awaited my arrival."

Isis sat up and leaned her head forward with interest as Valeria went on. "It told me all about you, Luther's coven, and the boy who ruined all her plans." Valeria looked up toward the ceiling. "I do not recall his name as there was no reason to commit it to memory. The other version of myself removed the boy from future events. Leaving me that letter was her last act before fading from this new reality she created."

"What did she do to remove him?" Isis asked. Valeria scoffed. It was worth a try, but the queen didn't bite.

"The letter explained how misguided you and your fellow witches were toward her mission, thanks to Luther's influence, of course. That's why I made sure to end his continued existence before sending your coven to that island." Valeria stretched out her arms. "She made sure I could create this utopia without interference. Yet I know firsthand that you are a survivor. I am sure you bear the spirit of my apprentice. I suspected you would somehow find your way from that world into mine. I just didn't think it would take two hundred years."

Before Isis became a vampire, she suffered horrible dreams. Almost all were based around Valeria. Each night, her mind raced through all the scenarios where they would lose and the consequences of Valeria succeeding. But this was even worse than her darkest nightmares. Valeria went back in time and created a reality where she did win. To the victor went the spoils. In this case, it was the entire world, which she recreated in her own image. Unfortunately, this wasn't a dream; this was a frightening reality.

"You call this place a utopia?" Isis exclaimed. "You've destroyed everything! You killed so many, human and witch."

"Foolish vampire!" Valeria stamped her foot. The entire floor shook. "There is nary a witch alive who does not live in luxury, as it should have been since the beginning of time. Throughout all the world, so long as they serve me when called upon, they sleep in comfortable homes and on comfortable beds. Their connections to the power assure they eat and live well."

"And for those who don't serve you?" Isis heard the venom in her voice. From Valeria's narrowed eyes, she caught it as well.

"There are so few of those left," Valeria said. "Witches who were foolish enough to stand against me and against their kind's best interests did not deserve to live."

"What about people without a connection?" Isis

asked. "How are their homes in your utopia?"

Valeria's eyes rolled. "Mother Earth has deemed them a lesser species, and therefore they do not deserve homes. Each morning, witches gather the mortals from the streets and give them assignments for the day. They build, they clean, they put their all into any tasks given to them by their superiors. If their production is satisfactory, they eat. If it is not, they die. This system has worked to benefit the Wiccan population of Earth for a long time now. Why would any witch want it changed?"

"There will always be those who will rally against you, both witch and non," Isis shouted in an act of defiance.

Valeria's eyes went dark. Two sharp fangs protruded from her mouth. Then, she smiled. Apparently, she was still crazy even in this new reality.

"There have been many revolutions by both witches and the inferior mortals over time," Valeria said. "I encourage them. Eradicating the attempts serves as a message to others, and they prevent me from growing bored of absolute authority."

Valeria raised a hand. Isis' body lifted off the floor, hovered in the air, then dropped. Isis landed on her feet, but the impact almost knocked her over.

"I think a demonstration of how this world works is in order, my new guest." Valeria looked up at the golden chandelier. Her eyes let out a yellow glow. "Apprentice, go to the dungeon, retrieve the New Salem president, and bring him to my throne room immediately."

"What are you doing?" Isis asked. She received no answer.

Valeria was right. Any mutiny against her reign, even from witches, was only good for a distraction with no hope for success. From what Isis gathered, Cindi had made an attempt, but it failed as miserably as expected. No one had Valeria's experience controlling the energy, not unless there was another immortal witch somewhere out there. That did describe Isis but, even then, she was giving up centuries of experience. She certainly couldn't stand up to her with the collar around her neck. Without the connection, Isis was as useless as a bee's sting against a giant flyswatter.

She did have the lockpick in her back pocket. With it, she could unlock and remove the collar within seconds. But if Valeria caught her reaching for it, all hope would be lost, and not just for herself. She'd have to wait for her opportunity.

The area behind Valeria's right side blurred. A moment later it cleared, and the other Isis stood in its place. Her skin was clear and burn-free. For Isis, it was now truly like looking in a mirror, except for the frown on her face. The other Isis had a tight grip of Doctor John's right wrist behind his back. Even though he towered over her, the apprentice yanked the doctor's arm downward, forcing him onto his knees. He looked up at Isis with eyes and mouth wide as grapefruits. "There are two of you?" he screeched.

"Silence!" Valeria strolled past Doctor John and stepped in front of the apprentice. Her eyes narrowed as she peered down at her. The apprentice looked up with only the slightest hint of defiance. "As I've told you countless times, my apprentice, vanity is unbecoming. Remove the illusion."

The apprentice dropped her head away from

Valeria's gaze. She shut her eyes and concentrated. The burns across her face and arms returned. Valeria threw a sly grin at Isis. She approached Doctor John with clenched fists. "Now, to address the powerless mortal who would rule over witches."

The doctor rose to his feet. "Unlike you, I was an elected official, chosen by my people to lead. All people, with and without the connection, living in harmony. That is what we had within our borders, at least until your people murdered us all—"

"You annoy me." Valeria raised a hand. In response, Doctor John's body lifted inches from the ground. His feet dangled while his hands reached for his throat as if something was clamped around it.

"I am giving you one chance to spare your own life by telling me what I wish to know," Valeria roared. "How did the witches of your village hide your existence from me for almost two centuries? Did it have to do with the shield your village ancestors conjured, or was it something more?"

Isis wanted to help the man she knew from the moment he was born and throughout his entire life…well, another life…but there was nothing she could do. She couldn't go for the lockpick. Valeria's back may have been to Isis, but one pair of eyes stayed on her. The apprentice's curious gaze never wavered. She had to wait for the right moment. Unfortunately, Doctor John didn't have that sort of time.

The doctor-turned-village-president dropped his arms against his sides, then straightened his back. He tried to look brave, and not in pain, but the half-open eyelids and gritted teeth were dead giveaways. Still, it was bravery Isis had never seen out of her reality's

Doctor John. Of course, New Salem lived in peace since before he was born, so this trait was never tested. He must have had it in him all along.

Doctor John closed his eyes in what was a blatant act of defiance. "We have shared the spell that hid us from you with others. As well, our plans to topple you." He sounded gruff from the pressure Valeria had on his throat. "Surely, you realize, no matter how you torture me, I will share with you absolutely nothing."

Valeria nodded. "I do." She held a hand in front of her face and twisted it. "*Collum confractus!*"

Doctor John's head swung right. Isis heard the snap. "No!" she screamed. "Why? There was no need!"

"Of course, there was a need," Valeria replied. "He dared defy his queen!"

The doctor's eyes went blank. His body dropped to the floor like a discarded toy.

Chapter Thirteen

Doctor John's body lay across the floor, the life snuffed out by Valeria for no reason other than to flex her pride and flaunt her power. Isis could see it in her intoxicated eyes. The queen was proud of what she had done. Valeria stared down at the corpse of a once-prominent leader and smiled. The satisfaction across her face turned Isis' stomach.

The one small consolation was that it gave Isis the distraction she needed, Doctor John's death would not be in vain. With Valeria focused on her latest conquest, Isis reached into her back pocket and pulled out the lockpick. She jammed it into the keyhole of the padlock around her collar. She felt around for the pins, then rolled the lockpick, pushing down each pin inside the lock. She worked it exactly how she and Zack practiced. Of course, he always finished long before she did, thanks to his experience as a magician, but Isis did get faster over the centuries.

So far, Valeria was oblivious to Isis' actions, but the other Isis—the apprentice—watched her intently. If she let Valeria know, the jig was up. But she didn't react. Then again, that blank stare of hers didn't react much to anything going on around her.

"Now, Isis," Valeria said, still focused on the corpse. "Where were we?"

"Um, you were about to tell me what you did to

Zack?"

Isis' answer solicited a laugh, at least from one member of her audience. Finally, the last pin inside the padlock pushed down. The lock opened with a tiny click. Valeria turned around. Isis covered the padlock with her hand, acting like she was making a failed attempt to pull it off the collar.

"Oh, no, not at all," Valeria replied. "The past is no longer a concern. I am about to inform you of your new future."

"What new future?" Isis asked. It was best to keep Valeria talking. There would only be one chance to catch her by surprise. "You're not going to kill me?"

"Killing you immediately *was* the advice I gave myself in that letter." Valeria moved a pace forward, which forced Isis to take one step back. "But, from the moment I sensed you outside my castle, a far better idea crossed my mind. I see the potential in you as an apprentice working for my cause." Valeria placed a hand under the chin of the other Isis. "With the proper conditioning, of course."

"You already have an apprentice," Isis replied. "Why do you need me?"

Valeria peered toward the other Isis, who stared back with wide eyes. In that moment, the doppelganger had the face of a vicious but frightened dog that suffered the upbringing of an abusive master.

"Creating a world meant for witches was not difficult," Valeria answered. "But maintaining it across the globe is time consuming and requires constant reminders in various locations. You have seen the success I have achieved with this one." She slapped the side of the other Isis' face, perhaps harder than necessary. "Imagine how much easier it would be with two of you instead of just one."

Valeria strolled away from the apprentice and wandered to the nearest picture window. She stared out with her hands folded behind her back. "I can sense your thoughts." She sighed in a disappointed manner. "You believe it's up to you to stop me. I'm actually happy to see you have a defiant streak in you just like your doppelganger long ago. I believe I will enjoy breaking it. I certainly did the first time around."

Isis had the power to read thoughts, too, but she didn't need it to realize what Valeria had now become. This version of Valeria had been in power with no real threat to her throne for two centuries. It made her complacent in her position as queen. She was less vicious, certainly less cautious. Those battle instincts were gone, and that meant Isis had a chance.

A plan quickly formed in her head. Hit Valeria with everything she had using all the control of the energy she could muster. Catching the queen by surprise would hopefully balance out Valeria's power advantage. But, even if Isis could beat her, what then? Valeria morphed the entire world into a horrible nightmare. Countless people had already suffered and died. Ending Valeria's reign wouldn't bring them back.

No. Isis had to stick with the plan. Focus on escape and going to the past. She already gained what she could, confirmation that whatever moment Valeria had changed, it had to do with Zack. It was clear that she killed him early on, but exactly when? Right now, Isis had to get away and figure it out.

With Valeria focused on the view outside the window, Isis removed the padlock. The collar opened and fell off her neck. The moment it was off, Isis' strong connection to the Earth returned. She was whole once again. Isis focused on New Salem. Even in its dilapidated condition, it was still home. From there, she could figure out at what moment in time she needed to fix to put everything back the way it was. Perhaps she could help Domina tap into her gift and help narrow down when the change happened.

"Teleport!" Isis shouted to focus the energy on her need.

Everything blurred, then came back into focus. Instead of the destroyed village, the same huge throne faced Isis. She hadn't gone anywhere. Valeria turned from the window and grinned. "Excellent," she said. "I wanted to see how you would handle the situation. I am not disappointed."

"You were just testing me?" Isis asked.

"No." The corroded grin grew wider. "Not you."

The apprentice lunged, clutching Isis by the throat with her right hand and slamming her to the floor. Her left hand lifted high up above Isis' face. A flame rose from the apprentice's palm. Isis struggled to free herself, but the grip had a strength to it she never thought her own body could ever muster. The heat from the flame grew. The apprentice lowered her hand near Isis' face. Isis felt the burn of each spark hitting her in the face. All the while, she couldn't help but gawk at the permanent blisters across the apprentice's cheek and chin.

Isis tried to pull herself free. She couldn't move. The other Isis stared off into space as her grasp strengthened. Isis didn't need air to breathe, so getting choked didn't faze her. But being set on fire would cause excruciating pain. She needed to somehow reach out and touch the other's mind with her thoughts. She certainly knew that mind better than anyone else's. Well, at least she had an idea of what that mind used to be.

Isis, please listen to me. She kept her thoughts loud, but clear. *I know you must have gone through hell, but none of it is supposed to be. You've always known that. I can see it in you because we were the same person. Valeria used the energy to go back in time. She changed our history. She changed all the good that has happened to us and warped it into...this.*

For the first time, the other Isis' eyes blinked. A sign that she was getting through?

"Kill her, apprentice!" Valeria shouted. "And be quick about it! We have much work to do today."

I can fix it, Isis said into the other's mind. *I've learned how to travel through time, just like Valeria did. I can find what she changed and stop her. I can save our family!*

The other Isis' head tilted. Her jaw trembled ever so slightly.

Isis continued. *I can erase all of this so it will never have happened. I just need one chance to get away. She won't be able to stop me in the past.*

The apprentice moved her enflamed hand in front of her face and stared into it. Her grip of Isis' throat loosened.

"Apprentice, why do you hesitate?" Valeria strolled over and peered over the other Isis' shoulder. "End this now. Your master commands it."

"Please trust me," Isis whispered. "I can undo it all." She had to, for the sake of everyone who ever lived.

The apprentice brought her hands together. In moments, they both became engulfed in the ball of fire. Her eyes went dark. Even Isis wasn't sure what the other her would do, not until the apprentice twisted her head and threw a slant-eyed glance over her shoulder.

The apprentice's mouth opened. Her fangs jutted out. Then, with the speed of a cat, she jumped up, spun around, and launched a straight burst of flame at Valeria.

The force of the fire knocked the queen into the picture window. Glass shattered and shot in all directions. "What are you doing?" Valeria screeched.

The apprentice lunged and created a wind that sent the queen careening through the hole in the window. Valeria should have fallen several stories. Instead, she hovered in the air, a look of death across her face. "Dirty little traitor," the queen growled. "And after all this time."

The apprentice sent another blast of energy at Valeria, who countered with one of her own. The two blasts launched sparks in the air that sounded like fireworks exploding in the throne room. The heat and brightness from the energy forced Isis to throw a hand in front of her eyes. Valeria's energy blast was stronger, which was clear from the lack of struggle on her face. The apprentice's legs, meanwhile, wobbled.

It wouldn't be long before the battle would end for the younger immortal. It was a sacrifice she chose to make so Isis could fulfill her promise. She had to get away, go back in time. It was the only way to get off the queen's radar and change what already had been done. But Isis hadn't been completely honest with her other self. Yes, she knew how to go back in time, but that wasn't enough. She also needed to know, specifically, when and where to go.

What moment did Valeria interfere with the timeline and send it on this crooked path? Isis needed to figure that out, and quickly. Right now, she didn't even have a guess. For all she knew, Valeria could have killed Zack's great-great grandfather as a baby. Rummaging through time randomly, especially when she could barely control the energy in that way, wasn't the answer. She needed a concrete plan, or at least a somewhat good idea. One formed inside her head.

Instead of focusing on a time or place, Isis could concentrate on specific people. It couldn't be Zack, not in this reality's past. Since his death was the catalyst, if she found him alive, it meant Valeria's interference hadn't happened yet. Even if she could ask him to help her solve his own murder, he wouldn't have the information necessary to crack the case. Isis needed the right people who were smart enough and knowledgeable about witchcraft that they could figure out Valeria's plan. She needed people who knew Valeria as well. Only then could Isis come up with a way to counter it.

Luckily, she knew exactly who those people were. Mom and Dad, the great Selena Quinn and Sebastian Santell. They always came up with the right answers. Hell, Dad never tackled a puzzle he couldn't solve. If anyone could outwit Valeria, it was them. A few times since their deaths Isis had needed them, but never as much as right now. This was the plan, to go back to New Salem at a time when they were still alive.

Isis focused on their faces, or at least best she could

remember them. A long time had passed since they all lived happily in that village. They kept an eye on everyone else's best interest just as much as they did for Isis and Zack. New Salem was their home until the moment old age claimed them.

"Go back in time," she chanted over and over, focusing on Mom and Dad. Soon, everything around Isis blurred. A sense of falling back took control of her body. Through the distortion, Isis glimpsed Valeria glaring her way. Based on the smoke emanating from her fists, and from the other Isis' body on the floor, unmoving, the battle must have been over.

Valeria floated back into the throne room. Isis shut her eyes tight, focusing on the energy. "Back in time, find Mom and Dad, Selena and Sebastian." She needed the energy to take her back, and it had to be fast. Valeria held out her palm. A bolt of lightning shot Isis' way. Upon contact, her body shook uncontrollably, but Isis endured it. Her focus was planted on her time spell. Everything blurred, then faded.

Isis' stomach twisted. It was as if everything inside wanted to tear a hole through her pelvis and gush out. The striking pain between her ears forced her eyes shut. She must have been phasing through time. Otherwise, Valeria's blast would have incinerated her. She hoped to find a safer environment once her eyes reopened.

Isis thought she was on her back, except she felt ground underneath her feet. She was standing, but not for long. Balance failed her, and she fell forward, landing on her elbows. Her body still shook, and it was sore, a consequence from Valeria's lightning bolt. Isis grabbed the top of her head and reopened her eyes, staring at the grass underneath her. At least she was no longer inside the castle. But did it work? Did she actually travel back in time? Or did Valeria kill her, and this was the afterlife? No, not based on the strong smell of fertilizer and the sound of cows mooing nearby.

Isis sat up on her knees. The four tall buildings that made up New Salem's quad were fully erect without a hint of damage. The farm had animals roaming around. It wasn't just cows; pigs and chickens were there as well, separated by fences. The dirt and grass under her knees were cared for. The sky was lit up by the bright sun high above.

She did it! Isis traveled through time and made it home. New Salem was alive and well. This had to be the far past, but at least it was familiar territory. Where was everybody? The quad was never so empty, even in her time, not unless there was a perceived threat. In that case, part of the safety protocol was everyone had to shelter in their cottages.

A peek revealed that Isis was not alone after all. There was one other person in the quad. This was someone Isis met when she first came to New Salem. Her name was Natasha, and she was a prominent member of their village's law enforcement task force. She was also one of the most powerful witches in New Salem, until Isis and her family joined their ranks.

Natasha watched Isis from several feet away with determination across her face. The gray and black streaks formed throughout Natasha's curly long hair somewhere around her forties. This must have been many years after Isis came to New Salem. Well, it wasn't her folks greeting her arrival, but at least it was a friend.

"Natasha, thank goodness it's you." Isis stood up

and scurried the woman's way. "I really need some serious help right now. I know this is all going to sound weird but—"

Natasha screamed something in Russian and threw out her arms. A wind snatched Isis and propelled her backward. Isis hit the ground, back-first. Her body flipped over and rolled her across the grass. Damn, her head was already spinning from getting shocked by lightning. Now her chest stung from Natasha's strong breeze. It felt like she had been punched in the gut by a cannonball. What made it worse was that she wasn't prepared for it. Isis pushed against the ground to bring herself to all fours.

Her vision cleared in time to see Natasha rise an inch from the grass and hover her way. Natasha's eyes narrowed with rage while her hands motioned, stating that she was about to access the energy again.

"Nat, why?" Isis mumbled. "What are you doing?"

"You first," Natasha barked in her thick Russian accent.

Isis' shoulders tensed at a clicking sound behind her. She had heard that sound before. It was a gun cocking. Then it pressed against the back of her head. Isis raised her hands up to signal surrender. So much for being safe.

Part Two

Chapter Fourteen

"I'm not a threat!" Isis shouted. She pulled her head away from the barrel of the gun.

"We will determine that," Natasha replied.

Natasha closed in with clenched fists. Electrical static spread around them. Isis would have been offended if she wasn't so confused. She was there for the birth of all three of Natasha's children, all of whom became powerful witches once they hit their teen years. Based on her current age, all three of those children would have already been born. Yet the woman appeared not to recognize her.

"Turn around slowly," said a male voice which no doubt came from the one holding the gun. It had been a long time since Isis had heard that thick, Scottish accent. But at the time, she heard it a lot.

Isis peeked over her shoulder to see the old man with a revolver pointed between her eyes. Despite the bald head, wrinkles, and the fact that it had been two centuries, Isis knew Paul's face almost as well as she knew her own. At one time, they were close. Paul, who was vice president and head of village law enforcement for a long time, played a huge role in getting Isis and her family acclimated into New Salem life. He was also one of the toughest men she'd ever known, even after Valeria used her power to give him a massive stroke.

The woman behind Paul with the huge arms and

buzz-cut aimed a rifle directly at Isis from several feet away. Isis remembered her as well, but barely. She hadn't known her long enough to remember her name. She did, however, recall the poor lady's death. She was killed by Valeria on the same day as Sacha. She was in her mid-twenties at the time. Now, she had to be closer to forty and very much alive. At least someone in this warped reality had a better fate.

"Don't move a muscle," Paul said. "You may be a witch but—"

"But you can squeeze that trigger faster than I can twitch my nose. I know."

"That's right." There was a dash of hesitancy in Paul's tone.

His eyes lifted over Isis' head to Natasha. Isis had to grin. Paul had used that phrase so often, Isis thought they should have engraved it on his tombstone once he passed away. Zack talked her into keeping that thought to herself. He insisted it would be seen as disrespectful. He was right, of course, but Isis didn't mean it to be disrespectful. She just thought it would be fitting.

Isis was suddenly lifted off the ground. She dangled in the air like a puppet being held by its strings. She could move her eyes, mouth, and head, but the rest of her was frozen in place. There were several inches between the grass and the soles of her sneakers. At least it wasn't much of a fall if they decided to break the spell.

"I'm not here to cause trouble," Isis shouted. "I know you may not recognize me, but you do know me. I've lived here for a long time."

"Here in New Salem?" Paul's gun stayed on Isis. "I don't think so."

"Please, I can explain," Isis said, "but I need to see my family. They should be somewhere in this village. That's the only reason I'm here."

Isis tried to move her hands, but they wouldn't budge. The energy held her in place, and she knew who was controlling it. Natasha was powerful, but she didn't have the experience Isis had. With a moment of focus, Isis could take over the energy around her and easily free herself. But right now, she needed to gain their trust, a trust they rarely gave strangers who entered the village uninvited. Of course, Isis didn't think of herself as a stranger, she lived in New Salem for longer than any of them. How could they not recognize her? It had to be the pale vampire skin.

"Paul, wait a moment!" shouted a high-pitched voice. A slightly rotund body with a cane in his hand wobbled between Paul and Isis. It was Simon. He looked over Isis like a mechanic examining a classic vehicle he was about to fix.

"Simon, what are you doing?" Paul roared. "Get inside and let us deal with this—"

"Take a good look at her." Simon tapped Isis' shoulder with the tip of his cane. "She's a vampire like me."

Paul's head tipped forward. His eyebrows rose. "This girl is clearly a witch," he said. "We saw her teleport into the village. She also displays signs of mindreading."

"I'm not reading your minds!" Isis shouted.

"Then she is a vampire, but with the Wiccan gift," Simon said. "Much like the one who has taken over the American continents."

"I did not know there were any others like that,"

Natasha called out from behind Isis. "As far as we knew, the vampire who leads the witches overseas is one of a kind."

Paul grimaced. "If that one is creating others like herself..."

"Her skin is faded, even more than Simon's," Natasha said. "She must be far older than when the Wiccan wars of America began."

"There are rumors," Simon explained. "Our esteemed president has heard them in conversation with other European leaders. They speak of a young witch turned by the queen and kept in a dark prison for years. Each day, she takes this witch to the brink of starvation, then gives her just enough blood to restart the process." He let out a long huff of air and said with a bit of disappointment, "Of course, they are just that, rumors."

Paul looked up at Isis. His gaze was softer, his eyes a bit wider. He took a step forward as his pistol lowered. "Is that you?"

"Um, kind of."

"Natasha, let her down," Paul commanded.

Isis dropped. She tried to land on her feet but ended up once again on her face. Isis pushed her upper body from the ground and wiped the hair from her eyes. She was relieved at the ability to move her arms again.

The tough looking girl finally spoke up. "If that is the case…" Her glare never wavered from Isis. "Then it's dangerous to let her stay."

"Paul." Natasha nudged her thumb to the left. "The president is here!"

A dark-skinned woman waltzed their way. Isis remembered how impressed she was by her. Tia was the nineteen-year-old president of New Salem when

The Witches of Vegas first arrived. She held that position for a long time before finally relinquishing it on her fifty-sixth birthday. After that, she served as an advisor. The Tia who had just arrived had to be close to, or past, the age of thirty.

"Caroline, I am surprised to hear you say that." She walked with a swagger in her step. "If the rumors are true, and this is her, then she is a witch seeking refuge from persecution. That is exactly the principle upon which New Salem was founded."

"Madam President, with all due respect, we have discussed this," Paul said. "The Wiccan war has already destroyed America. It will eventually make its way across the seas. Our only hope lies in that this vampire witch never discovers our existence. It is why our witches' spell covers our village."

"A spell that clearly does not work," Caroline replied.

"If this *is* her—" Simon said, but Paul threw a hand on his shoulder, cutting him off.

"First things first." Paul peered down at Isis. "Are you the queen's prisoner or not?"

"S-sort of," Isis answered.

"You didn't answer the question before, and you're not answering it now," Paul growled. "What do you mean by 'sort of?' Who are you?"

"None of this should be," Isis cried out from her knees. "We beat Valeria right here." She slammed a finger against the ground. "But she went back. She changed it all."

Simon leaned his entire upper body over Isis. "Went back? What do you mean, like, through time? Are you saying you're from the future?"

"Yes!" Isis shouted. I'm saying I traveled back in time, and now I'm here."

"We've heard crazier stories before," Tia said through a grin.

"Have we?" Paul's head shot her way. "Frankly, Madam President, I think this one takes the prize."

Isis felt the skepticism in each of them, which was understandable, even though it was the truth. One face showed compassion and sympathy. Of course, it was Tia's. The president kneeled next to Isis and placed a hand on her back. "Try to relax," she said. "You have our attention. Tell us who you are and why you're here. Please."

"And do elaborate on this claim that you traveled through time," Simon added. Isis threw him an annoyed glance. "You understand, young lady, it's a rather hard pill to swallow, especially without any sort of evidence to confirm—"

"You have a wooden leg under those sweatpants!" Isis shouted.

"Yes, I do," the vampire replied. "But any witch could sense that."

"Your man, Nikolas, made it for you before he died. That's why you never looked to change it. That leg was the last thing Nikolas carved before he couldn't use his hands anymore. You always said how it reminded you of him."

Simon leaned back. A look of wide-eyed surprise crossed his face. "Okay, I admit, much of that is quite true," he said in a low tone. "I don't believe I've shared that with anyone outside this village."

"You shared it with me. We've known each other for two hundred years." Isis picked up her head. "I knew all of you a long time ago."

"You said you were here to see your parents," Paul chimed in. "What are their names?"

"Sebastian and Selena," Isis answered. She said to all the blank stares, "They should be here!"

Tia placed a hand against the back of Isis' neck. "There are no residents of New Salem by those names. I don't believe there ever has been."

"Sebastian and Selena, you say?" Simon's eyebrows rose. "Tell me, does Selena have a sister?"

"Yes, my aunt Sacha," Isis replied. "She was killed here protecting New Salem."

"Oh, my goodness gracious." Simon cupped his hands across the top of his head. "I know exactly who you are."

"Care to share that information with the rest of us?" Paul growled.

"Yes. Sebastian Santell, Selena and Sacha Quinn," Simon said. "Those were Luther's wiccan charges."

"Luther." Tia stood. "That was the vampire who brought you here during my grandfather's presidency, yes?"

"That's exactly who he is…or was," Simon replied. "They became performers in Las Vegas under the guise of magicians. They were quite popular over there."

"We were The Witches of Vegas," Isis mumbled. "Until we came here."

"I stayed in touch with Luther for a long time, up until they all disappeared without a trace. It was shortly before Valeria destroyed Las Vegas, then Washington, DC." Simon waved his hand at Isis. "Luther told me about *her* as well, the child they rescued and brought into their coven. Her name is Isis Rivera, and she should be in her late twenties by now. She must have died, then turned while she was a teenager."

Isis pulled herself off the ground. Simon leaned in and looked her straight in the eyes. "Tell me, was it Luther who turned you?"

"No," Isis answered.

"Was it the vampire who took over the United States?" Paul asked.

"Not directly, no. Well, here it was directly, but not in the original time." Isis squeezed her eyes shut. Fatigue was setting in. It was a sensation she hadn't experienced since her turn. The blood in her system must have been running low. "Look, I just need to see my folks. I know they can help me fix everything." She threw a wide-eyed glance at the president. "Please, I know they'll vouch for me."

"I'm sorry, Isis," Tia said. "But to reiterate, they are not, nor have they ever been, here in New Salem."

Isis' gaze focused on the muddy ground. "That can't be," she said more to herself than anyone around her. "The Earth's energy brought me here, to this time and this place. It wouldn't have just been random."

"No one truly understands how time travel works," Simon explained. "Up until now, I didn't even know witches could use their connections to go through time."

"We cannot," Natasha replied. "I know this."

"My grandfather believed it could be done," Tia said. "Although no witch has ever been strong enough to control the energy on that level."

"But you are, aren't you?" Simon asked Isis.

"Hold on. We still don't know if any of this story is true!" Paul roared before Isis could answer. "We are assuming she was the Wiccan vampire's prisoner seeking refuge. She's claiming to be from the future. For all we know, she's really a scout who was sent to find us. This time travel deal could be her cover story."

"Or she could genuinely be in trouble," Tia said through her familiar grin. "If there is any truth to her tale, how can we just send her away?"

"We may not have a choice," Paul replied. "Whether she is a scout or an escaped prisoner, they will come looking for her. She will lead them here, intentionally or not."

"The girl is a security risk," Caroline shouted.

"Don't worry." Isis wandered away from the group. "I'm not staying."

"Isis, where are you going?" Simon shouted at her.

"I don't know," she muttered.

Isis asked the energy to take her to a time Mom and Dad were still around. Instead, it brought her here to a New Salem that had never heard of them. Why? It suddenly dawned on her. The energy, while powerful, was also at times literal. When Isis cast her time spell, she was focused on New Salem. It was her assumption that she'd find her folks here. She ended up in the location of her choice. But was this also a time her folks were around, even if they weren't in New Salem? It had to be. That's what she asked of the energy through her spell. They had to be somewhere out there.

Isis looked to the sky. She squeezed her eyes tight and focused directly on her folks. How she'd explain herself existing may prove to be a huge problem, but at least they'd know her. First, she had to find them. Mom…Dad…where are they, she asked the energy that had been her ally for two centuries. She just had to focus on two people in a world of billions. It was a tough task, but Isis was determined.

Nothing from Mom; it was if she didn't exist. But Dad, she sensed him. He was somewhere far, and he was radiating an aura of sadness, but he was out there. That was where she needed the energy to take her. Ignore the people shouting. Focus on the location of Sebastian Santell. That was who she needed to see. It had been so long. Would she even recognize him? How would she even explain how she all of a sudden appeared in front of him? Actually, maybe that wouldn't be so difficult. It may take him a minute, but he would understand.

"She's disappearing," Paul shouted over the murmuring.

Isis' body tingled, a clear sign of teleportation. Thanks to the power of the planet, she was able to connect with his location. A nervousness filled her body. If Dad wasn't in New Salem, where was he? What happened to Mom? Why was he so sad? Isis had a hunch she wouldn't like the answers to the questions.

Her nose itched from the strong smell of seaweed that filled her senses. She opened her eyes as a gust of sand-filled wind hit her in the face. The tiny grains pricked at her flesh. A small but familiar island filled with fruit-covered trees surrounded her. Waves splashed against the shore. She recognized everything about this island, including the older man standing in front of her with his arms folded across his chest. At first, she wasn't sure if this was him. He looked in a way Isis had never seen him before. But his deep blue eyes under all that hair were a dead giveaway.

Isis walked forward. "D…Dad?"

"Well," he said with a huge smile. "I had a feeling I'd see you today."

Chapter Fifteen

Seeing Sebastian Santell again brought back a lot of memories from Isis' childhood with The Witches of Vegas. They certainly had their moments—none of them were perfect people. But one thing Isis remembered best was the love she felt while in their care. She also remembered how intense Dad became during Isis' training sessions. Then again, he was intense with everything that mattered to him.

Among all those memories was how much her adopted father hated facial hair. He always kept his hair short and full of gel, and his face clean shaven. Yet here he stood with brownish-gray hair hanging down his back and shoulders along with a dirty beard that reached his chest. He had also never been so skinny. This was a man who spent time in the gym but could never turn down a good steak or dessert. Now, without a shirt covering his upper body, Isis could see his ribcage. The sight of it made her cringe.

Sebastian folded his hands against his chest and grinned under all that hair. "This isn't how I remember you with such pale skin," he said. "But I do understand why I am seeing you in this way."

"Wait, you knew you were going to see me?" Isis asked. How crazy; this was the second time Isis found herself somewhere she didn't expect to be, and yet she ended up face to face with someone who was waiting for her. At least he'd be a lot friendlier than Valeria.

Sebastian nodded, then walked past her. He stopped at the shore, inches from where the water hit the sand, then rolled back. "I knew one of you would visit me. You always do." He looked back at Isis. "I realize none of you are real, just hallucinations from a brain destroyed by years of loneliness and sunstroke. There's really nothing to do here but watch the waves. But I've come to appreciate the company, even if you are all figments of my imagination."

Isis had been on this island in the Caribbean a few times during their teen years. It was the place Valeria had trapped her family, along with Zack and his Uncle Herb. The island also became Herb's final resting spot after he made the ultimate sacrifice to save them. Isis walked to the exact spot they buried his body and rubbed the sand with her foot. The grave was conspicuously missing. That was strange, but not as strange as Dad being here by himself. He didn't have the power to teleport this far on his own, and it was clear he was living on the island and had been for a long time. What the hell happened?

This had to be a consequence of whatever Valeria did. But realizing that didn't bring Isis any closer to figuring it all out. It would help if she could figure out when Valeria changed history. She needed to ask more questions and find out some more about this timeline. It was best if she was gentle with her approach.

"Dad." Isis looked him up and down, from his long hair to his dirty feet and long toenails. "How long have you been here?"

"Now, why would I ask myself that question?" Sebastian lay back across the sand and folded his hands behind his head. "Okay, I'll play along, but I still don't know the answer. It was five years from the day we started leaving lines in the dirt for each sunrise. Then the tornado that ripped through this island wiped it out. It's been a long while since then."

Sebastian stood up and walked to the shoreline. He let out a sad laugh. "I haven't imagined you here in a while, and certainly never looking like a vampire. It's usually your mom who visits me. I figured my mind was avoiding you because I just don't know what happened to the real life you. If you're alive, if you're okay. Maybe I don't want to know because I'm sure it's bad."

Boy, he was right about that. After seeing what Valeria had done to the other Isis, "bad" was an inadequate way to describe it. Isis straightened her back. She hated to push anyone in the midst of a psychotic episode, and, in this case, it was the man who raised her. He deserved so much better, but she had no choice. She needed context. "Dad, tell me what happened to everyone else."

Sebastian shook his head. "Haven't I gone through this enough times? Why must my brain insist I relive it over and over?"

"Please?" Isis said in as soft a voice as she could.

Sebastian let out a deep sigh. "Okay, I suppose I have a reason for it. On the first day, we lost Luther. Valeria stabbed him twice with a wooden stake and, without blood, he simply expired. Soon after, we lost Sacha." He waved a hand toward the rest of the island. "Who could have guessed that the fruit on those trees we needed to survive—the only food we have in this damned Other World—Sacha was deathly allergic to?

She lasted only days."

Isis dipped her head. The frustration ripped through her like a hot knife through butter. They never realized that they weren't in The Other World. After all this time, her dad still didn't realize it. That made sense since it was Zack and Herb who deduced Valeria's lie. Of course, they did. They were magicians who could see through scams better than any witch. Plus, Zack had his phone which put him on the right path. Without them here, the family never would have figured it out. Apparently, they didn't.

Was this the change Valeria made? Did she somehow stop Zack from figuring everything out? Did she take his phone or kill him during the initial battle instead of stranding him with the coven? Maybe she changed her plans so Zack and Herb never met the witches. Of course, Isis could have been grasping at straws, but it did make sense. The magicians helped them escape. Valeria's best move was to remove them from the equation.

"What about Mom?" Isis asked. "What happened to her?"

Sebastian sighed. "Your mom, she held on a few years, but losing her sister and the guilt of what Valeria must have been doing to you, it was just too much for her to handle." Sebastian wiped his forearm across his eyes. "It drove her mad. Then her heart gave out. It was like she couldn't live with it. After that, it was just me and Herb, placing the bodies into the ocean water and letting it carry them out—"

"Wait." Isis' head lifted. Her mouth hung open. "Herb was here?"

"For a long while, yes," Sebastian answered. "Who

would have thought that a mortal without any Wiccan connection whatsoever would outlive two powerful witches and a vampire? Then again, he was used to living without the connection that doesn't exist here in The Other World. Of course, that was until the storm came and we found out The Amazing Herb Galloway wasn't so amazing, especially with only one working arm. While I clung to a tree for dear life, the wind dragged him off the island and sucked him under the water. I couldn't save the guy even if I tried."

Isis' entire body flinched. The Sebastian Santell who raised her was a hero; he was never the type to hang back while an innocent life ended. Even in a hopeless situation, he'd at least try. Well, that was the Sebastian Santell who didn't have to watch his entire family die while he could do nothing about it. Loss after loss, starting with losing Isis to Valeria, had destroyed the man's spirit. It was a horrible sight.

How interesting that Herb Galloway was here. Isis' thinking was off. She had assumed that Valeria never used Zack and Herb as pawns to get to Isis and trap the coven. Without them in the picture or on the island, Valeria would have won. But Herb *was* on the island with them. She did use them. In this history, Valeria's plan didn't differ as much from her own. But something was different, and it led to a different result.

"What about Zack?" The words rushed off Isis' tongue. "What happened to Zack?"

"Zack?" Sebastian asked. "Who is Zack?"

"Zack Galloway! Herb's nephew?"

Sebastian scratched the side of his head. Sand poured from his hair. "Herb must have mentioned a nephew somewhere along the line. Why else would I know the name? Unless I'm just imagining it right now?"

Ugh. Isis was back to square one trying to figure out what Valeria changed. She needed to take a chance in this conversation and push a little bit harder. "Zack was the one Valeria manipulated to meet me," she explained. "That's how she got us to his theater. He invited me to see his Uncle Herb's show. That's where Valeria snatched me. When you tried to rescue me, she sent all of you here."

Sebastian shot a confused squint Isis' way. "No, no, no, that's not how it happened at all. There was no Zack." Sebastian waved his arms like a referee signaling a non-catch. "It was Herb befriending Sacha, which led to Sacha taking you to see his show. That's where Valeria captured both of you."

Sebastian pointed a finger in the air as he faced Isis. "My brain is trying to change details again, but I remember this because I held a real long grudge against Herb. As far as I was concerned, he was Valeria's ally and our enemy. But, to his credit, he did redeem himself. He freed Sacha so she could come get us. He even tried to rescue Isis by himself before we arrived." He dropped to his knees. "We could have beaten her right at that moment, but then things went bad. Real bad."

Tears rolled down Sebastian's cheeks. "I'm so sorry, Isis. We went in cocky, and she tore us apart before stranding us here. Now, I can only hope she killed you. If not, I can only imagine how she may be torturing you even now."

Isis backed away. Not by choice, but seeing her hero break down like that made her wish she could cry, too. Right now, she wanted nothing more than to embrace him with the assurance that she wasn't a delusion. She wanted him to know that she was real and okay. She'd also love to let him know that he wasn't trapped in another dimension without any hope of escape. To let him know that he was actually on Earth. With little effort she could rip him from this isolation.

But she thought better of it. He had just spent years believing he was in an inescapable prison and watching everyone he ever cared about die, all with the same belief. To find out that they were home all along would literally kill him. The best thing Isis could do for him was to stop Valeria from ever creating this sick and demented world. Then he would have never suffered this lonely existence. Inside, her resolve grew.

At least one important detail came from this venture. Whatever Valeria did, it was before Isis met Zack. If it happened after, then her dad would have known about him. However Valeria eliminated Zack, she did it to him farther in the past. That's where Isis needed to go. But the exact moment was still a mystery.

Manipulating the energy for time travel wasn't easy, but she was figuring it out. She wanted to see her dad and, without direction, it brought her to this moment. In that respect, it took her exactly where she wanted to go. Now, she just needed a way to direct the energy in a more specific manner, not just in location, but also in time. To do so, however, would require control of the energy that was even beyond her two hundred years of experience. Without that control, she'd end up making random jumps through the timestream.

It suddenly hit her. "Of course!" Isis snapped her

fingers.

Sebastian wandered away from Isis, dismissing her as the delusion he believed her to be. Isis was ready to leave; she got all she could out of this conversation. Plus, seeing him like this broke her heart, at least metaphorically. But before she left, it was time to get some assistance with her jumps. Since the first time she tried it, they hadn't been accurate in either span or location. That assistance was on this island, and it wasn't from her parental figure.

Enchanted crystals heightened a witch's control of the energy, at least it did within the pentagon formed from five crystals placed at equal distances from one another. Valeria had a set of them surrounding this island. She used them to cut off her family from the energy so she could convince them they were on The Other World. Controlling the crystals in such a manner from an incredible distance away was impossible for witches but, as Valeria proved, anything was possible for one with four hundred years of experience.

With those crystals, along with the strength of her own natural connection, Isis could focus the energy so it would aim her time jumps with more accuracy. At least that's what she hoped would happen. But first, she needed to locate the crystals. On the island, Isis was inside the pentagon Valeria controlled. There was a good chance Isis' own connection was cut off depending on whether the spell within was for all witches or specifically aimed at the ones Valeria placed on the island.

Isis strolled into the ocean water. It covered her sneakers and pressed her wet jeans against her knees. Not a comfortable sensation, but the crystals had to be on dry land. Valeria wouldn't have taken the chance of one or more of them getting snatched by the waves and dragged out of position.

"Now I know for sure you're not real," Sebastian called out to her. "That water is explosive. It would kill anyone who touches it." Another lie Valeria told them which they figured out in her reality, but apparently not in this one.

Isis focused on the enchanted crystals. "Come to me," she chanted, over and over until she was sure the energy heard her plea. The sand spread out in five equally distanced locations around the island. Five small transparent pebbles, barely bigger than the sand, rose in the air. The sun shined off each as they hovered across the island and landed in Isis' open palm. "Yes!" she exclaimed, staring at the five shiny trinkets for the first time since New Salem's last batch burnt out over a century ago.

Sebastian's head popped up. He stared down at his body in awe. "I'm sensing the energy," he said to someone other than Isis. "Can you feel it as well, Selena? Is this real, or are we imagining it again?"

Isis ran from the water, back onto the wet shoreline's sand. She dropped her hand. The crystals stayed in the air until she willed them to land on five separate sides of her, creating a perfect pentagon. She took one last look at her dad, who reached out in front of him for someone who wasn't there. His eyes were wide with uncertainty. God, she hated the idea of leaving him behind in his own personal hell, but the best thing she could do for him—for Domina, and for everyone left behind—was make sure none of this happened in the first place.

"Goodbye, Dad," Isis said. "Soon, you'll be in a better way, I promise." He didn't respond.

Isis shut her eyes and connected with the energy. She felt it vibrating all around her within the crystals. It sounded like bacon sizzling on a skillet inside her head. "Take me to when and where I need to go," she whispered, putting her faith in Mother Earth to place her on the right path.

The plummeting sensation enveloped her body, as did the tingling and the sense of teleportation. Wherever and whenever she'd end up, Isis hoped to find the answers she sought.

Chapter Sixteen

The smell of seaweed and sound of waves splashing against the shore had been replaced by a diesel odor, car engines purring, and horns blowing from all directions. Isis let out a sigh of relief, happy to be in familiar and long-missed surroundings. It was the Vegas strip, many years before Valeria remade it into her queendom. The sidewalks were filled with people rushing from one side to the other. A few stopped in their tracks and looked down at Isis' sand-covered shoes and soaking wet jeans before continuing on their paths.

Isis picked up the five enchanted crystals that surrounded her and dropped them into her left front pocket. She looked up at the skyscraper as if it were an old friend. It was The Sapphire Resort and Casino, the place she had called home while being raised by The Witches of Vegas. They lived in one of the top floor's suites which gave them a nice view of the Vegas strip. It was the happiest time of Isis' life…but when during that happy life was this moment, exactly?

The answer came in the form of a brown leather couch crashing through the top floor window. The sound of glass shattering forced Isis, and all the people around her, to look up. Her eyes went wide at the sight of the couch hurtling down along the side of the building, picking up speed like a rocket. The screams of people around Isis were loud, as was the sound of traffic coming to a screeching halt.

Just like all the people around her, Isis ran back. One woman who looked barely out of her teen years stared up. She was seemingly frozen in place. Before Isis could react, the woman woke up and lunged out of the way. The couch hit the ground with a loud thud. The leather pillows tore from the impact while metal springs flew in all directions. Isis knew what was coming next. The top of the couch went ablaze, burning like a backyard barbecue.

A quick peek around confirmed no one was hurt or killed. Even the woman who had saved herself was shaken up, but unharmed. Isis let out a sigh of relief. It was a concern that weighed heavily on her mind when this happened. At least now she knew the exact timeframe the crystals had taken her. She was ten years old practicing with her Wiccan powers unsupervised. Sending the couch through the window was obviously not what she was trying to accomplish.

Isis focused on invisibility, then her "lighter than air" spell. She floated straight up, stopping in front of the square hole that used to be their hotel suite's window on the top floor. The suite was a horrible mess with broken glass everywhere. Each picture that hung on the wall was now on the floor and broken, as were the television and chandelier. A skinny ten-year-old Latina with light brown skin stood in the middle of the living room, frozen in terror. Isis knew her exact age and how frightened she was because that girl was her.

A beep came from the front door, meaning a keycard had unlocked it. Someone was about to enter the suite. The young Isis gasped. The door swung open.

It was Sebastian and Selena, Isis' newly "adopted" family. They entered the suite and stopped in their tracks. Their smiles were replaced with lower jaws aimed for the floor. Isis had forgotten how much she missed having them in her life, even in the worst of circumstances. This day certainly qualified.

"What the hell happened in here?" Sebastian shrieked.

It was a much younger and healthier Sebastian Santell than the one Isis saw on the island. His short brown hair was slicked back with gel. He had nary a speck of facial hair. His wide blue eyes shined, although they rarely blinked as much as at this moment. Next to him, Selena ran her fingers through her long red hair while eyeing every inch of the suite. "Sebastian, the window's broken, and our couch is gone."

Isis remembered well the feeling of dread she had in the pit of her stomach. It was at a time she was first learning how to control the energy. Isis decided to practice on her own. She was sure she could handle it. To no one's surprise, she couldn't. She was sure this new family that she was already learning to love and trust was about to toss her out of their home.

Isis had spent time in foster homes before these witches took her in. She had seen those families kick their foster children out of their homes for anything they saw as bad behavior. As kind as these people seemed, Isis had little reason to think they wouldn't react in the same way. Of course, she didn't know them so well at that point.

Young Isis' body visibly shook when the pale-skinned and egg-headed vampire, Luther, entered the suite. Without a word, he looked around the apartment, then leaned against the wall, folding his arms. Isis never understood why he always wore a black cape over his shoulders, but he did.

Luther threw Sebastian and Selena his slant-eyed "I told you so" look. Isis hated that facial expression, especially when it was about her. He believed they were far too easy on Isis during her training, and he rarely kept that opinion to himself.

Sebastian stepped in front of the younger Isis. "I-I-I…tried to move the pencil," she sobbed. "It-it didn't m-move…"

"You were using your witchcraft by yourself?" Sebastian's voice rose with rage. "Isis, what were you thinking?"

"The chandelier is in pieces all over the floor," Selena said. "Isis, you could have been cut or worse."

"Not to mention I'm pretty sure our couch caused that big hole where the window used to be." Sebastian glared down at Isis and repeated his question, "What were you thinking?"

The young Isis stuttered. "I, I...I'm…th-think…" She dropped to her knees and wept. Isis remembered trying to come up with an answer that wouldn't get her killed. Or worse, shown the door with all her stuff packed in a garbage bag. Crying was all she could come up with. She was ten, after all.

It worked. The rage on Sebastian's face extinguished. Selena sat on the floor in front of Isis and put a hand under her chin. The tension in her shoulders had disappeared. "You need to understand, Isis, the energy is not a toy for us to play with." Her voice was calm and sweet. "It is a responsibility we must take seriously, especially at your level of power. Do you understand?"

Before the young Isis could answer, Luther scoffed. "And now you coddle her." His voice boomed throughout the suite. "Why not just take her out for ice cream and roller skating as a method of discipline?"

"Luther, she's a child," Selena snapped. "Sebastian and I are working with her—"

"Hardly." Luther rolled his eyes. "Despite her age, she is a witch with an abnormally strong connection to a source of unlimited power and no experience or understanding on how to control it. Yet, instead of focusing on training, you play house with her."

Luther's comments made the young girl cry even harder. If she could, Isis would have let some tears fly as well, but for a different reason. She adored the life her adopted family had given her, but Luther wasn't wrong. They were really easy on her, and it left Isis unprepared when Valeria abducted her. Then again, had she fought back, Valeria may have killed her immediately.

A rhythmic whistle from the hallway forced everyone's attention to the open front door. "Hey, why is the front door open?" Sacha Quinn waltzed in, her red hair tied behind her head so all the freckles on her cheeks showed. Her head snapped back as if a stiff wind punched her in the face. "Whoa, what happened in here?"

"That's a great question. Let's ask the babysitter who was left in charge," Sebastian growled. "Where were you, Sacha?"

"I went downstairs for a quick massage," Sacha responded. "I was only gone for an hour."

"You were supposed to be here with Isis, Sis."

Selena stood up. "You can't just leave her alone all this time."

"I question in the first place why you thought it best to leave her in the care of *this* one." Luther waved a dismissive hand at Sacha. "How are you supposed to teach the girl responsibility when it seems none of you have mastered it yourselves?"

"Oh, be fair, Luther." Sacha slapped the vampire across the shoulder. "I think we've done well for ourselves. We live fancy. We have an amazing show that lets us train while keeping our secret. Isn't that showing responsibility?"

"That's assuming we don't get cancelled over this little mishap," Sebastian added. "We need to clean this up, and fast."

Luther's beady brown eyes focused on the broken window. He finally moved away from the wall. Isis thought he might have been looking directly at her, if she wasn't using an invisibility spell. "You figure this out," he said before storming out the suite's open door.

Isis tilted her head. It had been a long while, but she distinctly remembered Luther berating Sacha for her flippancy. She remembered it because, at the time, she had no idea what "flippancy" meant. After everything settled down and Isis' home schooling resumed, she asked Selena and Sebastian the question, "What is flippancy?" It led to a long discussion on Luther's role as mentor and how, despite his rough demeanor, he genuinely cared about the safety of their coven, which now included her.

But that's not what happened this time. If Valeria had already changed the timeline, why would it affect Luther's chastising them over an unrelated event? At this time, they hadn't yet met Zack or encountered Valeria. But even if they had, this moment should have played out the same way.

In the suite, Selena pulled the young Isis to her feet and wiped her tears. Sebastian joined them, with a far calmer and more soothing demeanor.

"Make me a promise," Selena said. "Promise me you won't try to access the energy without one of us present. Would you do that for me?"

"It's just like driving a car, Isis," Sebastian added as he leaned down and placed a hand against the young girl's head. "You can't get behind the wheel by yourself when you're still learning how to drive. Does that make sense?"

"Y-yes," the girl sobbed. "I promise."

Isis remembered the relief she felt in that moment as she realized they weren't going to kick her to the curb. She was part of their coven and part of their family. One mistake, even a massive one, such as destroying the suite and putting the show in jeopardy, wasn't going to end their relationship. These weren't the type of guardians who would try to abandon her or set her on fire. They had her back. God, she almost forgot how much she missed having them in her life.

All four in the suite looked to the ringing phone, knowing exactly who was calling. The resort's general manager was on the line demanding to meet. Sebastian gave the sisters and Isis a quick nod, then went for the phone. He was ready to handle it, and, in the end, he did.

As much as Isis wanted to keep observing the family she remembered so fondly, nostalgia was not why the Earth's energy brought her to this specific time and place. As Sebastian picked up the phone's receiver, Isis waved a silent goodbye then floated farther up, over The Sapphire Resort.

She landed on the roof, feet first, and peered out at the Vegas skyline from the building's edge. It looked beautiful as ever, but it didn't give her the answers she needed.

By using the enchanted crystals, Isis was able to communicate with the Earth's energy. She let it know exactly what she needed to find. The energy responded by bringing her here, but why? What would she discover now? Whatever Valeria did to Zack, did it happen around this time? Or did it happen farther in the past, or future? Was she here to gain more knowledge about that moment or directly stop it from happening—

"You are not the vampire I thought you were."

The deep voice nearly made Isis jump out of her skin. She spun from the edge to see Luther standing across from her, hands firmly on his hips. "Why are you here?" he growled.

Chapter Seventeen

"Invisible!" Isis shouted. Her hands in front of her face faded.

"There's no need for that. I know you didn't go anywhere." Luther's stare never wavered from Isis' position. "We can always sense our own kind," he said. "Even when they are on the rooftop, or outside the thirty-fifth-floor window, yet cannot be seen with the naked eye. And *especially* when they smell like the ocean."

Isis gulped and made herself visible. She didn't know why she thought turning invisible in front of the one vampire who hung around witches for five hundred years was a good idea. Definitely a panic move on her part.

Man, even with centuries of life under her belt, Isis still felt like a scared child around Luther. She wanted to just peek in on her old family and then move on, never having to face any of them. She forgot how sensitive a vampire's sense of smell could be. Luther's went even beyond that.

"You are obviously a witch as well." Luther took a step forward. His straight posture and angry eyes declared his intended threat. "I have known one other like you, both witch and vampire. Now another arrives here, where I live. I am sure that is not coincidence, therefore I ask again, why are you here?" Luther clenched his fists. His shoulders yanked back.

Isis wanted to mimic his intimidating posture, but she couldn't hold it long. Fatigue had taken over her body, which meant the blood supply from her last intake was running out. This was a sensation Isis hadn't experienced in a long time; she barely remembered how it felt. She reached behind with her foot to step back and felt only air. Damn, she was at the edge of the building. There was nowhere to go except down. She certainly didn't want to try to teleport, or leap for a nearby rooftop, not while her energy was so low. Isis only had one option: she had to come clean. So much for staying inconspicuous.

"You know me, Luther," she said. "And after all this time, you still scare the hell out of me."

"I know you?" Luther leaned forward with a suspicious eye. "I am sure if we met, I'd remember."

"The first time we met, it was the morning after they brought me home in New York. You berated them hard for not being ready to raise a child. I got so nervous that I threw up my breakfast all over your shoes. Then *they* yelled at you."

Luther paused. "What are you saying?"

"They said there was nowhere else for me to go. That's when you backed down and agreed I should stay." Isis looked up at Luther and widened her brown eyes. She stretched her mouth into a closed-lipped smile. It was the look Isis had on her face when she was nine years old and learned new ways to manipulate the energy. That wide-eyed smile was never aimed at Luther, but he observed enough training sessions from afar that she figured he'd recognize it. After that, she trusted his enhanced senses would kick in.

Luther studied her face as if it were a map for a lost driver. His eyes squinted to the point his eyebrows touched. "This is impossible." With a second glance, he said her name. "Isis?"

Isis threw out her arms, then let them drop to her sides. "In the flesh. Well, sort of."

Luther circled around Isis, looking her over from every possible angle. He stopped when he was once again in front of her. "How old are you?"

She shrugged. "I was sixteen when it happened. Since then, the time went by really fast, so I'm not too sure. I'm somewhere around two hundred."

"You can use the energy to travel though time."

Isis nodded. "I'm still figuring it out. But yeah."

Luther's eyes widened with concern. "Something happened. That's why you are here now."

"It's…" Isis nodded. "It's a really long story."

"I think you need to share it." Luther folded his arms. "But, first, tell me how you became undead. Was it I who turned you?"

"Not you." Isis spun around and sat at the edge of the roof. She didn't think her body could feel so fatigued. "It was Valeria. Well, not directly, but she started the turn. Although, I think with the girl down there in our suite, it will be directly."

"*Valeria?*" It was the first time Isis could remember hearing panic in Luther's normally stoic voice. "So, she does find a way to escape The Other World."

"Yeah." Isis raised two fingers. "Twice, actually."

Luther sat down next to Isis. His legs dangled over the edge just like hers. It was a closeness she had never seen out of him during her childhood. Not toward her, or any other member of the family.

"So, Valeria does escape, and it will be this coven that has to face her." Luther shook his head. "That is concerning since the three of them are clearly not ready for such a confrontation."

"We beat her," Isis snapped. "We sent her back to The Other World. But we had help. From Zack and his Uncle Herb."

"Zack and Uncle Herb," Luther repeated. "They are witches as well?"

Isis chuckled. "Not even. They were magicians here in Vegas. 'The Amazing Herb Galloway Show.' That was them until they got mixed up with Valeria. Herb gave his life to give us a chance. And Zack, he was big-time. He saw things we couldn't, figured out how to send her back. Dad made him part of our coven."

"Sebastian made a non-witch a member of the coven?"

"That non-witch earned it," Isis said. "And that was before he let himself get turned into a vampire so he could save my life. Then he helped us beat Valeria again. He distracted her so I'd have an edge."

"And you defeated her?" Whoa, Luther actually sounded impressed. "How?"

"I trapped her within enchanted crystals," Isis explained. "Then, I got rid of her. She went through our whole coven, but I was the one who beat her. Crazy, right?"

"Why are you here, Isis?" Luther asked, the sympathy extinguished from his voice.

"Somehow, she escaped by going back in time. Then she changed everything." Isis shut her eyes as she spoke. It felt like every part of her body wanted to shut down as well. "I think she killed Zack before we ever met him. Now, she's Queen of the world. She even destroyed New Salem."

"New Salem," Luther said. "She destroyed the village? Why?"

"Because they wouldn't give themselves to her cause." Isis rubbed her palms across her eyes. "She didn't need them—enough witches worked for her. She took over the whole world."

Luther stood from the edge. Isis felt his eyes on her even without looking back. "Is this the day Valeria changes events?" he asked.

"I don't know," Isis replied. "I used crystals to focus the energy. I asked Mother Earth to take me when and where I needed to go, and it brought me here. All I do know is that Zack and I have a strong connection, but I can't sense him anywhere in Las Vegas."

"I take it you and this boy are intimate?" Luther asked.

"Real intimate." Damn, she thought that was clear. Isis grabbed her forehead. It felt like a drum solo inside her brain. "I have to save the world from Valeria. To do that, I need to save Zack. But I don't know when, where, or how."

"Then that is exactly what we need to find out." Luther's voice rose. "If this boy, Zack, is dead, we must gather the details."

Isis peeked over her shoulder. "How are we supposed to do that?"

"By asking the one person in this moment who would know."

Luther gestured to the electronic billboards that

filled the Las Vegas strip's skyline. From The Sapphire's rooftop, they could see them all for miles. Isis stood up and eyed the one Luther was pointing at a few blocks ahead. It read "The Amazing Herb Galloway Show at The Felicity Hotel's Galloway Theater."

Isis wanted to kick herself. It was such an obvious answer, yet she needed Luther to figure it out. How did she not come up with this herself? Maybe because she was feeling weak—and a bit overwhelmed. Both of which kept her from thinking clearly.

"Luther, I-I think I need blood." With all the time travel, Isis had no idea how that affected her body. Or how long it had been since her last drink. She was sure it hadn't been twenty-four hours, but she couldn't really say that for sure. Maybe traveling through time was like going through different time zones in an airplane and it caused jetlag. Or would it be called timelag?

"Do you hunt animals in your time?" Luther asked.

"I do," Isis answered. "Never people."

"Good, then we shall make a stop at the Las Vegas desert where we will find a source of blood for you." Luther waved Isis along to follow him. "Then, we will speak with Herb Galloway."

Chapter Eighteen

In all the time Isis spent in Las Vegas, which was from the age of nine until sixteen, she never once visited the desert. She had no idea it was so spacious and peaceful. There were no people, congestion, or neon signs. There weren't even paved roads. It was all just mountains and empty space. No wonder Luther spent so many of his nights here. Isis found it hard to believe she was only a few miles away from the busy and congested strip.

She caught Luther shutting his eyes and opening his mouth, sucking in the cold breeze. He didn't need air, but he certainly appreciated it. Isis understood why; the fog around her brain was already clearing out from the peace and tranquility around her. Even New Salem was never so peaceful—the swamp jungles were filled with noisy animals. That included crickets and tree frogs which screeched all night. The best part of this desert was that the sun over their heads was bright, but not strong. Isis' pale skin appreciated it. Sunlight didn't kill vampires like the folklores claimed, but intense heat did make them uncomfortable.

Luther ran up one of the hills for a better view of the area. He placed his hands over his eyebrows like a visor. The one issue with this desert was that it may have been too tranquil. In the twenty minutes they had been here, not one single animal crossed their path.

Still, these twenty minutes may have been the longest amount of time she had ever spent with Luther even though he was the mentor for the entire coven. It was also the first time she recalled him treating her as an equal…or at least as equal as Luther treated anybody.

Isis wanted to give herself a chance to enjoy the moment. But when the pains throughout her body weren't distracting her, the thoughts in her head took over. What if Valeria was already here and sensed her? What if Queen Valeria from the future followed her through time? Was either scenario even possible? Isis took a peek from one end of the desert to the other. The coast was clear, at least so far.

Until recently, Isis didn't know time travel for a witch was possible, yet the evidence surrounded her. She was standing in the past, hunting with a man who had been gone for centuries. Isis also thought she was the first witch to accomplish such an impossible use of Wiccan energy. As it turned out, Valeria had done it two hundred years prior. Not only did she travel though time, but she also changed the course of history. God, Isis wanted to kick herself in the head. Why didn't she make sure that damn witch was truly gone after sending her into outer space? Maybe some of the pain she felt was well-deserved guilt.

Luther leaped from the top of the hill and landed next to Isis. "Let's keep moving," he said. "The desert is home to many beasts. I am confident we will come across one soon enough."

"I hope so," Isis replied.

"On our way, tell me about Valeria," Luther said. "When she returned, what was she like?"

"Totally mental. I remember she killed Sa…" Isis'

voice drifted off. There were some details about the future she didn't have the heart to share. "She…killed a lot of people. She's incredibly powerful."

"You were about to say Sacha, weren't you?" Luther asked. Isis replied with a nod. "Valeria was always driven, but never so violent." He had a sadness in his voice Isis had never heard from him. She almost forgot that he and the Wiccan vampire were an item back in the day. "The Valeria I knew wanted to save witches, not extinguish their lives."

"The Valeria I knew nearly killed an entire village of witches for no good reason."

Luther's sudden flinch made Isis bite her tongue. She didn't mean to be so flippant with him, especially while he was dealing with the shock of what Valeria became—or will become—from his perspective. But the lack of blood in her system plus the stress left her cranky.

"I'm sorry," Isis said. "I didn't mean to…I shouldn't have—"

"Over there." Luther pointed forward. A small four-legged animal trotted along several feet away from them. From the long snout and sharp ears, Isis took it for a puppy, although it wasn't a breed she'd ever seen before. Maybe it was a wolf? She threw a glance at Luther who answered her unspoken question. "That is a coyote."

"It's a baby," Isis whispered. "It must have gotten separated from its mother."

"Which means the animal will be easy to catch." Luther kneeled with his hands out. He was ready to pounce. "Leap in front of it. I will grab the animal from behind and snap its neck."

Isis jumped in front of Luther and faced him. He waved his hand, a demand to step aside. "Right now, you must feast, and that animal is the only source we have seen thus far." Isis stayed in place, her stare never wavering. The elder vampire rolled his eyes. "I will make sure it is quick and painless."

"That's not necessary," Isis said.

"Really?" Luther growled. "You have a better option for obtaining your life source from this creature?"

"I do." Isis grinned. "I have my own style of hunting."

Isis waltzed in front of the baby coyote. It picked up its head and looked at her with innocent confusion written all over its face. Isis pointed her palm at the animal and triggered her connection to the energy. "Coyote, sleep," she chanted. The animal's eyes shut. Then its body lay down and rolled onto its side. Isis dropped to one knee next to it.

She placed a finger onto the coyote's neck and focused. A small hole ripped open. Blood gushed out. Isis placed her open mouth over the hole and sucked. Once her mouth was full, she picked her head up and swallowed. The fresh blood almost immediately mixed with the old blood in her body. After a second big slurp, Isis' body felt stronger. The fog over her brain had all but gone away. She no longer felt sluggish or lethargic.

"That was certainly painless for the animal," Luther said. "A thoughtful use of your Wiccan abilities."

"Not done." Isis wiped the blood from her mouth with her sleeve, then focused on the animal. There was still one step left in her hunting technique. She held a hand over the cut in the coyote's neck. "Heal," she said to the energy. In response, the blood left inside the coyote multiplied as the skin around the cut came together and sealed. "Now, wake."

A yellowish glow shot from Isis' fingers to the coyote. The young creature's eyes opened. It rolled to its feet and ran off. Isis stood, keeping an eye on the animal which showed no ill effects from its generous contribution.

She peeked over her shoulder where Luther was observing her. His brows had risen over frozen eyes that looked almost dilated. "What is it?" Isis asked.

"It would seem I owe Selena and Sebastian an apology," he said. "They do instill a good sense of responsibility in you."

"They're great parents. In fact, they were the best. Sacha, too." The smile disappeared. "Now I have to make sure they have the chance to raise me."

"Isis," Luther said. "How adept are you at illusion?"

Weird question. "I've had experience with it. After two hundred years, I guess I'm pretty good."

"Then show me."

"Show you what?"

"Show me what you have seen," Luther replied. "If I am committed to helping you change the future of this timeline, I need to know what it is you are seeking to change."

"There's a whole lot to see," Isis said. "I wouldn't even know where to begin."

Luther marched forward until his chest was inches from Isis' face. "Start with New Salem's fate."

"Okay." Isis shut her eyes and focused on the

destruction that she'd seen in New Salem. A tingling engulfed every inch of her body. It was the energy that was now under her control. She reopened her eyes. The desert was gone, replaced with New Salem in two hundred years. Smoke rose into the sky from the rubble around her. She couldn't create the acerbic smell, but everything was exactly how she remembered it.

Luther's cape swung as he spun like a top, taking in every detail around him. "This is damnation. Valeria did all this?"

"Not exactly," Isis mumbled while biting down on her bottom lip. "But she did give the order when they wouldn't comply."

"If not her, then who would cause such destruction?" Luther asked. "Who would follow those orders?"

The answer clogged Isis' throat. "It was me…well, another me. The one Valeria made into a monster."

"I don't understand." Luther's gaze fell onto Isis. "The graves, all this death…it happened all because she eliminated this one boy?"

"He's really smart." Isis sniffled. "He also made me feel complete. With him at my side, I would never do…this."

"You *didn't* do any of this. Do not take on that responsibility." Luther's back straightened. "The Wiccan vampire who made sure that adolescent coyote suffered no pain and lived to frolic away would not extinguish the lives of all these people."

"I also wasn't in Vegas getting tortured into a submissive apprentice for two hundred years."

"Let me see Las Vegas," Luther growled. "I want to see what she did to it."

"You won't like it."

"I don't like *this*!" Luther threw out his arms and snapped. "But I must know."

Isis focused on her memory of the Las Vegas she experienced two hundred years from now. Everything around them faded into a blur. Pure grassland and the one solid road leading to Valeria's castle came into focus.

"What is this?" Luther roared. "Where are we?"

"This is it," Isis answered. "This is Las Vegas. Two hundred years from now."

Luther looked side to side with a scowl across his face. He walked past Isis, staring up at what used to be The Sapphire Resort. "So, this was your dream," he said, clearly not to Isis. "You've truly perverted this planet into something unnatural."

"She turned Sapphire's basement into a dungeon where she keeps non-Wiccan people," Isis explained. "Around the rest of the world, they're all slaves who sleep in the streets."

"Isis." Luther's head twisted her way. "What is my fate? What happens with me?"

"It's…" She still couldn't bring herself to tell him. "It's a long story."

"I am no longer among the living," he said.

"I didn't say that—"

"You didn't need to. It is the case, is it not?"

Isis threw her arms up, then nodded. "What gave it away?"

"Your emotional sentiments about our coven." Luther folded his arms across his chest. "When you talk about them raising you, I am conspicuously left out. I know I wouldn't leave them on my own volition, especially once you were turned. I would have stayed and taught you. The boy, as well. Yet I am not there."

Damn. Isis forgot all about Luther's annoying talent of deduction. The last thing she wanted to do was make this five-hundred-year-old vampire confront his own demise, so she purposely avoided it. Either way, the cat was out of the bag. He might as well know the whole truth.

"Did my end come during the confrontation with Valeria?" Luther asked.

"We reopened the portal to The Other World. You dragged her through."

"I see." Luther scratched the side of his head. "She killed me in The Other World?"

"No," Isis quickly replied. "Well, actually, yeah, but only when we reopened the portal to come back."

"I am certain that was done against my wishes."

"Pretty much, yeah, but they needed Valeria to save me," Isis explained. "It worked, except it led to Valeria turning Zack into a vampire, her escaping The Other World, and…well…"

"And that is when she ended my afterlife."

Luther knew enough. There was nothing left to hide. Might as well fill in the blanks. "She killed you, then Sacha. She almost killed all of us." Isis caught Luther's eyes fluctuate to black. "I beat her. We won. At least, that was before Valeria went back and changed everything. This time around, she killed you much earlier."

Luther stared hard at Valeria's castle. "I've seen enough. End the illusion."

Isis focused on shutting down the energy around them. Within moments, the illusion faded, and the desert came back into focus. She wiped away the insects that found their way onto her forehead with the back of her hand. There were a few on Luther's forehead as well, but if he noticed, he didn't show it.

"Luther, are you okay?" Isis asked, although she knew he was far from okay.

His head shook back and forth. "I am still amazed that this one mortal boy changed events that led to Valeria's demise, and on more than one occasion."

"I told you, he's amazing. He really is." Isis caught Luther sucking in his lips. This conversation was crushing him inside. "I'm sorry. Maybe I shouldn't have shown you any of that."

"Don't be sorry. I asked to see it, and you obliged. Now you're going to fix this." Luther's voice was filled with resolve. "You're going to save your friend and make sure this dark history never happens."

"That's all I want to do."

"Good. Then it is time we meet with Herb Galloway."

Isis took hold of Luther's arm, then concentrated on The Felicity Hotel. Everything around her blurred.

Chapter Nineteen

The discussion between Isis and Luther after teleporting in front of The Felicity Hotel was about how they'd confront Herb Galloway. They needed a good cover story that would not only gain a meeting with the magician but also solicit the information they needed from him. The hotel security officer would most likely stop two ghostly-looking strangers, with one wearing a cape, at the door.

As luck would have it, Herb was holding interviews this week for a new assistant for his show. The officer never even asked Isis or Luther why they were there. Without a word, he walked them directly to The Galloway Theater where six folding chairs sat outside the door. He motioned them to have a seat. "Mister Galloway will be right with you," he said in a clear, disinterested tone. He waved to the chairs, all of which were available, then marched off.

Isis dropped into a seat. Her left knee shook. Luther took the seat next to her. The two vampires sat for a good ten minutes without uttering a word. Luther finally broke the silence. "This will require subtlety," he said. "Perhaps I should do the talking."

"I'll be fine," Isis replied as a reminder that, despite appearances, she was not a child and Luther was never subtle.

One of the auditorium doors swung open. A young

lady somewhere around twenty years of age strolled out. Her long, purple-dyed hair swayed with each step. Isis covered the smirk on her face caused by the pink tank top and short-shorts that looked like they were painted on the woman's body. It really didn't go with the expensive white tennis shoes on her feet.

She was followed out by a man Isis recognized immediately. It was "The Amazing Herb Galloway" although she had never seen him quite like this. He was younger than she remembered, with dark-blond hair and a swagger in his step. His face was wrinkle-free, and his cheeks glistened. Was he wearing makeup on those cheeks? His white dress shirt and blue tie under a sparkling red vest were both ironed and pressed. It was in that moment Isis realized the toll Herb suffered in the next six years competing with and losing to "The Witches of Vegas." In all that time, they didn't even know he existed. Meanwhile, they were inadvertently ruining his life.

"It was interesting meeting you, Lily," Herb said with a huge fake smile, one Isis had seen Zack use numerous times. Now she knew where he got it from. "Thank you for coming in."

"You are so welcome." Lily's voice pattern said "valley girl," and it squeaked like a mouse. She placed a hand on Herb's chest. "Now, when is our first show? I probably need time to get ready and prepare myself mentally before I start."

"Um, Lily…" Herb gently grasped Lily's wrist and removed her hand from his chest. "You have so much talent and personality, I'm sure you will do well for yourself."

"I know," Lily said through a huge grin. "I hear

that all the time."

Luther grunted. Isis peeked over at him. The subsequent eye roll mirrored Isis' feelings perfectly.

"I'm sure you do. However, I don't think you're the right fit for this particular performance."

"No? Really?" Lily's head tilted sideways. "But I gave a great interview. What happened? What didn't you like?"

"I'll give you three reasons," Herb snickered. "The first is you came to an interview for a job dressed rather casually and provocatively. It is inappropriate, especially for a show that usually gets a good number of children in attendance. The second reason is that you spent the entire interview telling me the days you can't work and the things you won't do."

"I thought you should know all that before I start." Lily's response forced Isis to bite her bottom lip so she wouldn't giggle.

"I appreciate the courtesy, and your honesty," Herb replied. "That brings us to the third reason, which is the biggest of them all. When I brought up magic, the first thing you told me was how much you dislike magic." Herb's eyes squinted. "You do realize this is a magic show you're applying for, right?"

Lily sucked her teeth. "You are a very nice man, Mister Gallagher, but leading me on, getting me to think I was hired, that was really uncool. Good day!" Lily about faced and stormed off. Her backside jiggled with each step down the hallway.

"And the fourth reason is that you never once got my name right." Herb focused his gaze onto Isis and Luther. "I guess the two of you are next. I presume you're here together? I'm Herb Galloway."

"We know who you are," Luther growled.

"Um, I'm Isis," she said through wide-eyed embarrassment. "And yes, we are together."

"Okay, then. Please follow me." Herb motioned for them to come, then reentered the theater.

Isis and Luther followed Herb up the aisle. Isis scanned the entire auditorium. After two hundred years, she barely recognized it. She thought she remembered it being much larger. Then again, she may have been mistaking it for The Sapphire's theater where The Witches of Vegas performed. She suddenly paused in her step when she realized where Herb was leading them; it was the dressing room on the side of the stage. Her memory of Valeria keeping her tied to a chair in there hadn't faded as much as the dimensions of the auditorium had. Memories were flooding into her head like a tidal wave.

"Oh, God," she whispered.

Luther peeked over his shoulder. "Are you all right?"

"Yeah, I'm good." Isis pressed a hand against her stomach, then resumed her pace.

The room was used by Zack and Herb for changing outfits. She certainly had time to take in every detail while tied up in there. It wasn't a large room by any means. Once they were inside, Isis did a double take. It was different from how she remembered. For one, it was a lot less cluttered.

Although the table was still there, it was in the center of the room and not against the wall as it would be in five years. It was covered in papers topped with a picture frame that faced away from the door. Two metal folding chairs were opened and positioned in front while a vinyl office chair was on the other side. There were no magic items. The clothes were also gone. Herb maneuvered behind the table and sat. Apparently, at this time, the room was used as an office, not a dressing room.

Herb motioned them to sit. Isis obliged while Luther remained standing with his arms folded across his chest. Herb looked up at Luther with one raised eyebrow. "By any chance, do you two have a résumé?" he asked.

"We do not," Luther shot back.

"Sorry," Isis added.

"I figured as much." Herb folded his hands against the table and leaned forward. "So, let me start by saying I love the get-ups. Excellent makeup jobs with the pale skin and purplish tone with the lips." He motioned at Luther. "Especially you, way to go above and beyond."

"Thank you," Isis said.

"However, this is not that kind of show," Herb continued. "I do a standard magic act. The tricks and the talent, they are what drives this show. That is our gimmick. It is what Vegas likes to see on the big stage."

It sounded like Herb was ready to end this interview before it even got started. Somehow, they needed to find a subtle way to turn the discussion to Zack. Before she could come up with an idea, Luther spoke. "We are not here to audition for your magic show," he said.

"Really? Could have fooled me." Herb sat back and cupped his hands behind his head. "Okay, I'll bite, what are you selling?"

"This is not about making a sale," Luther answered. "We are here regarding your nephew, Zack

Galloway."

Herb's face changed. His eyes narrowed, and his smile disappeared. "Zack?" Herb peeked at the picture frame on the desk, then back at his guests. "How do you even know about Zack?" His tone had lost its jovial kindness. It was now filled with distrust. "What business would you have about *him*?"

"We need to know the details of your nephew's death."

"His death?" Herb stood from his chair with fists clenched. The smirk melted from his face. "Who the hell are you people, and what do you *really* want?"

"Um, we're detectives," Isis said. "We're conducting an investigation."

Luther tapped Isis on the shoulder while keeping eye contact with Herb. Isis, following the elder vampire's unspoken command, stood from her seat. She could only imagine how this conversation affected Herb deep inside. The man lost his nephew, and most likely in a tragic way. Isis didn't know how recently that loss happened. Was he still grieving, or did she and Luther just rip open an old wound? It sure didn't help that they both looked like death. This needed a delicate approach. Unfortunately, Luther had many strengths, but being delicate was not one of them.

"Detectives, you say?" Herb's eyes rolled. "I don't know what this is really about, but if it's some sort of sick joke or a demonstration—"

"I assure you this is not a joke," Luther replied.

"Herb—Mister Galloway, I promise we're not looking to hurt you." Isis leaned across the table with widened eyes. "I know this is hard to believe, but we are here for all the right reasons."

"Because you're detectives." Herb's leaned forward with his fists against the tabletop. "I don't suppose you have I.D., do you?"

"We do not," Luther said. "Nonetheless, we need to gather this information. We need to know when, where, and how."

"Oh, is that all you need?"

Once again, Herb's eyes darted to the picture frame. Isis had a hunch it was a picture of his beloved late nephew. "I need you both to leave immediately before I call hotel security," he roared. "I really don't get what game you're playing here, but I know I'm not interested."

Isis cupped her hands together. "Please, Mister Galloway—"

"*Out!*" Herb shouted. He pointed a finger straight at Isis. "Let me assure you my nephew is alive and well, so you can close your, ahem, investigation and make sure I don't see the two of you anywhere near my theater ever again."

"Wait. What?" Isis' mouth popped open. She propelled forward, throwing her hands on the table to keep from falling over. "What do you mean Zack's alive?"

"Just what I said, young lady." Herb's finger shifted between Isis and Luther. He was now pointing at the door. "Apparently, the information you received for this sweet little scam of yours was false."

"I don't understand!" Isis shrieked, her eyes dropping to the frame. "If he's not dead…"

Isis snatched the frame from the table and turned the picture side to face her. The boy in the photo was around ten years old, but she knew that blond hair and green eyes well. Also, the huge smile. It was Zack, but the other two in the picture she didn't expect to see. The man with his hands on each of Zack's shoulders had the same green eyes, dark-blond hair, and Zack's chin. The woman to their right with the light blonde hair also had Zack's nose and ears.

Zack and the man were bare chested while the woman wore a one-piece swimsuit. They were all dressed right for that amazing beach behind them. But what really stood out to Isis was the bulge in the woman's stomach. It didn't come from overeating.

"These are…his parents," Isis gasped.

"What the hell are you doing?" Herb shouted. "Put my picture back on the desk and get out of here!"

"This is a recent photograph?" Luther asked while looking over Isis' shoulder.

"What the hell business is that of yours?" Herb grunted.

Isis reached into Herb's mind. That wasn't a use of the energy she cared to use, but this time there was no choice. Isis needed to know. She saw through Herb's eyes a camera in his hand as he stood on a beach in California. His brother, sister-in-law, and ten-year-old nephew all posed for him. Herb took the picture during his weekend visit a month ago.

"You visited them a month ago," Isis whispered.

"Yes." Herb's tone was filled with surprise. "How do you know?"

The frame slipped through her fingers and hit the floor, shattering the glass plate. She didn't want to believe it, but Isis knew the picture was recent even if she hadn't entered Herb's mind. Two blocks away, Isis was ten years old, and Zack was only a few months older than her. The boy in the picture was the right age.

"This can't be," she sobbed. "This isn't fair." Isis looked up to the ceiling and screamed at the top of her lungs, "*It's not fair!*"

"What the hell is she talking about?" Herb looked at Luther.

"I haven't the foggiest idea," the vampire responded.

The room around Isis spun, and it wasn't caused by witchcraft. Her hands shook—the sign of a mental breakdown, but how else could she react? A horrible realization formed in her brain, and it was too much to handle. She had to find a way to fix it all. But how could she, especially now that she understood what Valeria had done?

"Isis?" Luther asked with concern. "Speak up. What is the problem?"

Right now, she needed space from the two men staring her down. Luckily she was a witch, and that meant she could get the hell out of this small and stuffy makeshift office.

"Teleport!" Isis ran to the door. Everything blurred before she exited the room.

Chapter Twenty

The alleyway next to The Felicity Hotel materialized around Isis. She found herself face-to-face with a green dumpster against the building's wall. Rage ran through her body like a tornado trying to pick up speed and burst its way out. "This isn't fair!" Isis screamed even though she was by herself. "I can't do this! How can I be expected to do this?"

Isis threw out her arms and fired a burst of pure force at the dumpster. It lifted off the ground and slammed into the side of the hotel. The dumpster dropped to its side. A ruffling sound from behind swung Isis around. A man sat up from underneath a dirty green blanket. The newspapers which had covered the blanket flew in all directions. He wore an overcoat even though it was a hot summer day.

"Wha' ya doin'?" he slurred. His long and unkempt beard which was covered in dirt made Isis think of her dad on that damned island.

"Go away!" Isis snapped. "Go now!"

Isis shot a burst of electricity straight up from her fingers. The air around the spark crackled. Taking the hint, the man jumped to his feet and ran through the alleyway to the street. Cars screeched to a halt to avoid hitting him. He kept running until he was out of Isis' sight. She would never have hurt the poor sap, but right now, she needed privacy. She didn't like being this upset in front of an audience, even if it was an audience of one.

Isis focused her thoughts on the dumpster. "Levitate," she shouted. The dumpster lifted up and hovered in the air. As Isis screamed at the top of her lungs, the dumpster ripped in half. Both pieces fell to the ground. Overstuffed garbage bags flew in all directions, some popping open under the exertion of power. None of it made her feel better.

The presence of another grabbed Isis' attention. She peeked over her shoulder to find Luther in the alleyway strolling her way. "Mister Galloway was quite impressed with your disappearing act," he said. "In fact, he offered us the magician's assistant job."

"This isn't right," Isis sobbed, dropping to her knees. She stared down at the cracks in the sidewalk. "It just can't be. I can't do this anymore."

Her veins streamed with frustration and rage. She wanted nothing more than to punch a hole straight through the ground, if only doing so would help. But it wouldn't. She squeezed her eyes shut and cringed. When she opened them, Luther's boots were under her gaze. "The boy is alive," he said. "Why is this not a good thing?"

"You don't understand." Isis rose to her feet and staggered away from Luther.

"You are correct. I do not understand." Luther's calm demeanor ripped at Isis' insides like a scalpel. "Perhaps you could explain it to me?"

Isis took a deep breath through her nose, held it in, then exhaled it from her mouth. She couldn't taste the air, but it was a technique she learned at a young age to calm her nerves whenever she felt anxious. The technique still worked during her vampire life, although at that point it was purely psychological. Right now, however, it wasn't helping; her brain was freaking out. If her heart could still beat, it would have shot out of her chest.

"I am waiting, Isis," Luther demanded. "Speak to me."

Isis faced Luther with a hand pressed against her forehead. "Valeria didn't kill Zack," Isis cried out. "She saved his parents!"

"Explain to me why this is bad." This time, Luther's voice was quick and rough. He was feeling the same frustration, but for a different reason, one of confusion. It was as Isis said—he didn't understand. But how could he without perspective?

Isis grabbed two clumps of her hair, one with each hand. "Zack's parents died in a car accident when he was six. It was the worst experience of Zack's life, but it was how he ended up living with his uncle in Vegas. Then, later, with us. But, if none of that happened—"

"Then he was never involved in your altercations with Valeria," Luther said, finishing Isis' thought.

She nodded. "The picture on Herb's desk…he looked so happy. He was so content with his parents. I…I don't know what to do."

"Untrue," Luther barked. "You know exactly what you must do."

"No, I really don't!" Isis threw her arms out and screamed. "I can't kill Zack's parents, Luther! I can't destroy his family!"

"They were already killed, Isis," Luther said. "It happened years ago. You know this."

"So what am I supposed to do? Go back in time

and stop Valeria from saving them? Make sure they die in a horrible car accident? "

"You need to pull yourself together, Isis—"

"No! I'm not destroying Zack's life!" Isis clenched her fists against her temples. "You can't tell me I have to kill two innocent people!"

Luther's eyes went dark. Fangs protruded over his bottom lip. He lunged forward. Isis staggered back until she hit the side of the building and was now sandwiched between the elder vampire and the wall. She stared up into his pitch-black eyes.

"After two hundred years of existence," he roared, "how can you still think like a child?"

"I'm not a child, but I'm also not a killer," Isis sobbed. "You saw. I don't even kill the animals when I hunt them for blood."

"You are an immortal, and you need to think like one." Luther planted his hand against the wall near Isis' face. "You are weighing the lives of two people, this one boy's happiness, and your own conscience against the fate of the entire world. History has been changed, and not for the better. If you do nothing, life will get far worse under Valeria's rule for every single person who will ever live. You must fix time, Isis. Put it back on track."

"Why me?" Isis shouted. "Why is this all on me?"

Luther retreated a step. The black in his eyes faded, revealing his deep brown irises. "There is no one else. The responsibility is yours. It is what Sebastian and Selena prepared you to do since the day they took you in."

"What, to go back in time and kill two innocent people? To murder the mother, father, and unborn sibling of my soulmate?"

"To make the hard decisions which will lead to the greater good." Luther's tone was now calm. "To protect this world from being damned by evil. Right now, you have the power to do that. We *all* need you to succeed. To allow that one family to live, how many will die as a result? What fate are you dooming us all, including them, to endure under Valeria's rule?"

Isis wanted to keep arguing. She wanted to refute Luther's statement. But she had nothing. Because he was right. Zack and his family would suffer, just as the rest of the world would. Valeria's corruption of history had to be stopped, and it was all up to her, no matter what she had to do to prevent it. Deep down, Isis already knew this, but she didn't want to admit it to herself.

"Hey!" a loud voice shouted. "What's going on over there?"

Isis and Luther looked toward the end of the alleyway, which led to the strip. Two men in black tank tops and exercise shorts stood side-by-side throwing nasty glares at Luther. One of them marched their way, his long and curly hair flying with each step. Luther's eyes narrowed, but they didn't go dark. He was clearly not intimidated, although from the enormous size of their sweat-covered arms and legs, along with the workout belts they were holding, there was a good chance the two men had just left the gym.

"Hey, kid." The buff and sweaty man creeped closer. "Are you all right over here?"

"Yeah, I am!" Isis responded. She looked up at Luther's face. "And you're right, I understand what I have to do, no matter how hard it will be for me."

"How hard it is for you does not matter," Luther replied. "Only that you succeed."

The guy stopped in front of them and paused. His eyes darted from Isis to Luther. "What the hell?" he squawked.

"We are street performers," Luther explained. "We are rehearsing our lines before our next performance."

"Is that true, kid?" the man asked.

"Yes, it's true," Isis answered. "He's my grandpa."

The man rolled his eyes and about-faced. "I swear, man, only in Vegas," he muttered on his way out of the alleyway and back to his friend.

"Grandpa?" Luther whispered.

Isis shrugged. Once the man and his friend were gone, Luther leaned forward. "Do you know the details of their deaths? The when, the where, and the how?"

"Zack and I talked about it a number of times," Isis answered. "We even visited the location where it happened along the Pacific Coast highway, about a mile away from the Bixby Creek Bridge. They were speeding, hit a slick spot, and lost control. The car flew off the ledge and crashed along the mountain miles below."

"Are you sure about all of this?"

"Pretty sure," Isis answered. "According to Zack, that's what the police report said. They gave him a basic idea of what time it happened."

"Then it is time for you to stifle your emotions and fix the damage Valeria has done to our history."

"Any chance you'd come with me?" she asked.

"You are the only one who can do this, Isis." Luther placed a hand on her shoulder, then he gave her a rare grin. "I will stay here and make sure the coven prepares you for this moment."

"Damn, that means you're going to be even more impatient with me, aren't you?"

"You can count on that."

Isis tilted her head. Did Luther just make a joke? Either way, she heeded his words. This was Isis' mission. It was one she needed to accomplish. After all, part of the blame did fall on her lap. An error of judgment by a sixteen-year-old changed history and doomed humanity. Now it had to be fixed, no matter what that meant.

She had to do this for her family, for Zack, and for herself. Not to mention the countless people she had ever known—or never knew. They all needed her to succeed, even if they didn't know it.

"Thank you, Luther." Isis pulled back her shoulders with a renewed determination. "I miss you."

"It is good to know that once I'm gone, I will be missed."

Isis grinned. "You definitely will be."

"Good luck to you, Isis."

Luther gave her a nod and backed away. It was an unspoken command that said it was time for her to go. Isis removed the enchanted crystals from her pocket. She tossed them in the air and gave them a mental command. They hovered, then landed on the ground around her, forming a perfect pentagon shape. Isis focused on the energy, pulling it in-between the five crystals. She expected this journey through time would prove easier as she wasn't looking to go back two hundred years. It was more like four years. Granted, she hadn't gotten it exactly right yet, but she did get plenty of practice over the last day.

Isis focused on the exact date and location. "Pacific Coast Highway, one mile from the Bixby Creek Bridge," she muttered under her breath. "To the moment I go."

Euphoria shot through Isis, which meant she was about to go through time once again. Before it could take her over, she gave Luther a quick wave. He returned the gesture with one of his own. Whatever happened next, she had a hunch this was the last time she'd ever see him.

Chapter Twenty-one

Isis found herself on a steep hill surrounded by tall redwood trees. The branches high above were so close they blocked off most of the sky. With so much shade, it was hard to tell if it was day or night. Plus, she had no idea if she was in the right time or place. Isis trusted the energy, and the crystals, but in truth, she could have been anywhere or anytime. Well, at least she wasn't in the swamp forests around New Salem. The sound of a vehicle's engine passing nearby assured her that civilization wasn't far off.

Isis summoned the five enchanted crystals. They disappeared from the ground and then formed a bulge in her jeans pocket. Isis navigated herself down the hill, moving in the direction she had heard a car roaring by. Once she passed several trees, Isis found herself facing a long, paved road stretching from east to west.

Across the road was a steep cliff with a long drop. For a quarter mile's worth, there was no barrier along the side that faced the edge. A vehicle could easily fly off if it wasn't steered properly. It was the only area along the Pacific Coast Highway's path where the cliff wasn't protected by fencing. Isis presumed it was still a work in progress. It had been a long while since she and Zack came here, but as far as she could remember, this was the spot. But how could she be sure? All life depended on Isis being one hundred percent right.

She widened her eyes at the sight of a yellowish-brown puddle along the road. It looked like syrup, but her enhanced sense of smell told her it was oil. That must have been the spill the Galloways' car hit and skidded off that long cliff. For the life of her, Isis couldn't imagine why anyone would ever drive this way, especially fast and at night. It was amazing there weren't more accidents, although Zack did tell her how the city finished the barrier a month later. Not that it helped his folks, but it did prevent future mishaps.

Isis swung her head from far left to far right. There were no signs of Valeria, at least not yet. She needed a place to hide. If she could stop her and avoid a big battle while doing so, that would be ideal. The last thing Isis wanted to do was match power with a witch who had two hundred more years of experience than her. If she lost, then all of history was doomed. Better to be discrete.

Her head swung to the top of the trees. One thick branch hung out high over Isis' head. It was surrounded by thinner branches, all of which were covered in thick clumps of needles. Perfect. Valeria wouldn't expect Isis to be here, no reason to try to sense her. Isis would be safe high above where she wouldn't get noticed. Valeria wouldn't think to check the top of the trees for another witch. At least that was Isis' theory, and she was betting the future of humanity on it.

"Lighter than air," Isis chanted. In response to the spell, her body floated straight up as if it were filled with helium.

She reached for the branch, threw her legs across it, then stopped the spell. The sunset gave off a blinding light that forced Isis to cover her eyes. From the height of the top branch, she had a good view of Bixby Creek Bridge standing in the far distance. It was simply gorgeous, especially with the sun's light shining off the cables. The bridge would soon bear witness to an event of major importance. But how soon would it happen?

So far, there were no cars driving by from either direction. No Valeria in sight either. Eventually, the Galloways would pass, coming home from their romantic getaway. Their plan was to pick Zack up from his Uncle Herb in Las Vegas. But would that happen tonight? Their fate, for better or worse, would determine mankind's direction for the next two hundred years and beyond.

Would the world carry on as it always had, progressing at its own natural rate? Or would it fall under Queen Valeria's rule? The answer would come in the moment that one car passed by. Depending on whether or not Isis was successful, either all of planet Earth would stay safe, or it would separate into two classes. One would be the superior and dominant species made up of witches, while the other would end up living as slaves. To think, neither Mister Galloway nor Missus Galloway had the slightest idea of their importance, or more specifically, of their son's value to the world.

The branch rattled, caused by Isis' knees shaking. Willing them to stop was even harder than using the Earth's energy to cast spells. It wasn't that she was anxious over a potential confrontation with Valeria—although that possibility did scare the hell out of her—it was the idea of what she'd have to do to win the day. She put on a brave face for Luther, and in the moment, she did feel brave. But bravery and compassion were two different things. She had to do all in her power to make sure her true love's parents were killed. The thought of this made her sick. When the time came, could she really do it? How long would it be before she'd have that decision in front of her face?

The sun fell below the horizon, and everything around Isis went dark. There were no lamp posts, no lights except for the full moon shining off the road, and headlights from the occasional car that drove by. So far, one of those vehicles slipped on that oil slick but then immediately regained control and continued its journey. As she waited, Isis worked her brain for another way, any other way, she could stop the damage Valeria was about to do that her conscience could accept. Was it possible she could save the world from the Wiccan vampire's reign while not letting Zack's parents die? No. Hard as she thought, any scenario that saw Mister and Missus Galloway survive changed Zack's destiny, and the world's.

If there was another solution, Zack would have figured out a way. After all the time they spent together, he understood Wiccan abilities even better than Isis did. Of course, she was able to know what he was thinking before he did, and that was without using witchcraft. It was part of what made them an amazing team. Zack would have figured out a solution that Isis could use her power to achieve; that was how it worked for two hundred years. This sort of situation was right up his alley. He was the one who analyzed the board and looked outside the box for answers. But he wasn't around. At the moment, Zack was in Las Vegas, and he was six years old. Isis had to figure it out by herself.

Unfortunately, Isis could only see one solution,

even if she didn't like it. Domina's words ran through her head. "Where it all began," she said. "The moment that opened the path to her queendom." That moment was almost here so…time to be strong. She couldn't think about what failure would do to the entire world. That was just too much for any mind, even one as old as Isis'.

Instead, she concentrated on bringing Zack back into her life. Maybe she couldn't save his family, but she could save their relationship. It was a selfish goal, but at least it was better than focusing on everything from the past to the future. The enormity of the moment wouldn't drive her crazy if she just fixated on one simple goal, bring Zack back—

The sound of grass ruffled. Valeria appeared a few feet in front of Isis' tree. She dropped to her knees, letting out a sigh of relief. Her body was covered in frost. Icicles hung from the ends of her hair. Valeria looked up to the sky. Her eyes were wide, like she had just seen her life, and afterlife, flash before her eyes. It was a state of disbelief that Isis had never seen on the normally cool, calm, and mentally imbalanced Wiccan vampire.

Valeria spoke in what Isis took for an old Latin dialect. Within moments, a red heat formed around the elder witch's body. The icicles dissolved to water. For Isis, their confrontation in space was ancient history. But for Valeria, it happened mere moments ago. That was a good sign. It meant she hadn't yet planted the letter for her former self to find. When the future Valeria inevitably escapes from The Other World, she wouldn't gain knowledge of events which she could turn to her advantage. She wouldn't know to prepare for

Isis' inevitable arrival. It meant Isis could put everything back right here and now.

Isis thought about attacking now, catching Valeria while she was still disoriented. She quickly changed her mind due to the risk. She understood how strong and experienced Valeria was in her connection to the energy. If they battled and Isis lost, then Zack, and the world, would lose as well. If Isis won, but Valeria escaped, she could come back to this moment and try again. Better to wait for her moment and take advantage of it. But she'd have to be sneaky. It was best to let Valeria presume she failed and couldn't change time than know she was sabotaged by another time displaced witch.

Valeria stood up and looked herself over. She walked to the edge of the road. Her eyes pointed east. As Isis expected, the four-hundred-year-old witch was focused on waiting for that one car to pass, and not on her surroundings. If she did, she'd sense another presence watching from high over her head. Then it would most likely be Isis' body the police would find at the bottom of that cliff.

A pair of headlights hit the road. A car's tires screeched their way from the east. It had to be doing at least sixty miles an hour. Valeria aimed a finger at the puddle of oil. Thanks to the moonlight reflecting off it, Isis noticed a clear platform form over the slick lubricant. Valeria jerked back her hand, which made the artificial surface evaporate.

"Not them," she said out loud.

Isis raised her eyebrows. It was a well-thought-out decision by Valeria, which was out of character for someone who was prone to rage-filled outbursts.

Valeria was focused only on saving Zack's parents. To remove the oil slick outright would have potentially saved the lives of others and changed history in either big or small ways. Smart move. Smart, and surprising. Maybe Isis didn't understand Valeria as well as she thought.

A red convertible sped their way. It came to a screeching halt, stopping in front of Valeria. The two guys in the driver and passenger seats were college age and wearing matching Hawaiian shirts. The driver's hair was bleached blond while the other guy sported a head dyed pure white and spiked.

"Hey, you need a lift somewhere?" the driver asked.

"No," Valeria snapped. "Keep going!"

"You sure?" the passenger asked. "You're a long way out all by your lonesome. You're nowhere near anything."

"You getting picked up or something?" the driver chimed in. "If not, we could give you a lift."

Valeria leaned forward. She looked directly in the faces of both men. "You never saw me here. Keep driving to your destination."

Without another word spoken, both men looked forward. The car sped off, neither of them realizing that they were just victims of Wiccan hypnosis. Valeria focused back on the road. Isis did the same, repositioning herself on the branch. She was careful not to make a sound.

The waiting continued…

Chapter Twenty-two

Isis heard the engine of another vehicle heading their way. She sensed there were two people in the car, and both were somewhat under the influence. One, the man, was thinking about Zack. It was the Galloways, and Valeria knew it, too. Her back straightened, and her hands came together. Her eyes fell onto the puddle of oil on the road. It was now time for Isis to make the most painful decision of her life.

There was no denying Valeria's ability to manipulate energy was far stronger than hers. That was clear just based on her journey through time. Isis had sat in that tree and waited for what felt like hours. But Valeria, who had only moments to formulate a plan and determine a location, arrived mere minutes before the Galloways' arrival. That was before freezing to death in space. God, she didn't even need enchanted crystals to accomplish this nearly impossible task.

The blue SUV closed in. It was traveling along this dark road near a cliff far faster than it should have. Zack's dad was behind the wheel while his mom dozed on and off in the passenger seat. His black suit and her fancy pink dress suggested they were coming back from a formal occasion. They had no idea this was to be their last night among the living.

Isis pushed herself along the branch she used as a seat. Valeria's head spun from the sound of the ruffling but put her attention back to the road. The car's high beams flashed against the concrete and asphalt, moving closer with each second that passed. Valeria held out a hand with her palm facing downward. Once again, a clear and thin platform covered the oil slick left in the middle of the road.

This was the moment Isis needed to act. If she waited any longer, it would be too late. But could she pull this off without alerting the much older witch to her presence? She focused on the tree to her right, which was directly in line with Valeria. Several feet separated them. It was exactly what Isis needed.

"Tree, fall," she chanted in as low of a voice as she could. She concentrated on an image of the tree being chopped down near its roots. "Fall…fall…"

The trunk creaked as it slowly tipped over, cut from its lowest point. The rustling from the leaves made Valeria spin around and look up just in time to find the tree plummeting to the ground and directly at her.

"What?" the Wiccan vampire shrieked. She threw up her hands, but it was too late. The huge oak tree crashed down, engulfing Valeria in its upper branches, many of which broke and scattered across the road upon impact. The clear platform disappeared thanks to Valeria getting sandwiched against the ground by Isis' huge and heavy ally.

The idea worked. Isis had stopped Valeria's interference in history. She allowed herself a sigh of relief, but it was interrupted by the sound of tires screeching across the blacktop road. The car swerved to the right to avoid smashing into the fallen tree. There was just enough road that, although it came close, the vehicle managed not to fly off the cliff. The car slowed to a speed where it would come to a halt just short of the oil slick.

The wheels slid but regained their trajectory as it came to a near stop. Isis shrieked. Two hundred years through time, hours hidden in a tree, and now, instead of Valeria, it was her own actions that saved the Galloways from their fate. She knew what she had to do, and the thought of it made her mentally sick. But there was no choice.

"Zack, please forgive me," she sobbed.

Isis held out her palm, focused on the SUV, and pushed. The vehicle flipped onto its side and dragged along the single lane's edge. It flipped again, but this time, there was no road underneath. The vehicle hurtled over the ledge. Isis cringed at each loud bang caused by the car hitting the rocks while it rolled down the hill. They sounded like a gun firing in the air. A pain shot in her chest around her dead heart. It felt like the strings around it were being tugged in every direction. She could only hope the Galloways died right away and didn't suffer on the way down.

The crashing stopped, meaning the car had hit the bottom. It was soon followed by a crackling noise which Isis was sure had to be the gasoline igniting. Her suspicions were confirmed by a huge ball of smoke which rose from the bottom of the cliff and spread out into the sky. The lives of the Galloways—Zack's mother and father—were over. Isis wanted to tear up, if only her ducts could release that sort of relief.

The downed tree levitated into the air and exploded. Bark chips shot in every single direction. Isis threw an arm in front of her face. Splinters smacked her forearm and wrist. She dropped her arm in time to see

Valeria hover off the ground and land on her feet. The vampire ran to the edge of the cliff and gawked downward. She twisted her head in all directions, an expression that almost always showed arrogance was now stunned and discombobulated.

"No!" she shouted at the top of her lungs. "How could this be?"

As a precaution, Isis focused on the couple in the car. She couldn't sense thoughts from either of them, meaning they were most definitely dead, their bodies burned to crisps. That was her doing, but it assured even Valeria with all her power couldn't heal them back to life. As much as that realization stung, along with the Galloways' demise went the future Queen Valeria. Isis put a stop to the wicked witch's plans without a confrontation she had little chance of winning.

Valeria looked to the sky and let out a loud scream which carried far into the night. Her plan had been demolished, and history was back on course. Zack would stay with his uncle. He'd be around to meet The Witches of Vegas where his ingenuity would lead to Valeria's defeat. At least that was the case for now. To assure it, Isis hoped Valeria would see it as destiny interfering and never realize that another witch meddled. She had no reason to suspect she was anything but alone.

Best not to push her luck by sticking around. She was ready to return to her own time. She missed her boring life in New Salem. Then again, maybe both she and Valeria would simply disappear, absorbed into the energy of an Earth neither of them belonged in anymore. Isis let out a silent prayer that if she could return, Zack would be there waiting for her. She dreaded the inevitable moment of explaining to him what she had to do to save reality. Would he understand? Could he ever forgive her? Should he? At least he'd be there, safe and sound.

Isis decided to make one last stop before the return trip. She needed to make sure the Zack of this time was okay. Well, she knew even if he were okay, he wouldn't be once he found out about what happened to his parents. But she wanted to see him, anyway. She owed it to him and to herself.

"Teleport to Zack," she commanded the energy in as low of a whisper as she could. She repeated, "Teleport to Zack." The sight of Valeria screaming over the cliff faded away.

Chapter Twenty-three

Everything around Isis came into focus. She found herself standing in a tiny dark room with buttoned shirts, slacks, and vests hanging on either side of her. She reached forward and gave the door a slight push, opening it just enough to peek through. It was the second bedroom of one of The Felicity Hotel's two-bedroom suites. A six-year-old boy, with blond hair, slept in a bed against the wall underneath a window that overlooked the Vegas strip.

The boy tossed and turned several times, meaning his sleep was anything but normal slumber. Isis wasn't surprised, not with the curtains wide open. How could anyone sleep with the bright neon lights shining through that window? He sat up, which gave Isis a clear look at his face. Even in the dark, she could make out the deep green eyes of Zack Galloway. The poor child had no idea he was soon going to get the worst news of his life.

Isis took solace in the knowledge that at least now they were destined to meet and have their relationship. She felt so horrible for even having that thought. She wanted to tell herself that it was because they'd save the world from Valeria, and that it was her time with him which gave her the strength to see this journey through. Should she make it back, she didn't want it to be a future where he wasn't at her side.

Zack fell back, letting his head hit the pillow. The bedroom's open door overlooked the living room where Herb Galloway stood over a long marble dining room table. There were blueprints spread across the surface which Herb studied seriously. He waved a hand from one end to the other and nodded. Isis was sure the blueprints depicted his next big magic trick, and discussing it with himself was part of The Amazing Herb Galloway's process.

"Yes, I believe this will work as a finale," Herb said, confirming Isis' suspicions. "What audience wouldn't go nuts over a great transmorph trick? Now, I just have to make sure at least one of my assistants can follow the routine."

Zack sat up again. This time his head looked directly at the closet. "Is someone there?"

Isis took a step back, knocking over a toy castle meant for action figures to roam through. It was surrounded by other toys all over the closet floor. Isis smirked. It turned out Zack was always a bit messy. The smirk disappeared when the boy climbed out of the bed and walked toward the closet.

Isis focused on invisibility. She had to hurry. What were the ramifications of Zack seeing her almost nine years before they were destined to meet? His approach was interrupted when the suite's doorbell rang. Zack shifted his attention to the living room where Uncle Herb waltzed around the table and opened the front door.

Two men in suits stood on the other side. "Yes, can I help you?" Herb asked, puzzlement radiating from his voice.

"Mister Galloway?" the taller of the two men

asked. When Herb nodded, the man pulled out a badge and flashed it. "I'm Detective Murphy. This is Detective Monroe. May we come in and speak?"

"Is there a problem, Detectives?" Herb waved them to come in.

Murphy placed his badge in his pocket and entered the suite. "Perhaps we should sit down."

Herb motioned them to the table. He clearly had no idea why they were here. How could he? But Isis did know. They were about to drop a piece of news that would change his life forever. Zack's as well.

Zack walked to the bedroom door. Isis stamped her foot in the closet to grab his attention. She never intended to reveal herself, just check on him, but the conversation outside was not one Isis thought he should overhear. Zack had told Isis that he never woke up to see the detectives. It wasn't until the next morning that Herb sat him down and explained it in a way that softened the blow as much as possible.

This time, Zack was awake and out of bed because he heard Isis in the closet. How would bearing witness to the conversation firsthand affect the boy as he grew up? Would it change his path and turn him into someone different or lead to him making decisions different from the first time? Isis didn't want to be responsible for changing his very being in this moment.

"Hey," Isis whispered, keeping Zack's attention away from Herb's meeting with the police detectives in the living room.

Zack walked to the closet and pulled the door open. His eyes opened wide as he looked Isis up and down. "M-monster?" the boy asked.

"Um, yeah, I guess I am." Isis had never seen a

picture of Zack at this age. His face was so sweet, so nervous. It probably didn't help that her skin had faded from being dead for two hundred years. Plus, she still had salt and sand throughout her hair and clothes from her brief excursion on that island.

Zack's eyebrows rose in a way only his could. He took a step back, but after a moment of consideration, he moved forward. "Are you a good monster or a bad monster?" Apparently, curiosity got the better of him.

Isis had to give that question some thought, especially with everything she had just gone through. Could she really look this boy in the eye and call herself a good person? Well, she did save humanity today, but what she had to do would haunt her forever.

"Good monster or bad monster?" he asked again.

"I think I'm a good monster," Isis finally answered. "But one who did a bad thing."

"You did a bad thing?" Zack's head tilted. "Why?"

Isis' head dropped to the floor. "For a good reason."

"Then it was a good thing?"

"I really hope so."

A quick peek into the living room revealed Herb standing from the table with his shoulders slumped. The detectives also stood, offering their sincere apologies. Herb waved a hand at the bedroom while looking at the watch on his other wrist. He was deciding whether to wake up Zack and tell him now or wait until the morning. Isis already knew his decision. He'd choose to wait until morning.

"Who is my uncle talking to?" Zack asked.

A chill flowed through Isis like a river of pain. "It's, um…" Man, this was hard. As a teacher and vice president of New Salem, Isis had plenty of experience talking to kids. What she didn't have was experience lying to them. Isis wracked her brain, trying to come up with a good answer that wouldn't tip off the boy. She knew Zack's curious mind well. Whatever she'd say would bring about a dozen more questions.

Isis barely noticed the bright light shining off half of her face. But it wasn't light. It was fire. A huge red and yellow fireball sped for the window. "What the hell?" she shrieked. Isis ran out of the closet, throwing herself in front of Zack.

The fireball burst through the window and the wall. Isis flew through the bedroom door and into the living room. It was like being trapped in a colossal tidal wave that she couldn't fight or escape. Everything in the suite was on fire. There was no time for Isis to get her bearings or even check on the others, but she couldn't imagine any of them survived. Another bright light forced Isis to turn her head. The sound of a sonic boom which shook the entire building was deafening.

The ceiling collapsed. Enormous chunks of plaster, wood, and concrete covered, then buried Isis. Her skin was on fire. She pushed against the hard chunks of ceiling that lay across her body, but it wouldn't budge. Each piece that fell on top of her sounded like heavy fists slamming against a punching bag. By the time it stopped raining ceiling, Isis felt like there was tons of weight on top of her. Another loud sonic boom caused the floor to rattle. "Don't panic," Isis told herself. "Stay focused." Easier said than done.

Isis blocked out the fear from her mind. Where once that would have been an impossible task, with two hundred years of practice, Isis was able to keep her emotions in check, even during times of crisis. She focused on the energy within her control, giving it one command. "Phase my body!" She suddenly fell, her body going straight through the plaster and rubble. Isis kept falling. She reached out, but her hand went through everything available to grab onto. The broken shards of plywood and plaster followed her down.

Isis slammed back first against something solid. The jolt running through her spine sent a message to her brain that she had lost control of the phase spell. It was also a reminder that a vampire could, indeed, feel pain. "Shield!" Isis screamed and threw up her hands. She conjured a clear shield which blocked all the debris that fell on top of her. The shield quickly evaporated. Isis was now buried under what used to be the building's upper floors. She had no idea how far she fell before she hit a solid surface that didn't collapse underneath her.

It all happened too fast. Did her body blast through only a couple of floors, or did she end up all the way at the bottom of the building? She couldn't tell, not in pure darkness. The smoke filled her eyes and nostrils. It cut her off from both senses. She also couldn't hear anything. The one thing she knew was that her body was being pressed against the floor by however much debris was on top of her.

Unfortunately, that was the second problem of the day. Her first problem was that she failed in stopping the seeds of Valeria's conquest. If anything, thanks to Isis' interference, all the death and destruction Valeria would cause started years earlier. How many people just died at this immortal maniac's hands?

Chapter Twenty-four

"Light!"

Isis held her right hand up in front of her face. It glowed like a lightbulb and lit up the pitch-black darkness surrounding her. A heavy cough shot a cloud of dust from her throat and mouth. There was probably a lot more where that came from. Isis tried to move her body, but the intense pain that squeezed around her thigh made it impossible. A long, narrow piece of wood stretched from the ceiling to the floor. It went directly through the lower left quadrant of Isis' abdomen.

Isis reached up with her left hand. The ends of her fingers touched the ceiling. She was literally buried alive, and despite being immortal, she was running out of time. There wasn't much that could end a vampire's existence, but there were a few things on the list. Wood inside the undead body was one of them. The chemicals within anything wood were poison to a vampire's anatomy. Isis' skin around the wound had already inflamed. So long as it was in her system, infection would spread. She had to get it out fast.

Isis wrapped her fingers around the long piece of wood. She gave it a slight tug. The intense stinging made her scream. It also caused the entire ceiling to shake like a tremor during an earthquake. She quickly let go. Apparently, this piece of wood was the only thing keeping Isis from an abrupt burial.

As a vampire, she was doomed with no hope of saving herself. But as a witch, Isis had options. She closed her eyes and focused. This was something Isis had trained for, although she never expected to need that training. "Phase my body," she chanted. "Phase my body."

Isis' midsection blurred. Her hand passed through. Isis no longer felt the wood. She laid her phased body down and rolled. Isis' left side screamed in pain with each movement thanks to the damage already inflicted, but it was worth enduring. Once she completed the roll, the wood still stood in place holding the ceiling at bay. She was now free, but the stinging pain from infection stayed with her.

A sense of nausea filled Isis' stomach. It felt like everything inside of her wanted to come out. That was a huge problem because the only thing running through her system was the fresh coyote blood mixed with much older blood. She couldn't afford to lose any of it, not when another meal was nowhere in sight. Isis clutched her gut. Nausea was something a vampire shouldn't have been able to experience—at least, she hadn't as far back as she could remember—which meant it had to be mental. Isis was in full panic mode. Then again, it could have been that the wood had already created an infection in her body. That was also something she had never experienced before.

"Stay calm, just stay calm," Isis chanted. She had never used the Earth's energy to control her nerves; who knew if that would even work? But right now, she was willing to try anything.

Isis crawled, keeping her lit hand in front of her. She couldn't stand, not with the ceiling so low and ready to collapse at any moment. She needed to get out before the sound of fire high above closed in. Isis was tired and in terrible pain, but she had to stay focused. The building had taken a lot of damage and wouldn't remain standing much longer. But even though escape would save her from the eventual collapse, it wouldn't mean she was safe. Valeria was out there. Who else could have been responsible for the fireballs that brought the entire hotel down around her?

A loud crash from high above made the rubble rattle. Somehow, it held, but it creaked, and the roar of flames grew closer. She pressed her left hand against the open sore on her stomach which felt like it had dug through her the way a worm tunnels through an apple. Ignore the pain, Isis told herself. She needed to take control of her body and the energy around her. Isis focused on the light shining from her right hand. It helped block out the smoke and damage that surrounded her. She opened her mouth, ready to speak the words that would teleport her to the outside of the building. Her concentration was suddenly broken by the sound of a loud female voice.

"Help me!"

Isis pointed her hand like a flashlight toward the voice. The woman's head and one arm stuck out from underneath a table with large pieces of ceiling piled on top. "You, with the light," the lady cried out. "Please, help me."

Isis wanted to help. She really did. But Valeria needed to be stopped before all of Las Vegas suffered the same fate as The Felicity Hotel. Soon after, her target would be the entire world. Isis had seen it with her own eyes. She didn't want to leave this one lady behind, but billions of lives were on the line, including those closest to Isis. She had to go back in time, figure out another way to end this nightmare. No choice. Time to leave—

"Please help me. I'm pregnant!"

Damnit, Isis didn't have the time. But in her pursuit to right the world, she had left behind both Domina and the man who raised her in nightmarish situations. She was tired of leaving people behind and suffering from the guilt afterward. Isis crawled back to the woman whose hair, once brunette, was now a dirt and sawdust-covered mess. "Stay still. I'm going to get you out of here," Isis said.

"H-how?" the woman cried out. "What happened?"

"Earthquake, I guess." Isis took the woman's hand. "Close your eyes."

"What? Why?"

"Trust me. Just do it."

The woman shut her eyes. Isis focused on teleportation. She was sure the building was surrounded by first responders and onlookers by now. Her best bet was to have them both materialize down the street behind the neighboring hotel. "Teleport to street." Isis formed a picture in her head of the alleyway. "Teleport to street."

Just as everything blurred and faded away, with a great earthly shift and metallic thunder, the ceiling fell. The side of the neighboring hotel appeared in front of Isis. The woman, who was, indeed, pregnant based on her stomach's bulge under the orange "Las Vegas" T-shirt, fell to her knees. She breathed heavily, taking in the night air.

"You're safe now," Isis said to her.

"How…how did we get out here?" From the look on the woman's frozen face, she was understandably traumatized.

"It's a gift," Isis answered. "Are you okay to stand up?"

The expectant mother did not answer. She didn't have to. Even if she was physically able to stand, shock had taken over her body. Isis stepped away from the lady, giving her room to recover from the ordeal. She ran to the front of the building which faced the Vegas strip. The Felicity Hotel was half a block away. What Isis saw, although expected, made her gasp.

The top four floors were collapsed inward. Smoke poured out the windows of the highest floor left standing. Isis smelled the fire even from down the street. The panic-filled crowd was made up of thousands, many of whom were using their phones to take pictures or video. It was as if every single hotel along the strip had emptied out and they were all around The Felicity.

Many people had made it out of the hotel in time, evidenced by the charred and dirty clothes, but there were also many who didn't. Everyone from those top floors were incinerated by Valeria's massive fireballs. That included Zack. His future would never be. Everything Isis did to put time back on course was a complete failure. Her reality would never happen, not unless she could outfox Valeria. But then what? She already foiled those plans, and the result was worse. She needed to figure this out, but right now, Isis' body was riddled in such agony, she could barely focus let alone come up with a new plan.

Metal rattled. Isis whirled at the sound. A nearby

green dumpster shook, then propelled forward at lightning speed. It shot at Isis, who raised both hands in front of her face. A clear block of force formed in front of her. It was an instinct she had developed from many lifetimes of training. The dumpster hit Isis' force shield like a speeding car slamming into a brick wall, and the impact caused a vibration that knocked her backward. Her body lifted high in the air, then dropped hard across the street's solid surface.

Isis grabbed the back of her neck. Her vision was filled with stars. She should have been able to stop that dumpster with no impact at all, but the pain in her left side had spread down her thigh and throughout her midsection. Isis felt it the moment she raised her arms. The sharp pain kept her from concentrating enough to strengthen the shield. Isis sat up and shut her eyes tight, trying to push through the fog in her brain.

Isis flung her head in every direction. It was obvious who attacked her with the dumpster. It had to be Valeria, which meant the four-hundred-year-old witch was aware of Isis' presence. There would be no sneaking up on her, no element of surprise, and no fixing things behind her back. No doubt, Isis wasn't ready for this fight. She shut her eyes and focused on an image of the Vegas desert. "Teleport," Isis shouted.

The sensation of teleportation took over her body, but it stopped almost immediately. Isis hadn't gone anywhere, and that wasn't her doing. Her connection to the energy was still working, but someone's control was stronger than her own. "Oh no," Isis whispered.

She opened her eyes in time to see Valeria floating in the air and landing directly in front of her. The elder witch's scowl told Isis that she was in a lot of trouble.

She was about to enter a battle she had no hope of winning.

Chapter Twenty-five

"Even here in the past, you are a deterrent to my plans to reshape the world. I will tolerate your interference no more." Valeria's feet touched the ground with purpose. Her words sounded calm, yet her eyes had turned pure black. Valeria's sharp vampire fangs showed.

Isis forced herself up into a seated position. The burning sensation in her stomach had extended to her thighs, meaning the infection from the wood had spread through more of her bloodstream. Soon, it would take over her entire body. She needed to replenish her bad blood with a fresh supply. Good chance Valeria wasn't about to let Isis call a timeout.

"You killed Zack!" Isis screamed. "You killed his uncle, all those people in the hotel. There was no reason for so much death!"

"That was obviously not my intention," Valeria replied in a calmness that overshadowed Isis' rage. "But your interference forced me to take far more extreme measures. Either way, the boy needed to be removed from my path. As do you."

Amazing Valeria spoke of the death of hundreds with such dispassion. To her, Zack was simply an obstacle she needed to move out of her way. What made this cavalier attitude even worse was that she blamed Isis for her actions. Life meant everything to

Isis. She would never want anyone to get hurt. In truth, she compared everyone she had ever met to Zack. There was, however, one exception. Valeria was the only one Isis ever truly wanted to murder, not from hate or anger, but out of compassion for the world. Despite her best efforts, she hadn't succeeded, and all of her concerns for humankind if she let Valeria live came to fruition.

"I don't understand why you feel you must stand in my way." Each step Valeria took toward Isis was slow and deliberate. "My goal is to create a peaceful world. One where witches like us thrive as the dominant species we are meant to be. You know this, yet you stubbornly resist. Are you truly so ignorant?"

"I-I've been to your future," Isis shouted. "It doesn't work out how you think it will."

Valeria paused mid-step. "Meaning what?"

"Witches are tortured and killed, just like everybody else. The only one who thrives in this new world is *you*." Isis jabbed a finger at Valeria. "Two hundred years from now, you are queen while the rest of the world burns. You destroy everyone's lives without mercy."

Valeria leaned forward. "You know this for sure?"

"I do. I was there." Isis glared at Valeria. "It was a horrible existence for everyone, including witches."

"I see." Valeria's head tipped up. Was she actually contemplating Isis' warning? "That does sound tragic. However, I always suspected the world would need a few hundred years under my rule before accepting its new path." Valeria's corroded teeth showed in what may have been a wide-mouthed smile. "It sounds like everything I planned is well on track in the future."

Damn, that was not the conclusion Isis hoped Valeria would come to, but she should have known. The ancient witch claimed her mission was for the betterment of the planet. Perhaps, at one time, that was true, but not anymore. Valeria had long ago lost all empathy even for her fellow witches. Her path had skewed into a dark, dangerous trip.

"You would allow all that death to happen? Death you caused?" The area darkened as Isis felt her temper rising. It meant her eyes had gone black as well. "Even all the witches who died horrible deaths because of you?"

Valeria's eyes narrowed. Then she nodded. "It will be over their corpses a new world will be built. Their sacrifices will not be in vain."

Isis had heard enough. The vampire inside was ready to assume command. Her muscles still felt sore from Valeria running her over with a dumpster. Time to return the favor. Isis focused on the dumpster. It levitated into the air. "Crush her against the building," Isis muttered. She never had such violent thoughts before, but she also never knew such evil. Isis now realized Valeria had no intentions of changing her plans. There was no reasoning with her.

The huge steel container flew at Valeria like a bullet fired from a gun. Isis waited for the thudding of metal on flesh…but it passed through the Wiccan vampire. The crash of the dumpster slamming against the building echoed like an explosion around Isis' head. Valeria faded away because she was never standing there in the first place.

"An illusion," Isis shrieked.

Isis lifted off the ground and then into the air. This

wasn't her doing. Something had taken control of her body. She propelled up three stories before finding herself face to face with Valeria who held out a glowing hand. Isis tried to flail her arms and legs, but they wouldn't respond to her mental commands.

"You sicken me," Valeria growled. "I see your coven's corruption stayed with you even in whatever time you come from. Such a waste."

Valeria pushed her hand forward. Isis flew backward until she crashed through a window. Glass splattered in every direction. Isis hit a cold tiled floor and rolled to the center of the room. Through the dim lighting, she saw unplugged slot machines lined up against each wall. Two gaming tables, one roulette and one craps, sat side by side in the back of the room, both covered in dust. One of the tables had stacks of multi-colored gambling chips along its surface. The room must have been used as storage for the casino. Every hotel on the strip had one to keep extra machines on reserve.

Isis stood in time to find Valeria materializing in front of her. On instinct, she backed against the wall. Valeria stared her down with a devious twinkle in her eye. Three of the slot machines lifted off the ground. They shook like spaceships revving up, ready to launch.

"I don't know how you found me here in the past." Valeria pointed a finger at Isis. One slot machine flew at Isis. With a wave of her hand, Isis changed the trajectory of the heavy slot machine and sent it crashing through the broken window. "I also haven't the foggiest notion of how far in the future you are from," Valeria said.

A second slot machine sprang Isis' way. This time,

she took control and ripped it in half. Both halves flew in opposite directions. They thudded into opposite walls. The last machine rotated sideways and pointed its head at Isis.

"One truth remains between us," Valeria continued. "You cannot best me. I have always been your superior."

Valeria was right. Isis couldn't match her in power, experience, or intensity. But, if she could take advantage of the cockiness and catch the Wiccan vampire by surprise, maybe she'd have a shot. It would only be one shot, so Isis needed to make it count. Time to think outside the box, like Zack. She focused on the energy around the slot machine. "Fire!" she screamed. The top of the machine lit up, but it stayed in place.

Valeria eyed it. She looked back at Isis and cackled. "After all this time," Valeria said through a smug laugh. "You still haven't mastered control, have you?"

But it was exactly what Isis wanted to happen. This was her one chance. The futile failure lowered Valeria's guard. Time to do something unexpected.

Isis ran at her, focusing on a teleportation spell. Her mind concentrated on the volcano she and Zack visited near the Fiji Islands years ago to rescue an abandoned witch. On Zack's request, Isis levitated them both high above the volcano so they could see it from an aerial viewpoint. It was a beautiful sight and, although it could certainly erupt, it hadn't since the early 1800s. But dammit, it would today. She'd make sure of it.

Isis wrapped her arms around Valeria's waist. "Teleport!" she screamed. Isis smiled at the frozen bewilderment on Valeria's face as the room faded.

Within seconds, they were falling directly into the volcano's crater. Isis pushed against Valeria's body, then willed herself to float in the air. With all the energy she had left, Isis pointed her arms downward, forcing the energy around Valeria to drag her into the volcano's throat.

"Erupt!" Isis' wide stare concentrated on the lava bubbling in the floor of the volcano. She heated the energy inside, which in turn heated the lava. It was like rubbing two sticks together to create fire. The lava churned like potion in a cauldron. Sparks shot into the air. Red-orange flames burst into life. "Erupt now!"

A loud explosion almost broke Isis' concentration, but she held her levitation spell firm. Smoke shot up from the crater. The intense heat burned Isis' arms and legs. She ignored the blistering from the heat and kept her focus. The lava itself must have been roasting Valeria alive, so she had to keep it going.

A second wave of steam shot up from the volcano's throat. It hit Isis in the face. This time, her concentration broke. Isis rolled in mid-air away from the crater. Her worry that she'd get sucked inside the mouth ended the moment her body hit the mountain, then bounced up and hit again.

A layer of dirt covered her arms and shirt, but it didn't cool the scalding burns throughout her skin. She'd heal, but for the moment Isis's arms looked much like the apprentice's. The legs of her jeans, meanwhile, were shredded.

"Ouch," Isis cried out. She lifted her head in time to see red lava rushing down the mountain on all sides. Every muscle in her body screamed in agony, which meant getting up and running would be a chore. She needed to throw the pain aside and focus on another teleportation spell. But that would take focus that she couldn't muster.

The lava stopped its descent just a few feet away. Talk about a close call. Any closer and Isis' body would have been covered in boiling lava. She whistled a sigh of relief. Isis was already sporting several bumps, bruises, and burns. Not to mention the infection caused by the wood fibers which ran through her body. Even if she could have stood up, she didn't have much of a chance to outrun the lava if it kept flowing. But, as much pain as Isis felt, she knew it was worth it now that Valeria was gone. The threat was finally over.

Or at least that was the thought running through her mind, until a distorted image appeared in front of her.

The distortion disappeared, leaving Valeria in its place. Her blackened eyes were enraged. Smoke poured out of every pore along her body. Her black overskirt dress was now scorched where there was little of Valeria left to the imagination. A shame that wasn't the case with the monster, herself.

Isis took her best shot, and Valeria endured. The witch now stood ready for their battle to resume. Isis, however, was not.

Chapter Twenty-Six

This time, Valeria didn't offer any quips, puns, or demeaning insults. This time, she raised her hands over her head while electricity shot between them, forming a ball of static. Isis wanted to jump out of the way, but her entire midsection burned like a hot chimney. She could barely move, which left her for dead. She'd have to dig deep and find a way. Whatever pain she'd endure had to be better than waiting to get electrocuted, or whatever this mad vampire had in store. Right now, to save herself, Isis had to get onto her feet and do something.

An idea hit her, but she'd have to be fast. Isis placed her hand against the ground. Dirt flew into Valeria's face. Isis made sure much of it shot directly into the elder witch's eyes and up her nose. The lightning faded as Valeria covered her face with her hands.

"Teleport!" Isis shouted.

Everything blurred, then refocused. Isis was no longer on the ground. She was now standing face-to-face with Valeria. This was her best chance to catch her off-guard and before the witch could take control of the energy to form a counter spell. But having the power and knowing what to do with it were two different things. So far, Valeria handled everything Isis had thrown at her. She got in close. Now Isis needed to hit her with something.

Isis focused on a single thought, wrapping Valeria in a cocoon of energy that would cut off her Wiccan connection. It was smart, and a ploy she hadn't ever tried on any other witch. If anything, it would lead to a battle of wills that Isis was determined to win. She took control of the energy around Valeria. Within moments, it would cover her like a blanket, leaving her powerless.

But she didn't expect Valeria, besides being an amazing witch, also had a hard right cross. It caught Isis across the jaw and knocked her off her feet. In two hundred years, Isis had never been punched so hard. The spell broke. She was surprised her jaw wasn't knocked clear off her skull.

"That was all you had, wasn't it?" Valeria scoffed. "An effort unworthy of immortals such as us. Your immortality, I shall end now."

A strong wind from below scooped Isis off the ground. She was able to move her arms and legs, but she couldn't stop the wind from carrying her into the sky. Valeria levitated off the ground as well. They were now inches apart, with the elder witch glaring down into Isis' eyes.

"I could have killed you long ago, but I chose not to," Valeria snarled. "I even helped your coven complete your turn. I did all this because I believed, once you overcame your naivety, you would be beneficial to my cause." Valeria's eyes were as bottomless as black holes. "I now realize that you are a hindrance to progress. The only way this world can be put on course is with you no longer on it! You have left me no choice. Now, it will be you who will float for eternity in outer space."

Isis certainly wasn't ready for her demise, not today. She reached out, wanting nothing more than to pull that cocky smirk from Valeria's face. Her right hand was just out of reach. Isis couldn't touch her, but she didn't have to. Another idea popped into her head.

"Light!" Isis screamed. In that moment, she thought about the brightness of the Vegas sun.

A bright light flashed from Isis' palm. Valeria's head shot back, breaking her concentration. Both Isis and Valeria toppled to the ground. Isis thumped on her knees and hands while Valeria landed on the soles of her boots.

Isis felt the lava's heat a few miles underneath the mountain. It was still boiling. Perfect. She pointed with both hands to the ground underneath Valeria's feet. "Open up, pull her down," she chanted. "Open up, suck her in!"

Obeying Isis' spell, the Earth ripped apart underneath Valeria. The ground around her dropped straight down while steam shot up through the newly formed hole. Isis commanded the steam to suck Valeria in like a vacuum. A great plan, had it worked. But Valeria didn't get pulled in. She hovered in mid-air above the hole.

Isis gasped. She needed to hit the evil witch with something, and fast. But she just blew her chance. Valeria whipped her hand in a violent fashion. A heavy blast of force rammed Isis in the chest, and she sailed down the mountain. Her body rolled, bouncing every few steps all the way to the bottom. The momentum once she landed sent her skidding along the rough terrain. The surface tore at her sleeves and jeans, shredding the pant legs further until they became shorts.

The force ripped through her skin. It was only seconds but felt like an eternity before Isis stopped sliding. Old blood rolled down her cheeks and forehead.

Isis shook her head to clear out the cobwebs. She sat up, expecting to find herself under attack. She looked back and forth. No Valeria. Did she get lucky? Did Valeria leave, thinking she was dead or—

Everything went bright as if the sun had risen out of the night sky. Isis looked up. What she saw made her gawk like never before. Valeria hovered, her arms over her head. A fireball had formed above her, and it was expanding. It had already grown to the size of the one that Valeria created to destroy New Salem. It would have done its job if Sacha hadn't absorbed the fireball into her own body. It killed her instantly. For all of Isis' power and immortality, she didn't expect to survive being incinerated, either.

Isis was out of ideas. It was clear she couldn't beat Valeria, at least not right now. The only strategy left was to get away and live to fight another day. Then maybe she'd come up with a new plan. She believed in her heart that there had to be a way, but what? Another time jump? Not as if this one worked out. But if she ran, there'd be a chance to figure it out, at least until either infection from the wood overtook her body or Valeria came looking for her.

Isis focused on New Salem. It was the first place that popped into her head, and it was far away from this volcano. "Teleport," Isis chanted.

Valeria's fireball grew. Isis waited for everything around her to fade away. But it didn't. Nothing was happening. "Teleport!" she screamed. The energy refused to respond. This time, it wasn't Valeria's doing.

It was Isis' own fear blocking her connection. The fireball was now even larger than the one that killed Sacha.

Sacha wasn't the only loved one Isis lost to Valeria's wrath. She lost everyone she had ever cared about. Was there really anything left to fight for? It was becoming clearer and clearer that she couldn't win, which meant she couldn't prevent Valeria's dark future from taking over the timeline. A destroyed Felicity Hotel in the middle of Las Vegas proved that.

It was time to accept the inevitable, that no matter what Isis tried, Valeria's power was just too much to overcome. In all their previous confrontations, Isis always had help, whether it was her family's combined power or Zack's ingenuity. Both had galvanized Isis in a way she could never do for herself. Hell, even in that horrible new future where Valeria was a pampered queen, Isis escaped only with the assistance of a tortured version of herself.

Now, left all alone, she could only wait for Valeria's fireball to end the nightmare, at least for her, but not for all of Earth. The fireball above Valeria's head had grown so bright it lit up the sky for miles. Even if Isis survived the fire's assault, she'd be left in a helpless state. Valeria pointed her hands down at Isis with her fingers stretched out. The fireball traveled with a slow descent. Valeria was taking her time, savoring the moment.

Isis pulled herself to her knees. She straightened her back and held her head high. After two hundred years, if her existence were to end at this moment, she wouldn't let it happen while quivering like a child. Isis dropped her hands to her sides, readying herself for what she expected would be a painful end to her existence. That's when she felt them, five small objects in her right jeans pocket.

"The crystals!" Isis screamed. Her hopes renewed.

The huge fireball moved closer, shining like a blinding inferno. Isis reached into her pocket and pulled out the enchanted crystals. Her confidence grew to where she could feel her control of the energy return.

"Pyramid!" She tossed the crystals in the air. They fell on five sides of her, each one at equal distances from one another. "Protect me with a shield! A strong, impenetrable shield!"

Sparks shot out from each enchanted crystal. They met at a singular point above Isis' head. Inside the crystals, the energy flowed as if it were a part of her. It was perfect timing due to the fire engulfing Isis along with a half-mile of the area. The inferno all around her was blinding. Smoke rose up and filled the sky. It was like being in the center of a nuclear explosion.

But the clear dome formed by the crystals held. Isis barely felt the heat. Moments passed, or maybe it was minutes, she couldn't be sure, but the fire dissipated. Soon, there was nothing left except for the smoke that filled the air.

Valeria floated to the ground, landing in front of Isis and her protective five-sided pyramid. The raised eyebrows on Valeria's face said that she was more than a little impressed, or pissed. Or both.

"Enchanted crystals. A clever ploy on your part." Valeria formed a small fireball in the palm of her hand. She threw it at the crystals' shield. The fireball splattered but didn't penetrate. "But I am sure you know well enough that the power enhancement of the crystals is not indefinite. And I certainly have the time to wait."

A second fireball slammed against the shield around Isis, and then a third. It rattled but stood firm. Isis held her focus on the crystals. They were her best protection. But Valeria was right—Isis couldn't stay in an energy shield for all of eternity. Eventually the crystals would drain. Then what? Everything Isis tried had failed, and she had no other plan. She even sacrificed her own set of morals by swerving Zack's parents and their car over the cliff to die.

The guilt ate at her insides like a parasite, but she had no choice. It was exactly what Isis needed to do, at least that's what Domina insisted she foresaw in her dream. "Go back, change it all, make things so it never happened," the girl said. "Where it all began. The moment that opened the path to her queendom." Isis did exactly that. She changed the moment, and it didn't hinder Valeria's plans at all. In fact, it led to an earlier start on the destruction of Vegas. Dammit, Domina's premonition was wrong, and now the world would pay for it!

Another blast of fire rattled the dome. Isis knew what Valeria was up to; she couldn't break through, but she could make the crystals work and eventually drain their power. It may take a long time—perhaps years—but, as Valeria said, time wasn't an issue to an immortal such as herself. More likely, the attacks were meant simply to taunt. The only thing that did penetrate was Valeria's loud cackle. Isis placed a hand against the clear shield. It vibrated with each fireball Valeria threw like a pitcher warming up the arm before a game. The shield held, at least so far.

Isis focused on her hand. Her skin had faded over the course of time. It now looked more like light brown chalk than a human being's tone. After a long and hard stare, her mouth opened wide. "Oh, my God, of course!" Isis shouted as it all came together. "How did I not see it?"

She wanted to kick herself so hard. Domina's words were right all along. Isis just didn't get it, until now. She had stopped Valeria from saving Zack's parents, but that wasn't the moment she was meant to change. Isis was so fixated on Zack's history that she never once looked to her own. The key to stopping Valeria wasn't at this time. In fact, the specific moment hadn't happened yet.

The dull pain in Isis' body ran from her chest to her legs. She had to block it from her mind. Nothing could distract her, not now. With renewed vigor, Isis reached out to the energy through the enchanted crystals. "Take me there," she said. "Read my mind and take me to the moment I need to go."

The crystals' energy sparked. Valeria's arm stopped in mid-pitch. The fire in her hand fizzled into pure smoke. "What are you doing in there?" Valeria's head cocked. "Why are you grinning?"

Everything blurred. The pyramid fizzled out. Isis experienced the sensation of falling forward. Valeria fired a blast of pure force at Isis, but it went straight through her body. The crystals sucked in the energy and responded to Isis' mental command.

"You fool!" Valeria screeched. "There is no moment in time that you can stop me. If you are trying to run, wherever and whenever you try to hide, it will not save you. I will find you and destr—"

Valeria was gone. So was the volcano. Isis was on the way to her last, and best, chance to end this nightmare for good. Hopefully, the crystals would take her to the right place, and the right time…

Chapter Twenty-seven

The sensation of falling forward stopped. Isis was on her knees with her back perfectly straight. Her ears appreciated the sudden quiet surrounding her. The ground was cold, meaning there was no pool of lava flowing underneath. The sound of fireballs smacking against her shield was gone, as was Valeria. The volcano had been replaced by high-rise apartments on all sides. The stench of wet garbage filled her enhanced sense of smell.

Isis pushed to her feet, ignoring the intense pain that wrapped around her body like an uncomfortable blanket. A look around told her she was in the right place. It was the neighborhood where, at nine years old, a scared mob tried to kill her. It was Isis' foster parents at the time who led their friends and neighbors on what they believed to be a righteous mission. After witnessing her Wiccan power, they believed Isis had been possessed by the devil. It was here, on this dark street, where Isis' coven and family, who would soon become The Witches of Vegas, saved her life and took her in.

Isis expected to never come back to this street. But she was wrong. Years later, Valeria brought fifteen-year-old Isis to this exact location and forced a confrontation with her foster parents. This was the exact spot Valeria started Isis' turn. That she was here now meant the energy and her own force of will took her to the exact place she needed to be. But was it the right time? God, it had to be. If not, she was screwed. She no longer sensed the energy flowing through the crystals. This last time jump drained them completely, and Isis could barely control the jumps without them.

Screams and the scampering of footsteps spun her around. Two people dashed past her in a panic. A memory from long ago helped Isis recognize them. It was her former foster parents, George and…something. This night happened two centuries ago, yet Isis remembered it all as if it happened last night. The frightened couple ran off after the Isis at the time turned her power on Valeria. What happened next was the exact moment in time Isis needed to change.

Isis watched the fifteen-year-old version of herself rush around the corner of the apartment building. She stopped, breathing heavily to the point of hyperventilation, and placed her back against the building's wall. The girl held her hand over the rip in her pants near her thigh, trying to use the energy to heal a burn created by Valeria. It was a futile struggle, attempting to focus the energy while her emotions were so erratic.

Isis wanted to yell at her younger self to run. Valeria was ready to attack. Isis would have known that even if she hadn't lived these moments before. She forgot how wide-eyed and inexperienced she was back then, with no idea how the next moment would change the course of her life. And the long-term course of the planet's.

Her insides felt like they were on fire. But Isis pushed past it, hobbling toward her past self. She needed to get there quickly. She only had a few seconds before—

Valeria burst through the ground and landed in front of the other Isis. The elder witch reached out with her right hand. Blood dripped from her long fingernails which were aimed for Isis' throat. Those sharp nails were about to thrust through the younger Isis' skin and allow the vampire blood to soak into her system. That was where the path started and would again if Isis didn't intervene.

With all her will, Isis lunged forward with both hands pointed at Valeria. The energy in the air sparked. "*Witch, freeze!*" Isis screamed.

Valeria's outstretched hand was inches from the other Isis' neck, but it wasn't moving any closer. Time had frozen around Valeria. Isis could kill her now, end the wiccan vampire's threat once and for all, but that wasn't the change she had to make. Everything still needed to play out exactly as it did the first time, but with one significant difference...

Lucky that Dad, the great Sebastian Santell, taught her how to use the energy to deliver hypnotic suggestions. He used it all the time on their sold-out audiences to keep them immersed in every moment of the show. Isis had never used hypnosis on anyone. She never thought she'd want to or need to. But he kept making her practice the spells in case of an emergency. Thanks, Dad, although he probably never had this sort of emergency in mind.

Isis limped in front of Valeria. She placed a hand across the elder vampire's forehead and looked deep into her darkened eyes. She focused on connecting with Valeria's mind. Once she felt the connection, Isis spoke. “Listen to my words. Hear them as your thoughts.” Isis kept her tone smooth and rhythmic, just as she was taught. “You don’t want to turn this witch. You thought she’d make a good apprentice, but you were mistaken. She’s more trouble than she’s worth. You’re better off killing her as a message to the world. She’ll be no good to you immortal.”

There was no movement in Valeria’s eyes. Of course not. She was frozen in time. But did the message get through? Did it sink into her brain? The only chance reality had was that Isis’ hypnotic words were now engrained and Valeria believed them to be her own thoughts.

Isis removed her hand from Valeria’s forehead and backed away. She ran a hand through her stringy and dirt-covered hair. If she read the energy right—and she was...almost sure she did—then the message did get through, and her mission was complete. Of course, that was a huge “if.” Valeria’s mind was strong, after all. But were her instincts strong enough to resist a hypnotic suggestion that she wouldn’t know was placed in her brain? Either way, win or lose, the war was over.

Isis put a hand on her stomach. The burning had been replaced by a dull numbness. One last problem arose. A voice behind her sobbed. “You…you want her to kill me? Why? Who are you?”

Isis slowly spun around. Damnit, in her anxiousness, she forgot to freeze time around her younger self as well. The other Isis slid down the building’s wall until she fell into a sitting position. Her arms and legs shook as if she were sitting in a freezer and not on an inner-city street. Isis dropped to her knees, so they’d come face to face. It was like looking at a photograph from her childhood. She forgot how overwhelmed she was back then by just about everything. That anxiety lessened over time, but it never really went away.

"Listen carefully," Isis said. "You need to convince Valeria to take you back to Vegas. You can't beat her alone, but you won't be alone. Your family will be there."

"My-my family? They're okay?"

"Of course, they are." Isis remembered knowing in her heart back then, that despite Valeria's lies, they were all still alive. "This battle is going to get a lot worse. But, in the end, you're going to beat her together. You'll be okay, all of you."

The younger Isis' head lifted up. Fear was replaced with a look of curiosity. "Are you…are you me?"

"Well…" That was a harder question than Isis realized. "I was. But I don't think I am now, not anymore." Isis' head pounded. Her vision slightly blurred even though she wasn't teleporting. The numbness now extended down to her knees. Hold off, she begged the Earth's energy. Just give me enough time. Please. "I don't think I'm going to exist much longer. I have to hurry and do this."

Isis held out her palm and concentrated. A ball of white light about the size of an enchanted crystal formed and rested atop her open hand. Both younger and immortal Isis stared at the round light as it shuddered, then split into two.

"What…what is that?" the young teen asked. "What are you doing?"

"All my history, everything I know. I've been through so much, it shouldn't all cease to be along with me." Isis looked up, directly at the past version of herself. "I'm going to share with you everything I've seen, everything I did. I get that's a lot to deal with by yourself. That's why I'm giving you two sets of my memories. So you can give one to someone else."

Isis laid her hand against her younger self's temple. "I ask you to think long and hard about who to share this knowledge with. Don't rush that decision. Make sure you've chosen the right person before putting this in their head. Do you understand?"

"N-no."

Duh, of course she didn't. How could she? "Don't worry, you will."

The two balls of light shot out of her hand and through the other Isis' skull. The young teen's eyes opened wide. Her eyes darted in every direction. She tried to speak, but no words left her lips. Isis couldn't imagine how the girl must have felt seeing so much history that she never actually lived through even though it was her in the memories. Then again, she could imagine just based on how she would have felt had she gone through this at the age of fifteen. They were, essentially, the same person.

A sharp pain drove through Isis like a scalding hot knife. Isis screamed out, wrapping her arms around her waist. Then, nothing. Her body was numb all over except for her hands and feet which tingled as if they had been asleep for weeks. Isis' every instinct told her that she was about to teleport, although she couldn't see a destination in her mind. She tried to use the energy to give her a little bit longer, but if it was still with her, she could no longer sense its presence.

"I…I think I'm losing my connection." Isis forced

herself to stand. Her feet wobbled. "I have to go. Get through this, then do well with the rest of our life."

Isis took one last look at her young self—the girl was still in shock, but she was getting her bearings, refocusing on Valeria. Isis willed herself to put one foot in front of the other. It felt like she had two-ton weights tied to her ankles. After the sixth step, she fell to her knees. Isis could no longer move her fingers or toes. She took what she knew would be one last look over her shoulder. The time spell on Valeria wore off. She lasered the girl in front of her with an angry scowl.

Valeria lifted the other Isis off the ground by the throat. Although the grip was tight, her fingernails weren't piercing the girl's skin. That meant no transfer of vampiric blood.

"I foresaw you making a great apprentice to my cause." Valeria's left hand ignited into flame. She lifted it over her head. "But now I see you are no good to me alive."

The younger Isis blinked her eyes rapidly. Her survival instinct took over, pulling herself back into the moment. "B-burn me…here." She barely squeezed out the words from the clamp around her throat. "No…one…to…see."

Valeria dropped her left hand. The fire dissipated into a puff of smoke. A devious smile crossed her face. Isis could practically see the lightbulb above her head. "You may have a point," she responded.

Isis' eyes closed. She felt herself losing consciousness. *Please, just a few moments longer.*

With all she had, Isis forced her eyelids open. Everything was still clear except that her vision had gone dark. Only the vampire in her was left, but it wouldn't last long either. It had to be enough. Isis fought the tug she felt around her body. Before losing what was left of her existence, she had to know it wasn't all for nothing.

"You wish to die in Las Vegas instead of in this decrepit neighborhood?" Valeria asked the younger Isis. "Very well, then, let us grant you your final wish."

"Good girl," Isis whispered.

It worked. Valeria decided not to infect Isis with her blood, and she believed it was her choice. That meant she wouldn't start the turn just to second guess that decision and leave her captive with vampire blood in her system. When everything played out and Luther dragged Valeria into The Other World, there would never be a reason to reopen the portal and find her. There would never be an opportunity for Valeria to escape, then go back in time after losing their second battle. In fact, there would never be a second battle. She'd never keep Zack from becoming part of The Witches of Vegas. She'll never kill him in the past since she'll never travel to the past.

Valeria and the younger Isis faded out. Their return trip to Las Vegas was complete. Isis wanted nothing more than to lay down and sleep, but her body no longer obeyed her commands. She couldn't even blink her eyes or move her mouth. This was it for her, yet she was okay with that. The future Isis knew, the one she cared deeply for, no longer waited for her. But neither Valeria's future as queen. The world was better off that way.

Bolts of lightning lit up the sky while everything around Isis faded away for the last time.

Part Three

Chapter Twenty-eight

Isis floated above the sold-out audience. Although she had only recently learned the "lighter than air" spell, it felt like she had used it thousands of times over the last two hundred years. Because in another reality, that was exactly the case. The memories didn't belong to her—well, not really her. Then again, maybe they did. Either way, they still bounced around her head competing with what she knew was real.

After a couple of flips and somersaults, it was time for Isis to return to the stage. She floated down and landed on her feet next to the host of their show, Sebastian, her adopted dad. There was a gleam in his eye along with a huge smile, both the result of her perfect landing.

"Ladies and gentlemen," he announced into the microphone. "I give you the future goddess of magic, *Isis!*"

"Future," Isis said under her breath. The thought still made her skin cold.

The audience cheered Isis' performance. A month ago, this would have thrilled her. The reaction was exactly what she strove for. But right now, it seemed insignificant, especially after all she'd seen. With Zack and her family, they saved the world, and themselves, from Valeria. But Isis' mind went beyond that. For the last month, she had sifted through the memories of all she had lived through in another life. Or had she lived through it? It was Isis' future—two centuries' worth—but now it wouldn't be her future. God, the whole thing was so damn confusing. It left her with a migraine that went on for weeks.

"Take a bow," Sebastian said with the microphone pointed away from his mouth.

Isis stared out at the thousands in attendance applauding. At least for the moment, these were people who didn't have a care in the world except to enjoy the show. After the final act, they'd all go back to their everyday lives. None of them had any idea what the future held. That in just two centuries from now, all their descendants would die from a nuclear holocaust. Or, in yet another reality, one where the final world war never happened, all their future relatives became slaves to Valeria. Isis didn't know which fate was worse. All she did know was that The Witches of Vegas show felt minor in comparison.

A hand pressed against the back of her head. It belonged to Sebastian, and it snapped Isis back to reality. He leaned down and whispered in her ear. "Hey. Are you all right?"

"Yeah, I am." Isis shut her eyes tight, then reopened them. "Sorry, Dad."

Isis hopped forward, took a big bow, then ran off stage. Sebastian brought the microphone back to his mouth and readdressed the audience. "Once again, ladies and gentlemen, the girl who is lighter than air. *Isis!*" The crowd once again cheered.

"And now," Sebastian continued. "Prepare yourself as the amazing Quinn sisters return to the stage for our grand finale, an unbelievable mind reading act! We will need a few volunteers…"

"Here we go," Sacha said to her sister while Isis walked through the curtain and into the backstage area.

Selena blocked Isis' way and put a hand under her chin. "Hey, you did well up there. Really well."

"Thanks, Mom." Each time Isis looked into her adopted mother's vibrant green eyes, she remembered how she died, guilt-ridden, on that island. Or she died of old age in New Salem, never fully getting over her sister's sacrifice. Isis wrapped her arms around her mom's waist and hugged her tight.

"Hey, it's okay," Selena said to her. "We're safe now. Valeria isn't coming back."

"I know she's not," Isis answered.

Except she did come back, but now she won't. Did any of it really happen? Was it real? That question had kept Isis up almost every single night for the last month. It had to be. Not long ago, the proof stood right in front of her and placed all these memories in her head.

"Mom." Isis released her bearhug. "I'm a little tired. Can I skip the final bow? I want to head upstairs and lie down a little."

"Are you joining us for dinner?" Selena asked.

"No. Can I just order something up to the room?"

"Of course, you can." Selena's eyes widened with concern. "Isis, you know we're here for you, always—"

"Hey, Sis," Sacha called out. "Your husband's introducing us, and the audience is waiting. We need to get into position, now."

"I know you're here for me," Isis whispered. "I'll be all right. I'm just tired. Some sleep should help."

"Go ahead, sweetie," Selena said to Isis. "We'll

talk later, okay?" Isis replied with a nod.

Selena moved to the front stage. Isis prepared to teleport herself to her bedroom when she caught Zack strolling her way. He was all decked out in white-collared shirt, blue tie, and slacks. He was the Witches of Vegas' opening act, but to Isis, he was so much more. If only he knew that, but how could he know? Their time together here was short, but they were long-time soulmates in a reality that never happened.

"Hey, Isis." Zack stopped his pace, keeping a step away. "Nice performance."

"Um, thanks." She still had no idea how to react to Zack. They had a relationship that lasted centuries. Although she never experienced it, the memories circled around her brain. In fact, there were two sets of memories, both replaying the same events. She was told to give one of them away, but she wasn't told the specific person, just to wait before deciding. It was all like a long dream that felt so real.

"Hey, do you want to head out tonight?" There was a sense of hope in Zack's voice. "Maybe we can go get some frozen yogurt or something?"

That sounded great, but what could they possibly talk about? Isis was now on a whole other level, knowing things about the world Zack couldn't. "I'm…real tired. I'm heading upstairs. Maybe take a nap. Um, raincheck?"

"Yeah, all right." Zack's eyes narrowed with what had to be frustration. "Another time then."

"Yeah, definitely." She put a hand against his arm. "I'm sorry, I really am."

"Yeah, me too."

Isis walked past Zack and out of the theater. Damn,

she wanted to kick herself. He was clearly reaching out to her, again. He knew she loved that yogurt place, while Isis knew everything about him. But knowing Zack as well as she did made the times they went out together awkward. Unfortunately, she could tell he was picking up on her awkwardness. Isis was sure Zack was the one she was meant to share the other set of memories with, but each time she was ready to commit, an image of herself sending his parents' car over that cliff made her pause.

Outside the theater was a hallway with four elevators. She decided to take one of those instead of relying on the energy. It was a much slower process, but she recently came to appreciate slow. Standing in the elevator while it moved floor to floor gave her a chance to get in touch with her thoughts and feelings…but were they her thoughts and feelings? Or did they belong to the other Isis?

The elevator doors opened. Isis moved down the hallway at a rapid pace and then into their suite. She didn't bother using her keycard to open the door. The hallway was empty, so she just phased in. She stood in place staring across the living room, from the long couch and easy chair to all the bedroom and bathroom doorways.

Her body was so tired, not just from the lack of sleep, but from the memories of the future that kept battering her brain like a flashing light. But that wasn't her future, and it never would be. Obviously, Isis wasn't going to turn into a vampire—the other her made sure of that—but were those still her experiences? If not, would that make the other, much older Isis, someone else? The answer to that question changed in her head more times than she cared to admit.

Isis walked up to one of the four mirrored pillars that were in each corner of the living room. Her reflection stared back at her with widened and stressed-out eyes. The others noticed them too, and her reluctance to talk about it, but how could she? She still had trouble recognizing herself. How could Isis explain to them that each time she passed a mirror, she expected to see faded skin? She remembered not needing to eat or breathe. Or sleep. She drank blood. Actual, real blood. It tasted like…well, she wasn't sure what it tasted like. Somehow, she couldn't remember the sensation, just that she did it, and so did Zack. That was the case with just about all of the memories.

Isis raised a hand, almost on instinct. It made the glass on the pillar crack. "Dammit," she cried out. At first Isis thought she was teleporting. But it was her eyes that had teared up which made everything around her blur. Isis dropped to her knees and pressed her palms against her eyes.

There were many times Isis thought about sitting her family down and telling them about what really happened and why she was in such a fog. So far, whenever she told them about Valeria taking her to her old neighborhood, she left out all the important details, like the other Isis. How could she share any of this with them? They'd think she was having a mental breakdown. Maybe she was.

She did have the power to get one of them to understand, at least that's what the other Isis told her. But there lay the problem—which one? Even if she could decide, then someone else would have memories the rest of the family hadn't experienced. Then two of them would look crazy to the others.

Eventually, she'd have to make that choice, Isis understood that, but the other Isis told her to make sure she knew for sure who it should be. Funny how her mind kept coming back to the same person she had already pulled from the running, the one non-witch of the coven. But what he'd find out, there was no way to know how he'd handle it, and that threw her back to square one. Isis was sure she never had as difficult of a decision in front of her at any other time in her life. Either life.

A knock on the door shook Isis from her thoughts. She sensed it was Zack on the other side. Isis wiped her eyes with the back of her hand, then peeked at her reflection in the broken glass. Her face was puffy, her cheeks red like strawberries. Great. No way could she hide the fact that she had been crying. Zack knocked a second time.

Isis stood up, scurried to the door, and pulled it open. She wanted to give him a huge hug but stopped herself just in time. She had to keep reminding herself that he hadn't experienced their relationship the way she did—he wasn't there. Well, technically Zack was there, just not as far as he knew. Ugh, the headache was coming back.

"Hey, Zack," she croaked.

"Are you okay?" he asked. "You ran out of the theater in the middle of our conversation. Now you look like you've been—"

"Yeah, I'm fine." Isis wiped her eyes again, this time with her arm. "What about with you?"

Zack stood frozen in place. He had something on his mind. In the far future, Isis' mind was connected with his. She knew what he was thinking in a way no one could ever understand. It wasn't her Wiccan abilities that connected them, but the fact that they were together for two centuries. Only now they hadn't lived those lives, and they wouldn't. She had to use the more traditional way of finding out what he was thinking. By asking.

"Um, what's up?"

"I was hoping we could talk." A huge scowl crossed his face. "It's kind of important."

Chapter Twenty-nine

"Please, come in." Isis stepped aside to let Zack walk through the doorway and into the suite. He took a slow march to the couch but didn't sit. Perhaps it was time they had that long talk. There was a tension between them since he joined the coven, and it was all her fault. She just hadn't known how to approach him.

"Is…everything okay?" she asked, although she could see on his face that things were anything but okay.

"Isis, I made a decision." Zack took a long pause. His eyes shifted away from her. "It's not one I came to easily, but it might be the right one. I thought I should let you know before I tell the others, but I think it would be best for both of us."

"Zack, what decision?" Isis asked. "What are you talking about?"

"Isis, I…" Zack's head tilted away from Isis' gaze. "I'm going to leave."

"Leave?" Isis gasped. "Like, for good? Where would you go?"

"I don't know." Zack shrugged. "There are places for someone my age without a family. There's a boys' home a few miles from the strip. I guess I could grab my stuff and go there."

"Is that really what you want to do, where you want to go?" Isis' breathing went heavy.

“Maybe not,” Zack replied. “I just…I don’t know if I belong here.”

“Of course, you do.” A tear rolled down Isis’ cheek. “My dad made you a member of our coven. You do have a family. You’re part of *our* family now.”

“Your family does treats me like I belong, that’s true. This isn’t about them. It’s about us.”

“Zack, please don’t leave me,” Isis sobbed. “You’re too important to my life. I need you—”

“Am I? Because it sure doesn’t feel that way!” The anger in Zack’s voice bounced against the walls. “Isis, I stayed because you asked me to stay. We both thought we have this great connection together—”

“We do!” Isis shouted.

“Yet since I’ve been here, it feels like you avoid me.” Zack’s hands flailed in the air. “Then, when we *are* together, you either shut down or you say things about me I’ve never told you. Hell, you’ve brought up thoughts and feelings I’ve never shared with anyone. I know witches can read minds, but you promised me you’d never read mine. Your whole family made that promise to me.”

“Zack, I’m not avoiding you. I’m also not reading your mind. It’s just—”

“Yeah, you are. I know you are! But, for the life of me, I just don’t understand why.”

“I swear, Zack, I’ve never...”

Isis bit down on her bottom lip. She hated lying, but the truth would be much worse. Maybe he did have a right to know. Everything inside Isis told her to share the memories with him. She only dismissed those thoughts out of fear. She didn’t want him to hate her. But that’s exactly what was happening. By hiding what she did, Isis was chasing Zack away.

For the sake of her own sanity, Isis needed to get that second set of memories out of her head, which is why she focused on her other family members. But she couldn't settle on any one of them. Because she was told to make sure she chose the right person before putting the memories in their head, and the right person was standing in front of her. She always knew that.

"It's you, Zack," Isis sobbed. "It's always been you."

"Me?" Zack looked back forth as if he was trying to find someone else in the room. "What in the world did I do? How could any of this be *my* fault?"

"No, it's not that. You don't understand." Isis' heartbeat raced. "I know it's crazy, but you just have to understand."

"Understand what, Isis?" Zack's voice sounded frantic. It was also the loudest she'd ever heard him. "Please, explain it to me, because I'm feeling lost."

"Zack." Isis stared into his eyes, a shade of green she knew so well. She took a deep breath to try and calm herself down. "I know I've been acting weird. It's because I have a secret. I have the power to share this secret, but with only one person. I wasn't sure if you were that person…actually, that's not true. I know you're the right person, I just wasn't sure if I should, not until right now."

Zack threw a hand across his forehead. "This explanation isn't making things any clearer."

"I know. I'm sorry, but it's the truth." Isis paced back and forth. "First, I thought about sharing it with my dad. He was the one who found me, the one who brought me into the coven. I know I can trust him. But then I thought maybe it could be Mom. She always understands me, and she is a really powerful witch. Maybe this would all make sense to her. I even thought about Sacha for about a minute." Isis looked back at Zack and held up one finger. "I couldn't choose between them, because the right person to share this with isn't any of them. It's you, Zack. I knew it all along, I just…I was afraid."

Zack opened his mouth to speak, but no words came off his tongue. It was one of the first times Isis recalled him ever being speechless…and that included as a vampire who lived for centuries.

"You're the one who went through it all with me." Isis stopped her pacing and threw her hands on Zack's shoulders. "You're the one I gave all my trust and my faith. You were always there for me."

"Isis, please slow down!" Zack screeched. "None of this is making any sense. I don't understand anything you're talking about."

"I know." Isis laid a hand against his cheek. "Before you make any decision about leaving, can I ask you to trust me this one last time? Please?"

Isis took Zack's arm and led him to the easy chair. There was a hesitation in his step but after a moment, he gave in. "Okay, Isis, I trusted you before, I want to trust you now." He let her sit him down in the chair. "What do you want to tell me?"

"Not tell, show." Isis sat across his lap, facing him. "I'm going to show you."

"What?" Zack asked. "Come on, Isis, my curiosity is dialed up to twelve."

Isis cupped her hand under their chins. A circular white light formed in her palm. "You said you trust me?" His nod made her smile. "Then please, close your eyes so you can see everything."

Zack gave her a perplexed look, but then did as she asked. Isis hesitated. What he would learn from seeing this other life, it had the potential to destroy their relationship before it even started. But her behavior toward him was doing just that, anyway.

She had to take the chance. Whatever the result, however he reacted, Zack had every right to know. Isis placed her hand against his temple. She took a deep breath and focused. The tiny ball of light shot from her palm and sucked into his head.

Zack's eyes fluttered under the lids. It was as if he was experiencing a dream at rapid speed. His eyes popped open wider than Isis had ever seen. She jumped off his lap and backed away. Zack's breathing became erratic. He gripped the armrests of the chair and squeezed. His head swung back and forth. It was everything Isis was sure she had gone through a month ago when the other Isis did this to her.

Zack took some deep breaths. His eyes opened, but they still had a gaze about them as if they were focused on an intense movie. His hands ran through his short hair. It was clear to Isis that he was taking in all that he had just seen. After a long minute or two, his breathing slowed.

"Zack, please, talk to me," Isis whispered. "Are you…"

Zack's head popped up at Isis. His bottom jaw shook. Finally, two words popped out of his mouth. "Holy crap!"

"I know it's a lot." Isis kneeled in front of him. "I'm sorry, I just…I thought you should know what we went through…"

Zack's wide eyes connected with hers. "We…we were vampires. Two hundred years. Valeria, a year from now. She poisoned you or something, with her blood." Zack dropped his forehead against his palms. "In my head, I remember…I was president of the village. We had friends, we watched them grow old, we saw their kids grow up, then get old. Oh man, there's going to be a nuclear war! Isis, we were *vampires*."

Isis stood and backed away. Give him enough time and space to come to terms with a long history that never happened…or did, but now wouldn't. When Isis first had these memories, she didn't have the time to deal with it, not with Valeria trying to kill her. But once everything calmed down, she had a month to process the memories bouncing around in her head. She still wasn't there yet, so how could she expect Zack to accept it immediately?

"Wow, just…wow," Zack said. His erratic breathing steadied, meaning he was already regaining his composure, which Isis had to admit was impressive. "Wow," he said again.

"Yeah, I know. Wow."

Zack's head tilted. "Isis, is this…is any of this real?"

Isis nodded. "It's all real. We lived it."

"How can you be so sure?" Zack shot up from the chair. "This could be some kind of witchcraft, like hypnosis, something Valeria did to you and you just did it to me—"

"I met her, Zack!" Isis snapped.

"Met who?" Zack's eyebrows rose. "The other Isis?"

"Yes. I looked right at her when she spoke. It was me, but it wasn't, not yet. Or not anymore, I don't know. But she was there." Isis felt her eyes tearing up all over again. "She froze Valeria, then told me to convince her to take us back to Vegas. She said we'd beat her there. That's exactly what happened. Then she put all this in my head. After that, I saw her fall down. I…I think she died."

"I believe you, but I don't know why. It's so crazy." Zack's widened eyes fell on Isis. "We were in love. Like really, really in love."

"We knew everything about each other." Isis walked up to Zack and wrapped her hands around his elbow.

"Oh, man." Zack clutched his forehead and massaged his temples. "This is what's been going on in your head all this time? Is that why you've been acting so weird around me? That's why you've been avoiding me?"

"Part of it." A sharp pain ran through Isis' gut. "Valeria won. She became queen because she kept you from being there. She made that happen by saving your parents from that car accident. I…the other me…I don't know how to tell you this—"

"I know what happened," Zack said, cutting Isis off. His voice croaked. "I'm pretty sure I'm seeing all of *her* memories of our lives together, not my own. The other Isis, she stopped Valeria from saving them, but it didn't work." A tear snuck out of Zack's duct and down his cheek.

"No, it didn't." Isis squeezed her eyes tight. She didn't want to lose her composure, but after seeing that tear, she didn't know how much longer she'd win that battle. "Zack, I understand if you don't want to be here now that you know. I don't think it's something I could ever make up to you."

"It also never happened." Zack placed his hand against Isis' moist cheek. "You didn't do it. She did it to try and save the world. Then she gave up her existence to make sure you never will. There's no reason I should hold it against you. Neither of us should."

Isis let out a deep exhale. That's when the tears rolled down her face like a waterfall. Her biggest nightmare for the last month was how Zack would react to finding out what she did in that other timeline. The guilt gnawed at her heartstrings, but so did the imaginations of all the possible reactions he'd have once he found out. But her worry was all for nothing. Zack handled it well. In fact, he understood and accepted the other Isis' actions better than she did.

Zack's arms folded across his stomach. "I'm also sure the mom and dad I remember would rather have died that day than raise me in that horrible world Valeria created."

"Thank you, Zack. Thank you so much." Isis lunged forward and wrapped her fingers around the back of Zack's neck. She tipped her head up to look up into his eyes, then kissed him, deep and passionately. It felt almost instinctive to press her lips against his. But would it to him?

"I'm sorry. I didn't mean to—"

"It's okay," Zack said. "It felt…familiar. Real familiar."

"And weird."

"Weird?" Zack asked. "Why is it weird? We were

together for two hundred years. I'm sure we've done that more times than we could count."

"Yeah. But in all that time I hadn't met you as a six-year-old. That makes it a little weird."

"Yeah, I get that." Zack's head popped up, with a gaze aimed at the ceiling. "I saw that memory of the other you talking to me when I was six. It was the night Uncle Herb found out about my parents. But I don't remember waking up and seeing you in the closet. I'm sure I don't remember fireballs blowing up the place. That's because it did happen, but now it didn't anymore. Is that right?"

"Something like that, I guess." Isis grinned, but once she looked into his wide-eyed and flustered face, her lips sank. "Zack, I'm sorry. Maybe I shouldn't have shared all that with you. I know I was supposed to, but to put you through this, it's so not fair."

"For what it's worth, I'm glad you did," Zack said. "We had a whole history together. I feel like I remember it, even if I didn't actually experience it."

"Yeah." That was exactly how Isis felt, too. Thank goodness Zack was okay about it, although she still couldn't look directly at him. That was something she needed to get over as soon as possible. He was, after all, her soulmate, in any reality. "Zack, it's been so hard keeping this to myself. I needed to share it with someone, and I knew all along that you were the one."

"I appreciate that." Zack's head cocked. "But why would we keep something this important to ourselves? At the very least, we need to share it with your family."

"How can we?" Isis spun around and walked to the corner pillar with the cracked mirror. Her distorted reflection stared back at her with swollen eyes and puffy cheeks. "This is beyond crazy, even for *us*. I want to tell them, but it's not like we have any proof that it ever really happened. They'd probably think I lost my mind. They'll think we both did."

Zack's hand clutched Isis' shoulder. Through the reflection in the pillar, she caught that confident look in his eye. It was the one that showed up whenever he had an idea. "You're wrong, Isis. We do have proof," he said. "We can totally prove this."

Isis' eyes blinked. She spun back to Zack with a scrunched face. "What proof? How can we prove something that never happened?"

The question made Zack's smile grow.

Chapter Thirty

Isis sat at the suite's kitchen area square table; her right foot performed a nervous tap dance underneath. Zack, who sat in the chair next to Isis, put a hand on her knee to try to halt its shake. Isis reached under the table and took his hand. The closeness shared was such that they could no longer hide their feelings for one another from Sebastian and Selena who sat across the table, eyeing them with scrutiny.

As far as her folks were concerned, they were together, but had only known each other for about a month. The first time they met, Isis and Zack were under Valeria's love spell. The spell had long since broken, but their love for one another was still strong thanks to two hundred years of intimate memories. At the beginning, Dad insisted they take that inevitable relationship slowly. Mom agreed. Both thought that was why Isis kept a distance from him, but that was far from the reason. They couldn't understand. But Isis wanted them to. That's why she asked to sit with them. Once Zack figured out how they could prove their memories were real, Isis was ready to fill them in on the entire story.

The unspoken tension was broken by Sacha entering the kitchen area. "Sorry, I'm late," she said between pierced lips. "I wasn't expecting yet another family meeting so soon after the last one."

"We didn't call this meeting." Sebastian nodded toward Isis and Zack. "They did."

"Oh, okay then." Sacha dropped into a chair at the table's end. "I wasn't aware anyone else could call a family meeting, but all right."

"We're all here," Selena said to Isis. "You have our full attention. What is this about?"

"You did say this was important," Sebastian added. "So, let's have it."

Sacha slammed her hands on the table like a police detective conducting an investigation. "You didn't get her pregnant, did you, Zack?"

"What? No!" Zack's entire body tensed up. His upper body snapped back against the chair.

"That's not funny. Let's not even joke like that." Sebastian's head turned from Sacha to Zack. "You *didn't* get her pregnant, did you?"

"I'm not pregnant," Isis screeched out of frustration. "My God, it's nothing like that at all."

"Then what is this about?" Selena leaned forward. "Go ahead, Sweetie, we're listening."

Isis opened her mouth to speak, but the words wouldn't roll off her tongue It wasn't that she was nervous around her adopted family, she wasn't, but it was the subject that was causing her angst. How could she cover this without being dismissed as completely insane? Since Zack had the idea that would prove their tale true, perhaps it was best he took the lead.

"Um, Zack?" Isis looked his way in order to divert everyone's attention. "You want to start?"

"Seriously?" Zack's lower jaw nearly crashed through the table. "You want me explain all of this?"

"Would someone please start?" Sebastian grunted.

"Okay." Zack straightened his back. He squeezed Isis' hand under the table. "So, Isis and I would like all of us, the coven, to take a trip."

"A trip?" Sacha asked. "You mean like a vacation?"

"Yes!" Isis jumped in. "Like a vacation."

"You realize we just returned to the stage after taking three weeks off," Sebastian said. "The hotel manager would have a fit if we ran out on him again."

Zack leaned his elbows against the table. "We wouldn't ask this if it wasn't important."

"It's real important," Isis said, her head still pointed downward.

"I get that sense from both of you," Selena said. "But I'm not understanding why."

"Do the two of you have a destination in mind?" Sebastian asked. "Or would any resort location on the map do?"

"We have a location in mind," Isis said. She and Zack gave one another a quick peek. Then, they answered at the same time, "Sweden."

"Sweden?" Sacha's face scrunched. "Of all the spots in the world, how did the two of you come up with Sweden? I'm sure it's a nice place and all, but really?"

Isis sat back. Zack gave her hand under the table a shake. "You need to tell them," he whispered to her but loud enough for everyone in the room to hear. "It's time."

"Isis," Sebastian said, his tone becoming one filled with dread. "What's going on?"

"You know you can tell us anything." Selena reached across the table and took Isis' left hand. "We're here for you."

Wow, two hundred years was a long time and a long story. Isis wasn't sure where to begin. Maybe she should have thought it all out before asking for a family meeting. Too late now, so might as well take it one step at a time and work her way up to the battle with Valeria. No doubt they'd have tons of questions, and that was only if they believed a single word of it.

"I have a story to tell you." Isis' voice shook. Zack put an arm around her shoulders. "I know it's going to sound crazy, real crazy. But I want to ask that you hear me out and consider the possibility that everything I tell you is real."

Sebastian's and Selena's mouths opened as wide as Isis had ever seen. Sacha's eyes did the same. After a moment of confused silence, Selena folded her hands across the table. "Our minds are open, Sweetie. Tell us your story."

"There's a village hidden in Sweden's swamplands. Zack and I were there for the last..." Isis paused. "Well, the next two hundred years."

"Two hundred years?" Sacha's head shot back. "I think I speak for all of us when I say...huh?"

A slight grin formed across Isis' mouth. "Maybe I'd better start over."

"That's a good idea," Zack replied.

Isis took a deep breath and spoke while the family listened.

****

Valeria crouched on a high branch of one of The Other World's many trees. It wasn't common that the animalistic creatures of this world separated from the pack. Yet, at times it happened, like now where the two she watched from high above had done exactly that. They walked side by side, letting their hooves drag across the grass with each step. They were young, naïve, and unaware that Valeria had followed them for over a mile, waiting for them to stop trotting. Finally, they halted simultaneously to munch some of the native grass.

The timing was perfect. The pressure throughout her body meant it had been close to a full day since Valeria's last intake of blood. The two animals were enjoying their breakfast, completely oblivious to their surroundings. Neither had looked up or reacted to the sounds of Valeria soaring tree-to-tree. They also showed no concern about reuniting with their pack.

The plan was to leap from the branch and throw her full body weight across the back of one of the beast's necks. That would kill the animal instantly. If the other attacked, Valeria was ready. She had fought these creatures every day for centuries. She knew their weaknesses better than even they did. If it ran, that was okay too. One had enough blood to satisfy for the next twenty-four hours.

Valeria squatted, readying herself to pounce. But then her senses went wild. A portal opened. It was near the ground to the right of the tree. Through it she felt the energy of Mother Earth. It called to her. The way back to Earth was here.

With a loud scream, Valeria hopped off the tree to greet this sudden transport. But there was nothing in front of her except more leafless trees and long grayish grass. She focused on the Earth's energy once again, but there was nothing. Did she actually sense it, or was she mistaken? Valeria's imagination had betrayed her before. Could that have been the case once again?

"I was sure," she shouted. "Or perhaps not."

The animals, finished with their meals, galloped away. Along with them went the opportunity for an easy blood feast. Valeria watched them leave, still unsure if what she experienced was real or simply a figment of her imagination.

"Valeria!" a deep voice called out to her. It belonged to Luther. "Are you okay? I heard you call out." Distracted by what she thought was a return to Earth, Valeria hadn't noticed his approach.

"I…" She tilted her head. "I thought…I was sure…"

"You were sure of what?" Luther asked.

Valeria once again examined the area with all her senses, both natural and vampiric. There were no signs of disruption, no indication that anything had been different. "Nothing," she answered. "I was mistaken."

Valeria had spent three hundred years alone on this plain prior to her escape, then abrupt return with Luther. The isolation caused similar hallucinations. Even then, they were momentary and quite possibly caused by the sheer boredom of hearing no other voice but her own. Now, she had someone with her. A love, turned enemy, turned…whatever this was or would become. As enraged as she wanted to be at Luther for his part in forcing her into a second exile, she had to admit, if this isolation was to last another three hundred years or forever, she did appreciate the company. The Other World was far more tolerable with companionship.

But what did happen? In the times she thought she saw or sensed a portal, it had never felt so real or moved by so quickly. It was almost as if everything had changed, then disappeared in the blink of an eye. It couldn't have been real. But if it was, it left nary a trace. Perhaps it was her imagination.

"It was a memory from the past," she explained. "Nothing we need worry about now."

"Then we should resume our hunt." Luther waved her along. "I saw four of the creatures grazing about half a mile down yonder."

Valeria straightened herself. She threw Luther a determined grin. "Then let's sneak up on the beasts and make sure we make a meal of at least one."

"Agreed."

The vampires took off for their next prey. Their business continued, as both knew would be the case for the rest of eternity.

Chapter Thirty-one

Isis leaned back against what was the most comfortable chair she'd ever seen in front of an office desk. It was cushioned with soft green pillows and even had a headrest. Zack sat to her immediate right in a similar chair. Despite the comfort, she was still nervous, although she didn't know why. It wasn't like the group of people looking at her in disbelief from across the desk were strangers. Well, technically, they were even though she knew them all by name and remembered many intimate details about their lives, including their families and friends.

Upon arrival into the quad, they were immediately "greeted" by the New Salem task force with all the distrust of strangers that resonated throughout the village for centuries. But Simon vouched for them. He recognized Isis and the family from the photographs he received years ago from Luther. Isis and Zack shared personal knowledge of each member of the New Salem task force, including history, likes, dislikes, and even Paul's favorite tough guy saying. Isis couldn't help but giggle when she mimicked his "twitch your nose" line. At least it earned them a meeting with the village president.

"I have to say, this is one amazing story." Tia had just turned nineteen, yet she sat comfortably in the president's oversized chair, which was clearly designed for someone of a much larger frame. "You say you were president of New Salem, or you will be after me?"

"A long time after you, over a hundred years," Zack replied. "Although, that won't happen now that we're not vampires anymore."

"Paul's daughter and grandson were both presidents before Zack," Isis said. "I know it sounds crazy—"

"I'd use the word suspicious," Tia shot back. "Yet your details and knowledge of New Salem make it hard to dismiss this as a simple ploy."

"We're not here to con you," Zack said. "It's all true."

"Then let's cut to the chase." Standing to the left of the presidential chair, Paul looked from Isis and Zack to their three adult escorts. Selena and Sebastian stood behind Isis' chair while Sacha leaned against Zack's.

"Why are you here right now, today?" Paul's blond ponytail swung as he looked back and forth. His eyes focused on Sebastian and Selena. "What is it you want?"

Natasha stepped forward, joining Paul at his side. Their uncertainties, despite Isis' and Zack's proof in the details, were justifiable. The first time the coven came to New Salem—it would have been about ten months from now—they had to earn trust, just as they had to now. At least this time they didn't come due to a desperate need for help. Isis wasn't sick or dying from Valeria's blood running through her system. Her power wasn't spiraling out of control. Thinking about that still made her stomach muscles scream out in pain.

The only one of the group behind that desk who had more curiosity on his face than suspicion was

Simon. He hovered to the right of Tia's chair. Simon watched and listened with a wide smile across his face as if he were hearing an amazing story around a campfire. The only thing he was missing was a marshmallow at the end of a stick.

"I can tell you why *we* are here." Sebastian waved his hands from himself to the sisters on either side. "We needed to find out if what our charges believe to be real actually is." Sebastian placed a hand on Isis' and Zack's shoulders. "Their story was so out of the realm of reality, yet it was also detailed. We had to know for sure."

"They described each of you like they knew you," Selena added. "Despite that, we honestly thought we were going to end up teleporting into the middle of a swamp. Yet, here you all are, just as they said you would be."

Paul turned his gaze to Sacha. "Don't look at me," she said through a smirk. "I still think they're all nuts."

Paul's stare dropped down to Isis and Zack. "Is this why the two of you are here? To find out if New Salem exists outside your heads?"

"That's part of the reason," Zack muttered. "Mostly, we wanted to prove to ourselves that we aren't crazy. That all we remember really happened. Although, I guess, technically, it never did, or never will. Even if we do remember it."

"And we are your evidence," Natasha said. Zack replied with a nod.

"You say that is only part of the reason," Paul stated.

"We're also here to say thank you," Isis explained. "I know for all of you it never happened, but for us, we owe you so much. Especially Doctor Mac and Simon."

"Me?" Simon asked.

"You taught us how to live as vampires," Isis replied. "You taught us how to survive."

"Oh, well, that was my pleasure, I suppose."

"Consider yourselves lucky," Sacha said. "Apparently, I was killed here." She ruffled both Isis' and Zack's hair. "It was tough getting that little piece of info out of these two."

"There is one more thing," Zack said. "We do need to ask a small favor. There's another member of the village we need to thank, although it's a little complicated."

"If that's all you're asking, it doesn't sound complicated," Tia replied. "Tell us who it is, and I'm sure we can arrange such a meeting."

"Um, that's kind of a problem," Isis said while biting her bottom lip. "She won't be born for another two hundred years."

The response was silence. It was finally Paul who spoke up. "Since neither of you are immortal vampires, how do you intend on passing this message of thanks?"

Simon raised a finger. "I'm an immortal vampire." No one responded.

Isis reached into her small black pocketbook which sat at her side. She pulled out an envelope and placed it on the desk. "This is a letter to her." Isis slid the envelope in front of Tia. "She's a descendant of yours and Jasper's."

"*Our* descendent? We don't have any children. We're not even yet married." Tia's hand hesitated, but then picked up the envelope and held it in front of her face. "There are two names and a date on here."

"That's the names of her parents and the date of her birth," Isis explained.

"We figure with so many witches in this village, you would find a way to preserve the letter without letting it become known and possibly changing the future." Zack straightened his back and grinned. "Then it can be given to her when she's the right age."

"We know it's a big commitment we're asking for," Isis added. "And we're sorry about that. But without her help, none of us would be here right now. We'd all be looking at a terrible future."

A cold chill blasted down Isis' chest to her stomach. She hated thinking about what Valeria did to this village, not to mention the people all across the planet. It was something no one else could understand. No one but Zack, and he only saw it; he did not live through it. Then again, neither did Isis, but she still had the memories and emotions running through her head.

"Isis? Are you alright?" Tia asked.

No, not at all. Isis' emotions were all over the place, as they had been since the battle with Valeria in the middle of Las Vegas ended. If not for the crystals that surrounded the room, cutting off the Wiccan energy, her witchcraft may have spiraled out of control.

"Yeah, I'm fine." Sebastian's grip of her shoulder tightened. Selena's hand touched the back of her head. "I'm sorry."

"So, thanking us, is that truly all this is about?" Paul asked. "Nothing else?"

"I believe we have what we came here for," Sebastian answered. "Proof. Now that we know, I'm honestly not sure what we should do with this knowledge."

"I guess we go back to our lives." Selena bowed her head toward Tia. "With your permission, of course, Madam President."

"Natasha," Tia said without breaking eye contact from Selena. "What is your take on our visitors?"

"They are powerful witches, all except the boy," Natasha replied through her thick accent. "More powerful than any in New Salem except, maybe, for Doctor Mac. If they wished our people any sort of harm, they would not need a charade such as this."

"What are your intentions right now?" Sebastian asked. "I know we are here uninvited, but we are clearly not here to cause trouble. Will you allow us to leave?"

"You certainly haven't committed any crime here in New Salem," Tia answered. "It is not our intention to keep you here against your will."

"Hold on," Paul's voice roared. He once again focused on Isis and Zack. "You told us there will be a nuclear world war in two hundred years that will kill just about everyone on the planet. We cannot simply walk away like we never had this conversation."

"I kind of agree," Sebastian replied.

"Is there anything we can do about it now?" Zack asked. "None of us will be alive then."

Tia picked up the envelope and examined the writing on it carefully. She stood and threw a quick nod at Paul, who returned the gesture. "Would you all please excuse us for a moment?" Tia and Paul strolled to the office's side door. Paul opened it, then followed Tia out. Isis almost forgot how easily these two non-Wiccan leaders communicated in an almost supernatural fashion.

As soon as the door closed, Simon dropped into the president's chair. "So," he said, "as a teacher, how was I?"

"You were great, Simon," Isis answered. "You taught us everything we needed to know."

"Although you were a bit sarcastic at times," Zack added. "A tad overbearing, and you bragged about yourself a lot. But your heart was always in the right place, I think."

Natasha laughed. "I would say these two really do know you, Simon."

"Yes, they do." Sebastian leaned forward. "How is it that we don't? You said you were Luther's protégé, yet he never mentioned you."

"I was wondering the same thing," Selena said.

Isis peeked over her shoulder at her folks with raised eyebrows. It was the same line of questioning they gave Simon the first time around. She expected Simon was about to give the same answer.

"It's not surprising he didn't," Simon responded. "As well as *you* know Luther, is it truly out of character that he didn't share his connections outside your coven?" Yup, she knew it.

"He's got a point there," Sacha answered. "Luther was never one for small talk or sharing."

The side door swung open. Paul cleared his throat, which was probably more a signal for Simon to get out of the president's chair. It was a message the vampire understood based on how quickly he shot to his feet. Tia sat down in the chair and folded her hands across the desk. She had the room's attention, especially that of her visitors.

"My vice president and I have spoken." She

glanced over at Paul, who stayed at attention by the side door. "Assuming everything you have said here is the truth, and you have certainly offered enough evidence—"

"It is all true," Zack interrupted. Isis tapped his calf with the tip of her sneaker.

"As I was about to say…" Tia held up a hand, a clear request to let her finish. "With all you've told us, we *do* believe you, which means you are already residents of New Salem. You are free to leave and return to your lives, but I am also inviting you to stay. In fact, the cottage you told us you lived in is currently unoccupied, as is the smaller one next to it. Your coven is welcome to both."

"Our only request," Paul added, "is that, either way, you share any future knowledge of upcoming or impending threats to New Salem security. Especially this war you say is coming two centuries from now. It is imperative we figure out a way to plant preventative seeds long before it happens."

"Meanwhile, if you can acclimate to our way of life, I believe witches of your level would offer huge benefits to our village, as we would for you." Tia offered her presidential smile. "What do you think? Are you interested in a change of location and lifestyle?"

Isis and Zack simultaneously flipped around in their seats and looked up at Sebastian and Selena. Isis took Zack's hand, awaiting the answer that would most likely determine the course of the rest of their lives. Sacha threw her attention on their coven leaders as well. "Your call, Sis, Sebastian," Sacha said. "What's it going to be, Las Vegas or New Salem?"

Sebastian's eyes met with Selena's. For the first

time in Isis' life with them—both lives—she saw her adopted parents indecisive. "That's a kind offer," Sebastian answered. "Um. I…don't know what to say. We'd need to discuss this as a family."

Tia scooped Domina's envelope from the desk and placed it in the top drawer. She leaned forward. "Perhaps you'd like to stay a few nights as our guests and mull it over?"

"Well…" Selena's gaze never left Sebastian's. "It certainly was a long trip, and it sounds like we have a lot to talk about. Both as a coven and a family."

Tia rose from her chair. "In that case, I'm sure Simon can escort you." Her head dropped to Isis and Zack. "Unless the two of you would like to show them the way?"

Chapter Thirty-Two

The next morning…

Isis would have rather spent the morning with her family getting the official tour of New Salem. But instead she agreed to be seen by the village doctor. Entering the medical center for her scheduled appointment shouldn't have made Isis so nervous, yet her heart sped up the moment she found herself outside the building.

She appreciated the fact that each member of the family offered to come along. But this was something Isis had to do alone. Besides, except for Zack, this was their first time in New Salem. They shouldn't spend the entire first morning in a doctor's office. It was obvious Tia was looking to give them the VIP treatment, and they deserved it.

Isis had walked through the medical center doors thousands of times and met with several head doctors…but that was all in the other timeline. Technically, this was Isis' first time in the building even though she knew it like the back of her hand. Ugh, the whole thing was still so confusing. The dull pain in her stomach didn't make it easier. At first she thought it was a lady cramp, but they only lasted a few days. This pain, which felt like someone grabbed hold of one of her stomach muscles and squeezed, had been going on for almost two weeks.

The hallway's first doorway on the left stared at Isis like an old and familiar friend. It was wide open and inviting. For a moment, Isis expected to see Doctor John working in his lab. Then she remembered Doctor John wouldn't be born for almost two centuries. The building's main medical room wouldn't be converted into a lab anytime soon either. The doctor Isis did see in there, from what she remembered, was far superior both in medical knowledge and bedside manner. Yet it bothered her that she'd never get the chance to meet Doctor John. In fact, there were a lot of New Salem residents she remembered yet would never get to meet.

Doctor Mac was inside scrubbing the metal examining table in the center of the room with a rag. Isis expected to see a head of wavy gray hair. She almost forgot how much younger he was when they first met. His hair was short, jet-black, and the skin on his face was smooth. If memory served, he used his witchcraft to keep from looking his age until his mid-seventies.

Isis also remembered the day he passed away and every member of New Salem attended his funeral. And how his future son and daughter, neither of whom had manifested a Wiccan connection, followed in his medical footsteps. Isis tapped her knuckles lightly against the door.

"Doctor Mac?" she called out.

The doctor stepped away from the examining table. A large gulp filled Isis' throat. She remembered being laid out on that gurney unable to move while Valeria's vampire virus poisoned her system. All she could see were Doctor Mac's deep brown eyes while he worked feverishly to save her life. Well, not exactly *her* life, or was it? The pain in her stomach intensified.

"Ahh, Isis Flores Rivera, good morning. I've really been looking forward to meeting you," he said in his calm and rhythmic tone. "Although, as I understand, from your perspective we've already met."

"Good morning," Isis responded. "I'm actually looking to go with Isis Quinn-Santell. In honor of my family."

"Unless your family decides to remain here." Doctor Mac gestured her to enter. "I'm sure you of all people are familiar with New Salem policies."

"Yes, last names stay behind." Isis took one reluctant step forward. "So, you know why I'm here?"

"Tia met with me yesterday evening, so I'm all caught up." The doctor folded his hands against his chest and flashed a kind and genuine grin. "Thank you for saving our future."

"Wow." Isis' head dipped. Her eyes opened wide. Doctor Mac was the first to thank her. She really had no idea how to respond to it. "You're welcome," slipped off her tongue.

"We should get started." Doctor Mac waved a hand toward the examining table. "Please."

Isis took a deep breath and tiptoed into the medical room. The appointment was Paul's idea, although her folks were quick to agree. Isis did as well, even if the idea of this checkup terrified her to the point she thought about it all night. It wasn't the doctor's examination that scared her, but rather the possible results of his exam. It was important to know for sure, but what if he ended up finding something? Isis understood the horrors the wrong result would lead to.

She didn't want to go through it again, neither for herself nor for the rest of the world.

"We don't get a lot of families that come to New Salem for a vacation," Doctor Mac said in what Isis believed was small talk to calm her nerves. "Has a decision been made if you will be moving here permanently?"

"We all went to bed early last night. We didn't talk about it much." Isis took another step forward. "It's a tough decision to just leave everything we built in Vegas."

"That it is," Mac replied. "I was once in that position having to make the decision for myself—"

"I know."

"Yes, I suppose you do."

Isis readied herself to hop onto the table.

Mac stopped her with a hand on her shoulder. He looked down with a face filled with concern. "I was told it wasn't that long ago you learned about this other history." Mac gently turned Isis his way. "I can imagine being back in New Salem must be strange for you. Maybe even overwhelming?"

Those were the exact words going through Isis' head since the moment they arrived. At first, she thought the doctor was using his Wiccan connection to read her mind, but Isis couldn't sense the energy crackling around her or him. She scanned the wall across from the door where six framed degrees hung. Of course, one of them was in child psychology. Maybe speaking to a therapist was exactly what she needed to do.

"It is definitely strange," Isis answered. "And, yes, overwhelming. I see people here that I remember knowing, but they don't know me at all."

"I see." Doctor Mac folded his arms across his chest. "How are you handling all of this?"

Isis let out a deep exhale. "At night, I have dreams, but sometimes I'm half awake, and it's memories going through my head. There are times at night when I forget for a minute which world I'm in. That's when I'm not waking up to find the room on fire. Either way, I usually can't fall back to sleep."

"What you experienced is certainly unique." Mac held his right hand up in front of his face. A blue glow formed around it. "I can't begin to imagine what it's like."

"Many times, it's not even a memory, but a feeling." Isis pressed her hands against her stomach.

"Hands at your sides, please," Mac said. "A feeling. Do you mean like déjà vu?"

"Kind of, yeah." Isis dropped her arms. "Like last week. I remembered Zack's birthday is coming up in about a month and two weeks. I want to do something real nice for him. An idea popped into my head. I'd teleport us to the island where my family was trapped by Valeria. It's also where his Uncle Herb gave his life to free them so they could stop her. We buried him there. I thought it would be nice for Zack to visit his uncle's grave on his birthday. Zack has said a few times he wished he could talk to his uncle again. I can't give him that, but if we go there, it would be the next best thing, right?"

"That's sweet." Mac eyed her, clearly enthralled in Isis' story. "I get the feeling there's more to this?"

"I asked Mom and Sacha to work with me on my teleportation so I could do this for Zack. It was during our first practice I suddenly had a sense like we had done it already. That's because I did, or the other me did. Now I'm wondering, well, I don't know how to explain it…"

"You wonder if you came up with the idea yourself or if it was one of the memories from the other timeline implanted in your head?"

"Yes! Exactly!" Isis flung a finger at Mac as an acknowledgment of his correct answer. "I see all these memories through her eyes. She was me. It was my face, my brain. Except she had confidence I don't. She made hard decisions I'm not sure I could. She had control of the energy I don't think I ever will. So, was she really me, and if she was, how could I ever live up to a version of me that saved all of reality?"

"That's an interesting question. I can see how it would keep you up at night." The lights dimmed. It made Doctor Mac's hand seem even brighter. "Keep in mind, Isis, even if you are the same person, you're fifteen. She was two hundred. I was told, she was the president of our village during a nuclear war?"

"Vice president," Isis replied. "Zack was president."

"Point is, you may be the same person, but with two vastly different perspectives and experiences. She may have been you, but you're not her. You may never be her, but that's okay. You have your own destiny to fulfill."

Isis took a moment to consider Doctor Mac's words. They did make sense. "Yeah, I think I get that."

"But the dreams, the lack of sleep. I'm going to say you're suffering from post-traumatic stress. I'm sure Zack is as well." Doctor Mac's hand glowed inches away from Isis. "Deep breath, please."

"That's the thing I don't get!" Isis sucked in a mouthful of air, then exhaled. "Zack is handling this way better than I am."

"And that bothers you?"

Mac held his hand inches from Isis' head. The blue glow shined so bright Isis had to squint. The doctor slowly moved his hand down to her chest, then her stomach. Doctor Mac's brown eyes focused on his hand.

"Zack's not even a witch," Isis went on. "He should be leaning on me to get him through all this, but it's me leaning on him…are you actually looking inside my body?"

"I am. Think of it like a Wiccan MRI." Mac's hand moved farther down to Isis' knees. He raised it back up to her chest. The light shining from his fingers engulfed her shoulders and arms. "You know Zack better than anyone else. Why do you suppose he is handling this experience as well as he is?" Mac rolled his hand from one of Isis' shoulders to the other. His palm hovered in front of her neck.

"We've talked about that," Isis replied. "According to Zack, everything about our world is brand new to him. He's had to wrap his mind around witches, vampires, and all this supernatural stuff." She let out a slight laugh. "The fact that we were immortal vampires in another realty that no longer exists, it's just one more thing on the list."

Doctor Mac held his hand near Isis' stomach. A slight tingle crossed her midsection. Isis knew that sensation. It was the effect of a witch's healing spell. The cramp in her stomach diminished. Then it went away completely.

"Did you just—"

"Try to relax," Mac said. The tingling stopped. "Zack makes a valid point. But he has also been through a lot recently, hasn't he?"

"That's for sure." Isis sucked in her stomach, which she was able to do with ease. It no longer felt like a boxer punched her in the gut. "Zack was almost killed by Valeria during that battle in Vegas. He also lost his uncle, moved in with a family of witches, then found out we lived a whole other life for centuries here in New Salem as the undead."

"That *is* a lot. Zack may be putting on a brave face, but there is no way he came out of all of that unscathed." Mac closed his fist and reopened it. The blue light faded. "It's more likely that inside he's experiencing the same stress and confusion as you." Mac tapped the table. "Hop on up."

Isis leaped off the ground and propelled herself backward. She landed in a sitting position at the table's end with her feet dangling inches from the ground.

A test tube from the counter floated across the room. Doctor Mac snatched it from the air and opened it. The sharpness of the needle he pulled out made Isis wince. "Is that…for me?" Isis gulped.

"I admit not having much knowledge on all things vampire, but I can say your body is virus-free. Just to confirm, I would like to take some blood and run a few tests. Is that okay?"

"Uh, sure. I guess."

"I picked up on a peptic ulcer formed on the internal surface of your abdomen. I healed it, but I recommend you avoid spicy foods and stressful situations for a while."

"Like that big needle?"

Doctor Mac held the needle straight up, then flashed Isis a smile. "Relax, I'm a doctor. I'm trained to be gentle with these things."

"Okay." Despite his assurance, Isis swiveled her head to the left and shut her eyes tight. She felt Doctor Mac's fingers wrap around her arm and stretch it out. Her elbow jolted from an instinctive flinch when something touched her inner crease. She quickly realized it was just an alcohol swab.

"I'd have thought my findings would have relieved you," Doctor Mac said. "But you still seem stressed, and I'm betting it's not just over the needle. I sense there's something else on your mind. Would you like to talk about it?"

Either Doctor Mac was perceptive, or Isis was being obvious. She didn't intend to unload all her problems on this kind man who had the responsibility of every single resident in New Salem. But there was still one lingering memory she needed to talk about. Zack was always an ear she could go to, but he didn't have the expertise necessary to be much help in dealing with this particular situation. Doctor Mac sure did, and he was offering.

"Just when I think I've sorted out all the memories from the other me, another one creeps into my head. Sometimes, they're about nothing. Other times, they're real bad."

"And you recently remembered a bad one?"

Isis nodded. "Yeah, last week. Mom was rubbing her stomach, and that's when it hit me. Early next year, she's going to get pregnant. She and Dad, they didn't—

they don't think it's possible, but it happens. I remember their excitement, Sacha's too. They called it a miracle—*OW*!" On instinct, Isis tried to yank her arm away, but Doctor Mac had a solid grip. Damn, so much for gentle.

"Almost done," Mac said. "What about you? Does a new addition to the family not excite you?"

Isis picked her head up and took a deep breath. Her eyes stayed shut. "Mom lost the baby. It happened a few weeks after she and Dad found out she was pregnant." Isis let out a deep sigh. This was harder to talk about than she realized. At least it distracted her from the needle jabbed in her arm. "I remember we were all devastated. But especially Mom and Dad. They didn't really have time to get over it before we…had to come here for me."

The needle slid out of Isis' arm. Her eyes popped open. Mac let go of her wrist and held his hand over Isis' outstretched arm. She felt a tingle around the needle hole. After a few moments, the sensation stopped. Isis held her arm up to see the hole was closed. There was no sign her skin had ever been pierced.

"I don't know what to do," Isis continued. "If I tell them now, I'm probably changing history. If I don't tell them, I know it's going to break both their hearts. Telling them now probably will too, but how can I keep this from them knowing the pain it's going to cause?" A throbbing formed in Isis' brain. She clutched her forehead.

"That's quite the conundrum." Mac placed a long test tube filled with red liquid on the counter next to the sink. The test tube stood vertically on its own. "But there is something you didn't have at this point in the other timeline."

Isis' head lifted. "What?"

"The first time around, you didn't know a physician who is also a witch." Doctor Mac corked the test tube. He then faced Isis while the test tube fell on its side. "Assuming history repeats itself, and your mother does become pregnant, I'll take her on as a patient whether your family decides to relocate to New Salem or not. If I find you are right, I will either do all I can to save the baby or break the news gently and soften the blow."

"Thank you," Isis said. "Really. Thank you."

"Meanwhile, let me test your blood sample and confirm that everything is normal—"

A knock on the open door made them turn. Isis waved a hand at their visitor.

"I'm sorry to interrupt. I hope it's okay."

"It's perfectly all right. We're almost done." Doctor Mac waltzed his way. "You must be the famous Zack Galloway. I'd say it's a pleasure to meet you, but I'm guessing you already know me."

"Word spreads fast around here," Zack replied and shook Mac's hand. "People all over the quad stopped what they were doing and stared at me when I walked through."

Mac snickered. "You will find here in New Salem, if you want a story to get around the entire village, just tell Simon. He'll share it with everyone whether they ask or not."

"Believe me, we know. I remember we were so careful about what classified information we gave him when we were—" Zack paused, then winced. "Um, never mind."

The doctor wandered past Isis and threw her a knowing nod.

"How is everyone?" Isis asked.

"They're good." Zack approached the examining table. "We had breakfast in the dining hall where Tia and Paul shared the history of New Salem with your folks and Sacha. Paul got a bit annoyed when I kept finishing their stories."

"I get that." Isis snickered.

"Paul is personally giving them a tour of the village. I think Sacha's out there scoping the singles' scene. I decided to come here instead."

Isis jumped off the table. She wrapped her left arm around Zack's lower back and placed her right arm across his stomach. "We don't really need the tour," she said while letting her forehead touch his cheek.

"No, I guess we don't."

Isis pressed her lips against Zack's neck. She gave him a tight squeeze. It made him grin. "What's that for?" Zack asked.

"For being there for me," Isis whispered. "I'm here for you, too."

They looked up at Doctor Mac who was eyeing them like they were a historic exhibit. His hands were firmly on his hips. "Two hundred years," he said. "Yes, I can totally see it."

Isis felt her cheeks turn warm as the doctor walked off and attended to the test tube on the counter.

"How are you doing, Zack?" Isis asked. "With everything."

"I'm all right. I'm dealing." Zack rested his arm around Isis' shoulders. His cheeks were slightly red. "Tia wants to meet with us after you're done in here.

She said she has a meeting set up with a trusted world leader this afternoon about the impending war. She wants us to tell her everything we know about how it all starts."

"Really? She's working on that already?" Isis asked, more than just a little impressed. "It's not going to happen for another two hundred years."

"Why wait?" Doctor Mac said from across the room. His eyes glowed while he stared into the blood-filled test tube. "No time like the present, right?"

"Yes." A huge smile crossed Isis' face. Her arms tightened around Zack, who returned her gaze and her grin. "No time like the present."

Epilogue

Dear Domina,

You don't know me. That's because I lived my life long before you were born. But, in another reality, I was there to see you grow up. I also witnessed all your ancestors grow up. In fact, although from your perspective we've never met, I may know you even better than you know yourself. I will explain what I mean by that in a moment.

What I am about to tell you won't make a lot of sense. In fact, it barely makes sense to me, and I lived through it. But I promise it is the truth, or at least it was at one time. In a reality that no longer exists, where I was a two-hundred-year-old vampire with a connection to the Earth's energy, I was charged with watching over New Salem much as New Salem watched over me. My boyfriend, Zack, was there with me through all of it, not as a witch, but also as a vampire. Crazy, right?

It was a good life, at least I thought so, until another Wiccan vampire named Valeria, an old enemy of mine and my coven's, went back in time and reshaped the world. Valeria's dark and grim reality formed over everything we knew. In fact, it would have sucked me in as well, if not for your timely warning. It was a warning you didn't give me much choice but to heed.

I needed to go back and put things right even

though I had no idea when, where, or how she changed history. It was in this horrible reality that I met another version of you, one who suffered yet survived the complete destruction of New Salem. It was there that your visions led me to the exact moment I needed to go to stop Valeria.

The fact that you are reading this letter is proof that everything has returned to normal. The world is a different place, and it's a much better place, thanks to you and your gift.

As I said before, I know you well. I know you doubt your ability to see the future and what it means when you receive those visions. It scares you more than you're willing to admit, and that is why you feel different around all the other witches in New Salem. You've always been hesitant to embrace that gift, in any reality.

I wrote this letter to thank you for your help. I couldn't have done what I did without you. But I also want to tell you not to doubt your connection with the Earth. Through you, it has already saved the world because you trusted it when we all needed you to the most. For that, I thank you on behalf of myself, Zack, my coven (which is also my family), New Salem, and all the world. That includes everyone in the past, present, and future.

Domina, I truly hope your life is a great one because, thanks to you, it exists. I will try to have a great life as well. I hope someday you can look me up and see if I kept that promise. Meanwhile, whenever those self-doubts creep up on you, give yourself a break. You've earned it.

All my love,

Isis

With assistance from Zack

Domina stared deeply at the framed letter on her wall. She had done so each morning, a habit that started a year and a half ago on her fifteenth birthday when her papa presented her with the letter. It was his determination that she was ready to read it. He framed and hung the letter on her bedroom wall. The story this letter told was farfetched, even for a village that was comprised of witches and other supernatural beings. Yet although its origin had been lost, her family had possession of the letter for generations before Domina's birth. It was saved for her over the course of two centuries.

The words spoke directly to Domina both literally and figuratively. The writer—a witch from long ago named Isis—understood the fear Domina felt since her first premonition at the age of thirteen. It was true that trusting her ability to see the future worried her. How could it not when every ancestor of hers who had that specific connection couldn't control it and could never fully understand the visions? Neither could she. At least, that was the case so far.

Yet, according to this letter, she saved all of time and reality by seeing what needed to be seen when it counted the most. This message from the past told her that she could trust her Wiccan connection. She did it once, and the world was a better place for it. How strange that her greatest contribution to New Salem, and to the planet itself, was one that neither she nor anyone else would ever know.

"Domina!" an adult female voice shouted from outside the bedroom. "Are you ready? It's time for school!"

"I'm coming, Mama!" Yes, she was ready to face the day, and the rest of her life.

Domina took one last look at the framed letter and skipped out through the door.

A word about the author…

Mark Rosendorf is the author of the award-winning young adult fantasy novels that make up The Witches of Vegas series. So far this includes: The Witches of Vegas, Journey To New Salem, and Witch's Gamble. He is also credited with other works such as The Rasner Effect.

When Mark is not writing about witches and vampires, he works as a high school guidance counselor for students with special needs in the New York City's public school system. Mark holds a Master of Science in Education from Long Island University. He is also a former magician and once worked in the hotel industry.

You can learn more about Mark and The Witches of Vegas, or get in touch with him through his website:

www.markrosendorf.com

The Witches of Vegas and their adventures will continue…

Thank you for purchasing
this publication of The Wild Rose Press, Inc.

For questions or more information
contact us at
info@thewildrosepress.com.

The Wild Rose Press, Inc.
www.thewildrosepress.com

www.ingramcontent.com/pod-product-compliance
Lightning Source LLC
Chambersburg PA
CBHW070055030726
47506CB00002B/478
9781509239924